ONE LONG WEEKEND

SHARI LOW

Boldwood

First published in Great Britain in 2024 by Boldwood Books Ltd.

Copyright © Shari Low, 2024

Cover Design by Alice Moore Design

Cover Photography: Shutterstock and iStock

The moral right of Shari Low to be identified as the author of this work has been asserted in accordance with the Copyright, Designs and Patents Act 1988.

Every effort has been made to obtain the necessary permissions with reference to copyright material, both illustrative and quoted. We apologise for any omissions in this respect and will be pleased to make the appropriate acknowledgements in any future edition.

A CIP catalogue record for this book is available from the British Library.

Paperback ISBN 978-1-83518-452-3

Large Print ISBN 978-1-83518-448-6

Hardback ISBN 978-1-83518-447-9

Ebook ISBN 978-1-83518-445-5

Kindle ISBN 978-1-83518-446-2

Audio CD ISBN 978-1-83518-453-0

MP3 CD ISBN 978-1-83518-450-9

Digital audio download ISBN 978-1-83518-444-8

Boldwood Books Ltd
23 Bowerdean Street
London SW6 3TN
www.boldwoodbooks.com

To my grandmothers, Sadie Hill and Betty Murphy.
Two irrepressible forces of nature who taught the rest of us how it's done.
Forever loved and missed.

NOTE FROM SHARI...

Dear you,

Hello again! Thank you for picking up another of my books, or, if it's our first meeting, welcome! I hope you enjoy the words that will fill the pages you're about to read.

I just wanted to say a little bit about how this book came to be, as it isn't the story that I thought I was going to write this time around. But, as with so many of my novels, real life threw in a curveball that consumed my mind and took my imagination off in a new direction. Most things that happen to me, good or bad, find their way into my writing, and, well, this was one of those events that chipped a little piece off my heart.

In September of last year, I was flying from my home in Glasgow to Los Angeles. I'd barely slept for days, because I was juggling lots of fun things – the launch of *One Christmas Eve*, edits on *One Year After You*, and writing two new books – while also dealing with some not-so-fun stuff: some family health issues, two devastating bereavements and building work on my home that had me living in cold, dusty rubble with only a microwave for company for almost a month. It's a (not so) glamorous life.

When the taxi came to take me to the airport that morning, I'd been awake for twenty-four hours, and I'd packed my case in a chaotic, sleep-deprived rush at some point between typing words, fulfilling promotion commitments for the new book, and chucking out all perishables from the fruit bowl and the fridge.

I say none of this for sympathy, only to set the scene for my huge mistake. *Giant.* One of the most colossal errors ever.

I never wear jewellery when I travel, so, as always, I popped the things I love most into a little black velvet pouch. Seven rings. Three of them were just costume jewellery, but they nestled beside the wedding set my husband bought me to celebrate our twenty-fifth wedding anniversary, another precious ring that I was gifted more than thirty years ago, and... I still can't even type this without tears... a smoky Quartz stone on a gold band that belonged to my late and oh-so-beloved grandmother, Betty. I'm not materialistic. I'm not particularly a jewellery person. But those four rings were among the few possessions in life that I truly adored.

I tucked the pouch into the back compartment of my handbag and that's when the mistake happened – I didn't zip the pocket. Instead, I chucked in my passport, purse, hairbrush and a dozen other things, closed the magnetic catch, and off I dashed to the sound of the taxi-driver's beeping horn.

You can probably guess what happened next, so at this point I'm going to hand this story over to one of my favourite characters, my darling Val. It seems fitting that she tell this tale.

Over the years, Val has popped in and out of most of my books and her huge, fierce, loyal heart was inspired by the gran who wore that smoky quartz on the hand that once held mine. What unfolds in these pages is Val's journey, not mine, but I'll share my own ending in the final chapter.

In the meantime, I'll let Val take it from here. And, dear readers, if you're travelling with anything precious, zip that handbag.

With love,
Shari xx

ON THIS JOURNEY, YOU'LL MEET...

Val Murray – a much-loved mother, grandmother and pal, blessed with broad shoulders, a huge heart and an endless supply of empathy, care and caramel wafers.

Carly Morton – Val's niece and one of her favourite people. Happily married to her second husband, Sam, but struggling with a nest that was abandoned when her sons Mac, 22, and Benny, 20, flew off to chase their dreams.

Carol Cooper – former model turned social media influencer, wife to Carly's brother Callum (and, yes, their names are all way too similar – it causes no end of confusion for their elderly relatives) and mother of their twins, Charlotte and Toni, 23.

Sophie Smith – primary school teacher, daughter of an overprotective dad, Sid, sister to Erin, and currently single – although she has plans to change that relationship status this weekend.

Erin Smith – Sophie's sister, works in marketing and social media for a London-based lingerie brand.

Ash Aitken – Sophie's ex-boyfriend, the only love of her life so far, and the one that got away.

Alice McLenn – mother of Rory, wife of Larry McLenn, a cleaner who does two shifts a day and somehow manages to find glimpses of joy in a solitary life with a husband she despises.

Larry McLenn – Alice's husband, a former politician whose public disgrace destroyed his career and devastated his family.

Rory Brookes (McLenn) – Alice and Larry's son, forensic accountant at the Fieldow Financial Group, married to the very glamorous Julia, currently weathering yet another personal storm.

Julia Fieldow Brookes – Rory's image-conscious, estranged wife and daughter of his boss, Roger Fieldow.

Roger Fieldow – Rory's esteemed boss, mentor, founder and CEO of the Fieldow Financial Group.

Albie Pratt – fledgling stand-up comic and Rory's friend since high school.

Dr Richard Campbell – chief of the ED (Emergency Department) at Glasgow Central Hospital.

FRIDAY

3 MAY 2024

1

VAL MURRAY

I wondered if dropping my phone into the biscuit jar and ramming on the airtight lid would make it stop ringing. Some kind of mental block meant I couldn't remember how to make the damn thing switch off (why wasn't there just a simple on/off button?) and I'm not one to make dramatic gestures like throwing it at the wall or crushing it under the heels of my blue furry mules, because then I'd need to buy a new one. Wasting money like that is against my religion. Thoust shalt not spend hard-earned savings or pension on modern tat like swanky phones or designer bags. However, ludicrously expensive tickets to see Tom Jones in concert on the other hand... Well, those were an investment in personal wellbeing.

The thought brought a memory that sent a lump straight to my throat. My husband, Don. At a million parties. Over forty odd years of marriage. Singing 'It's Not Unusual'. With actions, that deep sexy voice of his, and a cheeky sparkle in his eye because he knew he was making me laugh. A sparkle that had been dimmed by Alzheimer's disease a few years ago, and then extinguished altogether just over a month ago, when he passed away in my arms.

Suddenly, the pain of the memory was more brutal than the dread of talking to someone, *anyone*, on the phone, so I answered. 'Hello?'

'How many times did you think about throwing the phone out of the window before you answered, Aunt Val?' My niece, Carly, had always had an uncanny ability to know what I was thinking and she wasn't far off. I've been this lassie's official aunt since Don and I married more than four decades ago. I was more than happy to take the daughter of his older brother under our wing. She wasn't even in high school then, and now she's in her fifties, so the dotted line between blood family and in-law has long been rubbed out.

'None,' I answered, sliding into my usual chair at our well-worn oak slab of a dining table. Nowadays, they'd call it 'artisan' or 'reclaimed', but the truth was, it was just much loved and ancient. 'I was going to put you in the biscuit jar.'

'I gained two pounds just visualising that,' Carly shot back, making me smile.

My niece was one of my favourite people left on this earth, but for once, hearing her voice didn't de-escalate my feelings of anxiety by a single racing heartbeat. That's how it had been every single day since my Don died. Thudding heart, sleepless nights, interspersed with paralysing dread that would shut down my body and mind cell by cell until I could barely function.

In my adult life, there had been three losses that had almost broken me. The first was when my daughter, Dee, was mowed down by a drugged-up driver when she was barely thirty. The second was when my best pal, Josie, died suddenly, only hours after we were dancing up a storm, drinking champagne and giggling our heels off at a wedding. And the third was right now, only weeks after saying goodbye to the love of my whole lifetime.

Don passed on the first of April. April Fool's Day. Even then, he had to have the last laugh. Ever since, well-meaning folk have repeated all the clichés. That grief is the price you pay for love. That time will heal. That it's better to have loved and lost... But all that stuff just makes me grit my teeth and scream inside my head that they obviously didn't know Don Murray, because none of that trite stuff applies here. Instead, there's just an agonising, brutal hole in my heart that physically aches, even when I'm doing my best to go through the motions of day-to-day life.

'Aren't you in the taxi yet?' Carly asked, causing a fresh ripple of tension to creep across my shoulders. The taxi. That one that would take me to the airport for the flight to London, where she'd lived since she was in her twenties.

'No, I'm all packed and ready, but I'm still in the house.'

Her question sent my gaze to the clock on the kitchen wall. Ten minutes past eight o'clock. Bugger. The taxi was booked for eight o'clock and I'd completely lost track of time.

'They usually text to say the taxi is here, but hang on...' The heels of my peep-toe mules clicked on the laminate floor as I bustled down the hall of the terraced home I'd lived in since we tied the knot. It wasn't unusual back then to get married when you were barely out of school. In those days, most of my pals had swapped their parents' house for their teenage marital home. Changed times now and that was a good thing. There weren't many of those teenage marriages that went the distance, and some of the ones that did were just two people locked in a contract that they didn't have the strength, the energy or the resources to leave. I'd been one of the lucky ones, got a good man that I'd adored until the day he died, and a house we'd managed to buy off the council back when Spandau Ballet was top of the charts. It wasn't anything grand, but it had been the happiest of homes when we were raising our family here and I knew I'd never swap it for anywhere else.

I immediately felt the heat of the unusually warm May

morning as I pulled open the front door and looked down the path to the left, to the parking area at the end of the terrace, where a stout, red-faced bloke was clambering out of a red Skoda with a taxi sign on the door. Damn it, he'd probably been there since eight o'clock right enough. And he didn't look pleased to have been kept waiting.

I'd lived all my days in Weirbridge, and it was the kind of village where everyone knew each other, so nine times out of ten, I recognised the local taxi drivers. Not today. I'd never seen this bloke before.

He put his hand to his eyes and squinted as he peered along the path, then gave me a wave and pointed at his watch.

'Been here ten minutes,' he bellowed, and I immediately mentally deducted a couple of pounds from his tip for the edge of aggression in his voice.

'I'm sorry – I'll be right there,' I hollered back, before hurrying back inside.

'I just lost an eardrum,' Carly groaned, still on the other end of the phone. 'I'll let you go, Aunt Val, but I'll see you in a couple of hours. I'll be in the arrivals hall. And, Val...' She occasionally dropped the 'Aunt' and I didn't mind in the least. 'I'm so glad you're coming.'

'Me too, pet,' I said, and hoped it was convincing. Sometimes the truth was just better left unsaid. I wanted to tell the rude taxi driver to bugger off. I wanted to go back inside. I wanted to go upstairs and climb into my bed. And I wanted to stay there until the skin grew back over the open wound in my chest, caused by the violent removal of my heart. But I couldn't do any of those things because I'd promised everyone in my world that I'd go to London. 'I need to go. I'll see you soon, pet. Love your bones.'

'Love you back,' I heard, right before I clicked the phone off and dropped it in my bag on the console table in the hall.

I could feel my pulse racing, my hands shaking, and the dull headache of too many sleepless nights. I tried to drown it out by having a strong word with myself. *Right, Val Murray, get organised. You're not going to sit here and wallow. You can do this. Pull your big strong woman knickers up and let's go. Because, really, there are no good options.*

In the kitchen, I put my mug in the dishwasher, checked the back door was locked and the heating was off. Although it was May, I still kept it on timer to come on for an hour in the morning just to take the chill off now that I didn't wake up to the warmth of my Don's big arms around me.

Back in the hall, I grabbed my coat from the rack at the door, a pale blue jacket to match my heels and my trademark eyeliner (the eighties and Princess Diana's make-up style would never be forgotten as long as I was alive), set the alarm my son, Michael, had installed a decade ago, slung my bag over my shoulder, grabbed my large check-in case, my small cabin trolley case and steered them out the door, locking it behind me.

I hadn't even reached the end of the path, when a glance caught the Neighbourhood Watch sign attached to the street lamp post a few metres away. My pal, Nancy, had put it there years ago, as some kind of ninja-psychological deterrent after some toerag had broken into Don's shed and stolen our Christmas decorations and his brand new Flymo. I may or may not have expressed a fleeting hope that the thieving bugger would take his toes off with the damn thing. Okay, I did.

Suddenly, a domino line of thoughts collided into each other in my mind. What if someone broke into my home while I was in London? Those nasty bastards could override all sorts of alarms these days. What if they took my valuables? Not that I had much. Just the big telly Don bought to watch the football, and a few pieces of jewellery and...

Stop. Rewind. A few pieces of jewellery.

'Are you coming or not?' the taxi driver barked, as he spotted me frozen to the spot at the end of the path. Another couple of pounds off his tip. Especially as I knew that, quite rightly, he'd already have added a waiting charge on to the fare. I didn't mind that in the least as it was only fair and the man had a living to make, but there was no excuse for rudeness. In better days, I'd have been more than a match for this bloke, but today I didn't have the energy for conflict. Sod it.

'Just coming, sunshine,' I shouted back with a hint of sarcasm and then, leaving my cases where they were, I bolted back into the house, reversing my actions from a few moments ago. Door unlocked. Alarm off. Handbag dropped on the console table. Back along the hall. But this time I veered to the stairs on the right, and went up them at the speed of a caffeinated ferret. It was suddenly inconceivable to me that I'd even been thinking about going anywhere without the people I'd loved most in my life. Or, rather, the pieces I had left of them.

I opened the lid of my old mahogany jewellery box that had been my mother's before it was mine. Not that either of us had ever had anything of value to put in it, but still. Lifting a tangle of multi-coloured beads and costume earrings that dangled to my shoulders, I unearthed the little pad with the four rings I treasured more than any other material possessions in my world. Burglars could have the telly. Hell, they could have the ten-year-old sofa or the air fryer that I still couldn't work. But they weren't getting the ring Don had first proposed with, when we were barely out of high school. Or Don's wedding band. Or the beautiful white gold ring with the diamond D that we'd been paying up for months after we bought it for Dee for her twenty-first. Or the emerald cocktail ring that had belonged to my beloved pal, Josie.

I spotted a little black velvet pouch that contained a pair of earrings someone had bought me last Christmas, and I emptied out the flashing snowmen, popped the rings inside, and pulled the little strings tight to close it. I heard a horn beeping outside and didn't have to deploy my detective skills to work out who it was aimed at. I resisted the urge to make a gesture out of the window that would shock my lovely neighbours. Instead, with the little pouch in my clutches, I ran back downstairs, flipped open the flap on my handbag and tucked the pouch in the back section of the bag, then threw my hairbrush back in on top.

Another beep of the horn. Bugger. I pulled the strap up on to my shoulder, banged four numbers on the alarm keypad, and was out of the door and down the path before the long beep that told me the alarm was set.

'Good of you to wait so patiently,' I told the driver, whose face turned an even deeper shade of puce.

I took back what I said earlier. Now that he was up close, he looked vaguely familiar, but I still couldn't put a name to the face. After he grudgingly helped me put my two cases in the boot, I climbed into the taxi, and yes, as expected, there was already a six-pound waiting charge on the meter. I'd have happily given him seven if he'd been civil.

He drove the whole twenty-minute journey from Weirbridge to Glasgow Airport in stony silence, which suited me just fine, because if he'd made small talk, he'd have no doubt stumbled on the reason I was going, and I didn't trust myself to tell him without bawling. Not today. Not when I was leaving home for the first time since Don...

I blocked the thought and ran a different internal monologue. Don wouldn't want me to sit at home alone, especially as so many of my closest people were away right now. My son, Michael, had left last week for a month in Australia, on a trip that had been planned by his gorgeous Aussie wife for almost a year. He'd wanted to cancel it right up until he left and, in the end, he'd only agreed to go because I was going to London to be with Carly.

It was a similar situation with my pal, Nancy. We spent most days together, but Nancy was away on a holiday with her partner, Johnny, that they'd booked months ago, and I had been adamant that she had to go. Besides, Nancy's fortnight in the sun had been timed to coincide with a break in our childminding schedule. Nancy and I usually looked after our friend Tress's two-year-old son, Buddy, a couple of days a week, but he was on a week-long trip with Tress and her partner, Noah, to see the little one's grandparents in Cyprus. In the end, like Michael, Nancy only went ahead with her holiday because I told her I was taking up Carly's invitation to spend two weeks in the Costa Del Chiswick. Sure, I could have cancelled after Nancy's flight to Malaga was in the air, but my niece was no pushover either.

'Either you come down here, or I'm coming up there to stay with you, Aunt Val. And you know I drive you mad when I rearrange your drawers and eat all your biscuits. And I'm not even going to mention the last time, when I accidentally erased a hundred and two episodes of *Special Victims Unit* from your TV planner.'

That had made me roll my eyes, but the truth was that maybe there was something to be said for getting out of my house. At home, Don was in every room. In every cushion and corner and cupboard. Even after all these weeks, his mug still sat on the draining board because I couldn't bear to put it away. When I opened his wardrobe, I could smell the scent of him in the clothes that still hung there. Yet another part of him that I couldn't let go. Just like his slippers, in their usual place at his side of the bed. I couldn't imagine a time when I wouldn't need the comfort of seeing them there.

And maybe there was something to be said for leaving Weirbridge for a while too. Somehow, my daily walk always ended up at the cemetery, where I'd sit on the bench opposite his grave. He was buried with our Dee, so I'd have a wee chat to them both.

When Nancy and I were on our childminding days for little Buddy, we'd go to the park, or maybe up to one of the cafés on the High Street for lunch, but everyone in the village knew Don, so there was always a succession of sympathetic faces and well-meant words. It all just made me want to send a message up to Don to call off the condolences because every one of them was just a brutal reminder of the man I'd lost.

The taxi driver interrupted my thoughts. 'Bloody ridiculous. Six pounds just to get in here for five minutes. Scandalous. This bloody government...' he ranted as we drove into the drop-off zone at Glasgow airport.

I zoned him out, too busy trying to force my anxiety back down from my chest to the pit of my stomach, where it had been in residence for months. As soon as the car pulled to a stop, I grabbed the strap of my handbag and climbed out, pulling it behind me.

After my foul-tempered knight in Skoda armour grudgingly retrieved my trolley cases out of the boot, I put my handbag on top of the smaller one and wrapped the strap around the pull-up handle. I handed him cash for the fare, including a lower tip than he would have been given if he'd had a pleasant bone in his body, then I steered my cases on either side of me across the road to the terminal building.

At the check-in desk, I dug into the front pouch of my bag for my ID and phone, checked in my larger case and then headed to security. This was it – my last chance to change my mind. I could turn around. I could go home. I could hide. But I knew it would just bring a whole lot of worry to the people who loved me, so I kept on going. Through the barrier. Along the security queue. Kindle out. Toiletries too. Handbag and cabin case on tray.

Thankfully, the security scanner approved because I didn't have it in me to hold it together if I had to have a chat with a kindly security guard. I could just picture it. He'd tell me my genuine plastic handbag was being subjected to a random drug test and I'd end up wailing in his arms, disclosing every sadness I'd experienced since the seventies. It was all just sitting in my throat, ready to spill out to the first unsuspecting friendly face. Probably just as well I didn't have time for a coffee.

As soon as my bag and case were out of the tray, it was an Olympic speed walk through duty-free and down what felt like a mile-long corridor to the British Airways hub for the flight to Heathrow. As I turned the corner to gate 19, harassed and panting, I noticed my handbag had tipped forward on top of the case, so I righted it, then joined the end of the queue of passengers that had already been called to board.

A few frantic moments later, I was on the plane and in my seat, next to a very serious businessman whose avoidance of eye contact made it clear that he wasn't open to chatting to random women on planes. Probably just as well. He'd never know he was just a polite smile away from a torrent of grief. Although, a wee hand putting my case and handbag up into the overhead bin wouldn't have gone amiss. Not because I'm some defenceless, hapless woman, because I'm very far from that, as the bugger who stole Don's Flymo will find out if I ever catch him. However, the overhead storage was an issue because I'm five foot two and stretching a heavy weight up that high made my bra strap ping. Chivalry was well and truly dead this morning. My Don would have helped anyone in a heartbeat. Just thinking that brought a wobble to my chin that I tried to hide as I sunk into my seat.

The flight from Glasgow to London was barely an hour, and I passed the whole time with my eyes closed, psyching myself up for what was to come. The very act of being around someone else, of being seen, even by someone I adored, was making my chin wobble even more.

When Dee passed away over a decade ago, I felt the same. Worse maybe. That had been such a violent act that I didn't sleep for months, yet I couldn't face the concerned faces of the people I loved either, so every night I'd sneak out and spend hours walking up and down the faceless, deserted aisles of our local supermarket, carrying a basket that I barely filled, grateful that no one even cared to glance in my direction. Not even the security guards, who got so used to seeing me that I became invisible to them. Back then, I'd wished I could be that way to the whole world. It had been tough, and it had taken a long time, but eventually I'd found a way through that restored my strength and rebuilt my love of life. Not a new life. Just a different one. But the difference was, throughout every single day of that grief, and of the last forty-odd years, Don had been with me. And now he wasn't.

A gentle thud told me we'd landed. I somehow managed to pull my case down by myself and wasn't too gutted when it swung like a pendulum and skelped the unhelpful suited chap next to me on the arse. I pretended not to notice, too busy holding my ground in the usual 'elbows out' shuffle to the door.

I'd come to visit Carly, her brother, Callum, and his wife, Carol (yep, their names were way too similar), many times before, so I made my way to the baggage reclaim on autopilot, pulling my cabin case, with my handbag reattached to the top of it, alongside me.

For once, my big suitcase was one of the first off, and I gave an admittedly smug glance to the gent who'd been sitting next to me, and who was now eying the conveyor belt impatiently. Sometimes karma was real, I decided, as I went through the doors to the arrivals hall in record speed, thinking perhaps I'd have to wait for

Carly. But no, she was there, arms wide open, a Starbucks drink in each hand.

'Are you happier to see this cup of tea or me?' Carly asked, grinning. It was the family default position. Use humour to get through every emotion. Fake it until you make it.

My grin was automatic. The lass had gone to such an effort for me, persuaded me to come, booked the flight ticket and now showed up and was opening her home to me, so there was no way I was going to allow myself to pitch up here and fall apart.

'Definitely you, ma love,' I answered, hugging her, but being careful not to bump the drinks.

'I'm so glad you're here, Aunt Val,' Carly whispered into my hair, and I gulped.

Do not crumble. DO NOT CRUMBLE.

I cleared my throat. 'I am too, sweetheart.' There was a part of me that meant it. Carly was one of those life forces that was good for the soul and at any other time I'd feel thrilled to be with her, and excited for the days ahead. Right now, under my fake smile and fake chirpiness, all I felt was broken. And, God love her, even though I could see her concern in her tight smile, she cared enough to go along with the pretence.

'Right, give me that big case and follow me. The car park was really busy, and I'm pretty sure the space I eventually got is nearer to Cornwall than London, so we have a bit of a hike.'

She wasn't kidding. Almost twenty minutes later, my bunions were screaming in my furry mules when we finally manhandled my luggage and ourselves into Carly's car, some big fancy vehicle that said Evoque on the back.

'I know, don't judge me,' Carly pleaded. 'I held on to my ancient old Mini until bits started falling off it and I know I've gone to the other end of the flash scale with this, but... Okay, I'm just going to be honest. I fricking love it. It has seats that heat my arse.'

'In that case you're forgiven for being flash,' I quipped. 'Because warm buttocks are important.'

Carly chuckled, leaned over, hugged me again. 'We're going to be okay, Aunt Val.'

'I know, pet. I know.' I felt my throat tighten. *Don't cry. Don't cry. You've got this.*

Yet again, I cleared my throat, pulled my shoulders back and, more as a distraction than anything else, pulled down the passenger mirror and checked my reflection. It looked exactly the same as it had when I left home. My platinum blonde bob, cut just below my chin, was sprayed to the consistency of brick, so it never moved. My fringe was still sitting perfectly, just above eyebrows that were pencilled because I'd over-plucked them in the seventies. Who knew that bushy brows would make a comeback? My blue mascara and eyeliner were un-smudged, and my lips were still Avon Twinkle Pink. Nonetheless, I needed a distraction to avoid the emotional moment, so I pulled my handbag up onto my knee, flicked open the magnetic catch and released the flap, tossing it over the back of the bag. I stared at the two separate sections, my mind telling me something was wrong, but unable to pinpoint what it was. Finally, it came to me.

'Och bugger, I've lost my hairbrush.'

'I've got one in my bag, if you want to risk potential botulism by diving in there. I'm sure there's a Coronation chicken sandwich from last week lurking in the bottom.'

'I'll take my chances.' I laughed and was about to close my bag when a wrecking ball of realisation slammed into the picture and hit me right in the stomach. Oh dear God, no.

My eyes searched as my hands frantically began to pull out every single thing from the bag. Phone. Purse. Perfume. Lipstick. Electricity bill. I had no idea why that was there, because I was sure I'd paid it. Make-up compact. Boarding pass. Hair bobbles.

Don's comb. A plastic spoon I always carried in case little Buddy needed an emergency yoghurt. Assorted tissues. A packet of mints. Some loose change.

No brush.

The wound in my chest burst wide open yet again.

And no little pouch.

My precious rings were gone.

2

SOPHIE SMITH

Sophie saw the taxi at Glasgow Airport's drop-off/pick-up zone and made a beeline for it. The queue outside the terminal for the official airport taxis had been huge, and she remembered that it had been just as long the last time she'd arrived here, two years and one month ago. That day, her ex-boyfriend, Ash, had crossed from the terminal building to the ground floor of the car park and summoned an Uber from there. Today, she'd decided to do the same.

After following the same path as before, she'd just been about to open her Uber app, when the red Skoda had pulled up, and a lady with a blonde bob and a weary expression had got out and trundled off in the direction of the main building as if the weight of the world was on her shoulders. Sophie was pretty sure she recognised the sentiment because she was feeling that way too.

She leaned down so she could speak into the open slot at the top of the passenger window. 'Hi, can you take me to Glasgow city centre please?'

'I'm a private hire – can only pick up prior bookings here. It's the law,' the driver replied sharply, barely even making eye contact.

Slightly taken aback and irritated in equal measure by his rudeness, Sophie knew she should let him go, but there wasn't another taxi in sight, and she just wanted to get where she was going. Her irritation took charge of the situation. 'So if I call your company and book you, then you can pick me up?'

'Listen, I don't have time for this,' he grumbled. It was obvious he was edgy, his eyes darting around as if checking to see if anyone was watching him.

'Me either. Forget it. I'll call for someone else.'

As she began to stretch up, she heard, 'Thirty quid. No meter. Take it or leave it.'

Sophie's instincts told her it was a bad idea. This bloke was already being an asshole. But thirty quid, and he was right here? The alternative of standing around waiting for who knows how long had no appeal.

'Done,' she said, jumping into the car.

She wasn't entirely reckless, though. The first thing she did was take a sneaky photo of the driver's badge and send it to her dad.

In this guy's car. If he kidnaps me, channel Liam Neeson and come get me. x

The answer came back almost immediately.

I will find you. I have skills… But I might need help because I'm not the best at beating up kidnappers. Not since I put my back out on the golf course. Have a great time at the concert. Stay safe. x

Sophie felt an immediate flush of shame creeping up her neck. A concert. That was the reason she'd given her dad for coming up to Glasgow. If he knew the truth…

She shook it off. Focus on the important stuff. One step at a time. Step one. Get to the hotel and dump her bag. That was as far as she was going to let herself go right now. Anyway, these feelings of guilt were ridiculous. Her dad was hundreds of miles away, in the bungalow he'd lived in with her mum on the outskirts of their home town of Reading. He couldn't see her, and he couldn't know from a simple text message that she was doing anything other than what she said. He hadn't even asked her what concert she was going to or who she was with. It was fine.

She texted back.

Will do, Dad. Call you later. Love you. xx

Then immediately texted her older sister, Erin.

Dad is suspicious.

The reply was instant. Her sister worked in marketing, managing communications and social media for a lingerie brand based in Camden, so her phone was permanently glued to her hand.

Do you know that for sure or are you being paranoid?

Definitely paranoid.

I rest my case. Why don't you just tell him? You're twenty-six years old and you're a strong, independent woman who is in charge of her own choices and destiny.

Sophie's thumbs moved like lightning.

Have you told him you smoke and have a tattoo on your buttock?

Touché. Need to go. Writing a press release about gussets. Living the dream.

Smiling, Sophie put her phone on her lap and gazed out of the window for the next few minutes, staring at the sky over a city that she'd adored when she'd come here with Ash.

Actually, tomorrow it would be exactly twenty-four months since she left. The date was ingrained on her memory, because tomorrow was also the two-year anniversary of the day that Ash Aitken had proposed to her, after knowing her for exactly four months.

They'd met on a backpacking trip around Asia, and if anyone had told her she'd go all the way to Bali and fall in love at first sight with a guy from Glasgow, she'd have thought they had something dodgy in their hookah, but that's exactly what had happened. They'd immediately connected, and not just because they'd both recently qualified as teachers and had taken time out from covering temporary posts to travel for a few months. What were the chances of that? It was almost as if it was meant to be. Or, at least, that's what they'd told themselves. They'd changed their plans so that they could travel together, and been inseparable from that moment on. After three months spent falling madly in love on hot balmy beaches and chaotic, busy cities, she'd come with him to his home city of Glasgow for a blissful, glorious stay that had been cut short after just four weeks. Seemed like a lifetime ago now.

She'd been planning to stay for longer, but her mum had called to break the worst news Sophie had ever received. Even now, Sophie could only remember some of the words her mum had said. She'd felt poorly. Had tests. Hospital. Doctors. Diagnosis. Pancreatic cancer. Sophie hadn't even understood the severity of it, or the prognosis, but she knew she had to get back to her. To go home immediately. And that meant leaving Ash behind.

The next day, before they went to the station for her train to London, then on to Reading, they'd gone to George Square, in the centre of the city, and every detail of that afternoon still played like a movie in her mind.

The lawns and benches inside the square had been packed with people, and several of them had stopped to watch, as Ash pulled out a ring, a silver and jade band that he'd seen her admiring on the Beijing stop of their trip. Unconventional, but she'd adored the sentiment and the thoughtfulness behind it.

Thankfully, he hadn't gone down on one knee, because that was the kind of stuff that made it on to social media websites and stayed there forever. Instead, he'd leaned down, put his forehead against hers, holding the ring between them.

'Sophie, I know this is soon, and probably grounds to have me arrested for stalking, but I don't ever want to be without you. Every single moment since we met has been better than the one before. I am so incredibly happy with you and I never want it to end, so, Sophie Smith, please, will you marry me?'

'Aw, hen, say yes!' That came from two elderly ladies eating Greggs pies on the bench nearest them, who definitely deserved to be on social media for ever. Once Sophie got past the gobsmacking shock of the proposal, she was tempted to be rash, wild and romantic and say yes. She really was. For many reasons. The first was that she'd felt exactly the same way since her gaze first met his on a Balinese beach at sunset. They'd struck up a conversation and corny as it sounded, it was as if they'd known almost everything about each other instantly. Over the next few days, weeks and months, the stuff they didn't know just added even more layers of excitement and fun. She'd adored him. He was the first – and hopefully the last – man she had ever been in love with. But...

'I can't,' she'd whispered, answering his question, her voice cracking on the words. 'Because if I say yes now, I'll always remember that it was sad because I was leaving you.'

It was too much of everything. Too much emotion. Too much confusion. Too many people needing her. 'Can I take a raincheck? Can you ask me again later? In a while, I mean. When my mum is better?'

He'd sighed, smiled, kissed her forehead. 'I tell you what... Promise me you'll come back, and I'll ask you again in a year. Right here. And if you say no, I'll ask you again the next year, and the next, and the next... I'll ask you every year, on the fourth of May, until you say yes.'

'I promise,' she'd whispered, not sure if her heart was breaking or swelling so big it could burst.

That's when she'd realised that the two women on the bench had frozen, pies in mid-air waiting to hear her answer. And another four or five random people nearby were watching them, waiting for the big moment. She'd already disappointed Ash, and now she was about to disappoint them too.

'But Ash...' she'd continued, so quietly only he could hear. 'We have an audience. So you're going to cheer, and snog my face off, so that it doesn't look like I said no. Because I didn't. I just said later.'

And that's what they'd done. She'd nodded with joyous exaggeration, he'd punched the air, picked her up, swung her around, and then they'd kissed until the cheering from the audience stopped. The last thing she remembered hearing before they walked off into the sunset (actually only to Central Station to get her train) was one of the elderly ladies with the pies saying, 'Och, Daphne, no wonder I comfort eat. This place is an emotional roller coaster.'

As the train pulled out of the station, Sophie had no idea what was in front of her. She didn't know the awful things that were about to happen, or that the pain of what was to come would force her to cut off all contact with Ash just months later, that they wouldn't speak again, or that for too many reasons that she didn't want to think about right now, she wouldn't make it back to Glasgow until this weekend.

Even as late as last night, she wasn't sure that she would make the trip, but then she'd decided that it was now or never. School had closed yesterday for the half-term break, so what else was she going to be doing anyway? This was the second year in a row that she'd taught Year Two, so she already had the lesson plans for the next term organised and ready to go. Her class of six- and seven-year-olds were so excited about their break and it had been contagious. At least, if all this came to nothing, she'd be able to tell them about her trip to Scotland, and drop in some stories about castles and legends of monsters that lived in lochs.

Not that there would be any sightseeing this weekend. She was here for only one reason – to find Ash. Although, now that the taxi had left the airport and joined the slip road on to the motorway that would take her into the city, the doubts and fears were kicking in again. Did anyone ever find happiness chasing a regret? And would she be too late to make it right? All she wanted to do was to say sorry, to ask him to forgive her, to find out if he still felt the same, still loved her, still wanted her. And if he did, this time she wasn't going to be stupid enough to let him go.

The taxi driver grunted in the front. 'Where in the city centre are you going to?'

'The George Square Grand Hotel.'

That brought on an exaggerated sigh. 'Right in the centre. Of course it bloody is. The traffic round there is insane now, especially with all the ridiculous twenty miles per hour limits. I'd be quicker getting out of the car and bloody walking. All that bloody green nonsense. Speed restrictions and low emission zones. Arsehole councillors, they're destroying this city. Idiots, every last one of them.' He was agitated, and even from the back seat, she could see that his face had reddened with irritation. Maybe if he opened a window or put on the air con, he'd get rid of the sweat that was glistening on the back of his neck too.

Sophie sighed. She should have waited in the original taxi queue. Or found a bus. Or walked. Fricking anything but this. Her mum used to tell her that she attracted waifs and strays. When there was a new kid in school, Sophie brought them home for tea. If there was a dog wandering in the street, she'd pick it up and spend her pocket money on a tin of food before smuggling it into their kitchen. Apparently, she also attracted intolerant, mean-spirited blokes who wanted to rant about anything and everything. She briefly contemplated telling him that she was Greta Thunberg's big sister to see if his head exploded, but she didn't want to cause a motorway pile-up.

Twisting around, she was about to slip her phone into her bag on the seat beside her, when her eye caught something on the floor behind the driver's seat. The button of her jeans groaned as she stretched down, then almost immediately recoiled when her fingers touched the bristles of a hairbrush. Since the driver's greasy, straggly hair looked like it hadn't been brushed in a while, she figured it was a safe bet that it wasn't his. Someone must have dropped it. She pulled it up, and it was only when she got back to a seating position, that she realised there was something tangled in the bristles. Two thin black strings, attached to a little black velvet pouch.

Curious, she picked the strings out of the brush, and opened the pouch, then emptied it into her hand, letting out a gasp as four rings tumbled out.

Her reaction caught the driver's attention. 'Something you want to say?' he challenged her, meeting her gaze in his rear-view mirror. He clearly thought she was still on his conversation about

Glasgow City Council's green policies. His face was even redder now. She thought about suggesting he get his blood pressure checked, but decided her input wouldn't be welcome and it would probably send him off on a rant about the NHS.

'No, it's just that... I found something on the floor back here. Has anyone reported anything lost?'

In the mirror, she could see the suspicion written across his brow. 'No,' he answered, cagily. 'What is it?'

'A hairbrush. And one, two, three, four rings,' she said, peering at them more closely now. The plain gold band was definitely a man's ring as it was bigger than the others. Two others were also gold – one had a trio of diamonds, and the other, a single large rectangular emerald stone. They both looked pretty old, so maybe they were vintage. The fourth ring was silver or white gold, she couldn't tell, with an exquisite little cluster of diamonds. At first glance, she'd thought it was a circle, but now she could see that it was a D. That made something in her head ping. Diana. That was her mum's name. If she believed in cosmic signs, this would be considered a pretty big one that she'd been meant to come to Glasgow. As for the rings... It wasn't a stretch to work out what had happened here. The brush must have fallen out of a bag or a backpack and taken the rings with it. Someone, somewhere, would be missing these.

'Right then. Just toss them into the front seat here and I'll report that I've found them to our control room, then hand them in to the police.'

There was something in his tone, or maybe it was just the fact that he'd been the height of rudeness since she'd clapped eyes on him, but hackles of distrust were rising on the back of her neck. 'Can you radio into your control room right now? Just in case someone is worried and has already phoned to ask about them.'

A pause, and she could see that he was irritated at being challenged. 'Meter's not on,' he said, enunciating every word, as if he was speaking to a child. 'I'll radio in later, when they think I'm back on the clock.'

He was lying. She was aware that she had absolutely no evidence to back that up, and emotional perception wasn't her strong point, but she just had a feeling. An intuition.

In most of the confrontational moments in her life, she'd backed down and gone with the easy option, but something in her wasn't giving in today. There were cars whizzing by, so the fact that his gaze kept going to the rear-view mirror to see what she was doing was making her nervous. She'd be much happier if he was concentrating on the road.

'I tell you what, just drop me at a police station when we get to the city centre – I'll pay the extra fare – and I'll run in and drop them off. I'm sure someone will be desperate to get these back.'

He didn't like that suggestion and his low, pedantic tone made that clear. 'I said just toss them into the front. This is my taxi, sweetheart – that's how it works. Something gets left here, I decide what to do with it.'

Shit. Shit. Shit.

Sophie closed her eyes, took a breath. What did it matter? These weren't her rings. She had no idea who they belonged to. They could be stolen. Or maybe someone was on the way to a pawn shop to swap them for drug money. Or maybe...

No. She stopped herself. Even though she was a twenty-six-year-old woman, in times like this she always heard her mum's voice, nudging her on, encouraging her to fight her corner.

'Well, you said you were going to hand them over to the police, so come with me then. If there's a reward, you can have it. I just want to make sure they get put on a database or something, so they're returned to whoever lost them.'

'How fucking dare you... Are you suggesting I can't be trusted to do that on my own?'

'No!' she lied. She popped the rings back into the pouch and pulled the strings tight, then tugged on her seat belt, which suddenly felt uncomfortably tight. This car ride was taking a turn she really didn't like. She'd ask him to stop and let her out if she weren't on a four-lane motorway.

'Bitch.'

It was almost inaudible. Almost. He whispered it under his breath, but Sophie heard it loud and clear. The hard shoulder was suddenly a safer and more appealing option than sitting in this car.

How the hell had this happened? On her previous visit here, she'd encountered nothing but lovely people and taxi drivers who liked to have a chat and came out with entertaining anecdotes about the people they'd picked up and great suggestions for places to go. This time, she'd been in the city for less than an hour and she was in a full-blown dispute with a guy who'd just called her a bitch while driving at 70 mph on a motorway.

If Erin were here, she'd soon put him in his place and she'd blow the roof right off this car, but that wasn't Sophie's way. She'd always been the peacemaker. The quiet one. The one who stood back and thought things through – usually for far too long.

Well, not today. As soon as they got off this motorway, she was going to insist that he stop at a police station. In fact, she was going to look for one so that she was prepared. She pulled her phone back up in front of her. A quick glance to the mirror told her that the driver's eyes were now firmly on the road in front of him, but the scarlet face and the pulse on the side of his jaw made it clear he was furious.

Her thumbs worked overtime as she consulted Google for the location of the nearest police station and she worked out that they were just about to come up to one in a place called Govan, a couple of slip roads ahead. Even if he came in with her, she could ditch him and call another taxi from the police station. There was no way she was getting back in this car. Yep, that's what she—

'Idiot!' came a hiss from the front.

Sophie's head jerked up, just as the car swerved to the side, in an aggressive move, accompanied by a snarl in the direction of the white transit van that had just overtaken them. It was the kind of thing that happened on the roads every day, but this taxi driver seemed to be taking it personally. This was the worst morning ever. She'd come here with the intention of putting her heart on the line. She'd lied to her dad about why she was coming to Glasgow. And now she felt like she was in the next *Fast & Furious* movie: Lethal Taxi.

She'd barely finished that thought, when she saw the driver's head fall back. Felt the car begin to slide. And sway. And then, oh no, no, no, they were spinning.

There was a bang.

The thud of a collision.

The terrifying sensation of being thrown to the side, then forward, then back.

Then the pain. The awful, searing pain.

Sophie had the instant realisation that this wasn't going to end well.

Her dad would never forgive her for this. For lying about why she was here. For coming back for Ash. For dying on him.

Those were the last thoughts she had before everything went black.

3

ALICE MCLENN

This was Alice's favourite time of the day. She'd just come in from her dawn shift, cleaning over at the local school in the centre of the small town of Bankston, about fifteen miles from Glasgow. As always, she'd walked the mile from her dilapidated home in a run-down housing scheme through the town's streets to her work and back: at 5 a.m. on the way there it was deserted, at 7 a.m. on the way back it was busier. Not that she had a choice, because her car-owning days were long behind her. Anyway, according to the fitness thingy on her wrist, she already had almost half of her 10K steps done for the day.

As always, the solitude had relaxed her, and now she got to have her morning coffee in peace. At least, that's what she'd planned. She'd barely flicked the switch on the kettle when the phone rang, and through the cracks in the plaster on the ceiling, she heard the sound of her husband's disgruntled muttering as he answered the extension that sat on the ancient bedside table next to his head. Peaceful morning interlude ruined.

She listened for more signs of movement upstairs and heard his footsteps as Larry got out of bed, then drawers banging shut, wardrobe doors squeaking as they opened before thudding closed. Yes, he was getting ready to go out. He must have been called in to work and agreed to go. She could do nothing to stop the sigh of contentment that gave her. The house to herself for even longer today. Every hour without him here was an absolute treat. Maybe she'd go down to the swimming baths and do some laps. Or perhaps go over to Weirbridge, a lovely village only a couple of miles away, visit the library or treat herself to a cup of tea in one of the little cafés on High Street. Or maybe she'd just go for a walk and get the rest of her daily steps in, before it was four o'clock and time to go to her early-evening cleaning shift down at the Town Hall.

She worked six hours there, then returned home and slept for five hours until it was time to get up and do it all over again. It wasn't the career of her dreams, but she liked the women she worked with in both places, appreciated their non-judgemental camaraderie, and the hours didn't bother her. She'd never been much of a sleeper. And anyway, it was worth it, because her unsociable hours meant that she and Larry were ships that passed in the night, rarely in the same place at the same time. This tiny house only had one bedroom, but by the time she got home at night he was often sleeping, and she was up and away again before he woke up. She'd trained herself to sleep on the edge of the mattress so that they never touched, and she never glanced in his direction unless to check that he was already asleep. Although, his snoring usually gave that away.

If she were lucky, they only crossed paths once or twice in the day – for a brief few minutes when he was on his way out in the morning, and then on the occasional nights he was still up when she came home from her evening shift. It was more than enough, and it was only made bearable by her absolute certainty that she'd soon be in a position to leave him. As long as she kept her mind on the fact that her freedom would come, then she could tolerate sharing this space with a man she utterly despised.

After flicking on the kettle, she added Larry's travel mug to her large pink cup on the counter. By the time he came downstairs, her coffee was made, and she was pouring boiling water into the cup that he took in his car every morning.

'Bloody imbeciles down at that taxi office. Couldn't run a raffle. They're short this morning, so they need me to go in early to help. What the hell would they do without me?'

Alice knew that most people would say that as a joke, but she was depressingly aware that Larry McLenn absolutely meant every word. Neither self-confidence nor arrogance had ever been in short supply when it came to her husband. Although there had been a long-term drought on love, affection, decency and kind words. There was no point answering his question because they both knew he didn't care to hear anything she had to say.

He grabbed his coffee from the counter and put the lid on it before taking a sip. 'Urgh, you forgot the bloody sugar. Understandable. It's not like I haven't taken it the same way for thirty-odd bloody years. How hard can it be?'

Actually, she hadn't forgotten the sugar, but he'd snatched it up before she could stir it, so that's probably why he couldn't taste it yet. She watched as he opened the cup back up again, added three more sugars, then replaced the lid and made for the door, throwing out a snarky, 'I'll be back by five-ish. You go and lie on the couch and watch all that daytime TV shite while I'm out earning a living,' as he left.

She closed her mind to unkind thoughts about the sugar rotting every tooth in his head, and instead, simply lifted her mug, then slipped her notebook out of her bag, grabbed a pen and took it over to the French doors that led out into the tiny garden. Once upon a time, she would silently seethe when he treated her like that. Now she just fantasised about him walking out of that door and never coming back.

It wasn't that she didn't understand his rage – after his downfall over the last few years, it was only natural that he was angry. Dissatisfied. Frustrated. But, of course, he wouldn't blame the person responsible for destroying his life, because it was all down to himself.

As a city councillor and then a Member of Parliament, Larry McLenn had tasted power, adulation and success and he'd loved every second of it. But that was in a previous life. That was when he was someone, a politician who was feted by the great, the good, the wealthy, the dodgy and anyone who wanted something from him. That was when he used his position to enrich himself. To bully. To exploit. To extort. That was when he took bribes and drugs. Until just over two years ago, when a national newspaper broke a story both online and in print, with a video and photographs showing Larry McLenn, MP, clearly high as a proverbial corrupt kite, agreeing to accept a hundred grand bribe to use his influence in awarding a government contract worth millions to one of his cronies. The scandal had cost them everything.

Months of legalities, of clawing on to power, of denials and claims of political persecution had followed, but ultimately they'd lost it all: their beautiful home in the West End of the city, their jobs, their reputations, their dignity, their friends and, most crushing of all, their son, Rory. That was the only loss Alice cared about, yet it was the one that Larry cared about least. So, yes, she saw what Larry's own actions had done to him, but he deserved it. And Alice refused to let his denial of accountability and consequential fury with life have an effect on her, because the grief over losing the only family she had was like a shell of protection against his bile. None of his rants or rages mattered in the least so she just inhaled, exhaled, let it go and tried to stay... numb. Yes, that was the best word to describe it. Numb to him. It was easier that way. At least for now, until she was the one who could walk out of that door and never see his twisted, miserable face again.

Meanwhile, she filled her day with as many lovely moments as possible. Having her morning coffee in the garden, overlooking the roses she'd planted herself when they'd moved in here a little over a year ago, while jotting her memories, thoughts and observations in her notebook was one of them.

Closing her eyes, she turned her head up to the early-morning sun and focused on the wonderful feeling of the heat on her face. Another life-affirming moment. So many people took small things like this for granted, but when it was all she had, she'd learned to appreciate it. This was the tiny sliver of joy that had replaced the days when she had friends. And a hectic schedule. And places to go, obligations to meet, a son to take care of. Her life had been full and chaotic and some parts of it had been wonderful, but not now. Now, all she had was the sun on her face in the morning. And today, like yesterday and tomorrow, it would have to be enough. For now.

Coffee finished, Alice picked up her mobile phone and texted.

I love you son. Have a good day.

She'd done that every single morning since she last saw Rory, then waited for the inevitable reply and it soon pinged in.

Your text could not be sent.

Of course it couldn't. His number was no longer in service, but somehow, it made her feel better just to put that out there into the world. Wherever he was, whatever he was doing, she had to keep believing that he knew she loved him.

She wrote in her journal for an hour or so, before deciding she was ready to face the rest of the day. Ritual over, she went back inside, rinsed her cup, lifted her handbag and went upstairs.

Their bedroom was overcrowded with furniture, because Larry had refused to throw out the wardrobes and dressers from their previous house when they'd moved. They'd spent over twenty years in that four-bedroom, architecturally stunning, A-listed Victorian townhouse in the city's West End, and the one-bedroom, terraced ex-council house that they now rented could have fitted in the lounge of their previous home. The rent for these mouldy walls, the damp patches on the ceilings, the draughty windows and the seventies décor had been all they could afford after Larry's career was gone, the lawyers were paid, their savings cleaned out. Add on the debt he'd run up on their credit cards, and their two current jobs – his taxi driving and her cleaning – barely covered their outgoings.

She'd thought about leaving him back then, when he'd cost them everything, but she was in too deep, their lives, their debts, their reputations too entwined. The truth was, she had nothing left, nowhere to go, no family, no remaining friends, and he'd threatened to destroy the only thing she cared about if she left – their son. So she'd made a choice. She'd cut Rory out of her life to protect him, and she'd stayed. And on every day since then, she'd listened to Larry's grandiose, arrogant delusions of power and importance while plotting her escape.

'It's only temporary,' he'd spat, the day they'd moved in here. 'I'll show those bastards. I'll get it all back.'

Alice had said nothing, for fear of lighting a spark on another tirade. His fire and fury had been trademarks of his time as an MP and they hadn't subsided now that he had an unwilling audience of one. Better to keep quiet.

Hadn't that been the story of her life? For all of her fifty-four years, she'd been doing what she was supposed to do, with very few exceptions. Actually, marrying Larry had been one of them. Her parents hadn't approved of her choice at all, disliking his manner, his attitude and his politics, and she'd realised too late that they'd been right. Not that she'd ever have admitted it. Her father was the type of man who believed that you stood by your choices in life, and she'd done just that for over three decades now, long after both her parents had passed away.

Routine. That helped to stop her mind wandering to every what if, every mistake and regret. Just like every morning, she put her handbag on the bed, took off her cleaning uniform and dropped it in the white plastic washing basket in the corner of the overcrowded room, then took her robe from the back of the door and slipped it on. After brushing out her hair, she twisted it up under the shower cap that had been dangling from the same hook as her robe. The final step in the pre-shower routine was the same every day. She opened her wardrobe and ran her fingers along the suitcase that sat upright at the back, partially hidden by her winter coats. She always thought of it as her parachute. It was there, fully packed with everything she would need when the time was right to jump.

Larry had once asked her what was in it and she'd told him that it was the clothes that were out of season – her winter clothes in summer, and her light dresses and sandals in the cold months. She wasn't sure he'd even listened to her answer and that was fine, because it meant that he was entirely disinterested and that was the best possible scenario. The truth was that the case contained many things: some clothes and shoes, the few pieces of jewellery that Larry hadn't sold, her photo albums from when their son was a child, her insurance policies, cash. This was her escape capsule. Ready when she was.

She pulled the case out, opened it, took twenty pounds from

her handbag and slipped it into the envelope that was nestled between two bras and a packet of tights. She had no idea how much was there, but it wasn't enough. Not yet. Larry didn't know she'd been given a wage rise months ago, so every week when she got her pay packet, another twenty quid went straight into the escape fund.

Money secure, she took out one of the large white bottles with the gold trim and the black top, that were squeezed between her shoes, then closed the case, locked it, and slid it back into the wardrobe. As long as the case was safe in there, that was the courage and security she needed to get through another day here.

Patience. If being married to Larry McLenn for more than half her lifetime had taught her anything, it was patience. One day, she would pick that case up, and she would walk out of the door without looking back. But it wouldn't be today because she didn't have enough saved up to support herself yet. Patience.

In the bathroom, with its ancient green wall tiles, and burgundy toilet and bath, Alice caught sight of herself in the mirror above the sink as she placed the white and black bottle there. Gone were the days of expensive facials and meticulously applied make-up, and now, all she saw was fifty-four.

She averted her eyes quickly, switched on the shower taps, then dropped her robe and climbed into the bath, just as soon as the water from the stained white hose above it was warm enough to be bearable. They didn't switch on the heating unless temperatures dropped to freezing, and the boiler was only on for ten minutes a day to give them a tiny drop of hot water, so she didn't want to waste it first thing in the morning. She soaped, rinsed, then switched it off as quickly as possible, before pulling the rough grey towel from the bar next to the shower, wrapping it around herself, and then lifting the white and black bottle she'd brought from the case. Chanel No. 5 body cream.

In their wealthier days, Larry had his assistant buy it for her for every birthday and Christmas, because he didn't have the inclination or the imagination to look for anything different. When their worlds had come crashing down, and they'd moved in here, she'd had four bottles in that suitcase. Now, two years after the scandal broke, and just over a year since this became her home, she was down to her last one.

As she did every morning, she squeezed out the tiniest drop, then rubbed it on her arms and face, letting the expensive aroma fire up her senses, remind her of who she was and give her the kind of high that some people only ever got from a different type of chemical substance.

Back in her room, she pulled the suitcase out again, replaced the bottle, and put the case back in its place. She used to leave it out while she was in the shower, but one morning, when it was lying open on the bed, Larry had come home unexpectedly and if he'd come upstairs, he'd have found it. Lesson learned.

Dressing quickly, she pulled on a lilac linen shift dress, added a pale pink cardigan, white sandals, a slick of lipstick from a tube that was almost done, and transferred her purse and phone into a little pink bag. All these clothes were from her previous life, so she took meticulous care of them and only wore them when she left the house. For the next couple of hours, she was going to feel normal and that was going to get her through another day.

Dressed and organised, she went downstairs, checking her watch as she reached the hall. It was after eleven. Larry usually came home around five o'clock, later if there were extra bills to pay, so she still had plenty of time before she had to get back, change into her house clothes and pretend that she'd been here the whole time. Or before it was time to pull on her cleaning clothes and head back to work.

She'd just opened the front door, when the landline rang. She thought about ignoring it, but changed her mind. She'd only worry that it was important.

Taking a few steps back to the hall table, slowly, hesitantly, she picked it up.

'Hello?'

'Hello, Alice? It's Sandra here.'

Sandra worked at Larry's office. Or, rather, his control room. That's what they called the office at the taxi company. Except Larry who sneeringly referred to it as, Imbecile Central. Alice had spoken to the office secretary a couple of times when Sandra couldn't get hold of Larry on his mobile phone and called him on the landline instead. Usually it was to ask him to do an extra shift if they were busy, but he was already there. Wasn't he? He'd bolted out of the house and she'd watched his red Skoda go off down the street.

'Hello, Sandra. I'm afraid Larry isn't here. Someone at the office called him in earlier, so he should be out working.' Alice was puzzled – surely Sandra would know that already?

There was a pause, then what sounded like a choking sob.

'That's what I'm calling about. Oh, Alice, I don't know how to say this. The police have just called us. I'm afraid there's been an accident. Somewhere on the M8 around Govan, I think, because one of the other drivers called in to say he was stuck because of a crash there. The police notified us that Larry has been taken to Glasgow Central Hospital.'

'Is he... is he okay?'

'I don't know, Alice.' Sandra sounded so upset. Much as it was difficult to believe, maybe they thought highly of him at the taxi company. 'But I'm sure they would have told me if it was really bad or...' Definitely a sob this time. 'Worst-case scenario.'

Alice wasn't quite sure how to react to this weeping woman,

but she understood what Sandra was saying: she didn't know for sure if Larry was alive or dead.

Before Alice had time to process any of this, Sandra went on, 'I'm sending a taxi to take you to the hospital and it will be there any minute. Please let us know how he is.'

'I will,' Alice agreed, as the strangest feeling of calm came over her. She should be panicking. Frantic. Upset.

Yet all she felt was that maybe today, her life was going to change after all.

Perhaps all her patience was finally going to pay off.

4

RORY BROOKES MCLENN

Rory had barely slept a wink and it showed on his face as he leaned towards the mirror to get a closer view of what he was doing while he was shaving. Pitching up this morning with a blood-spattered chin wasn't going to be the best look given the circumstances.

Behind him, his mate, Albie, popped his head in the open doorway. He was naked from the waist up, and from the waist down there appeared to be some kind of pyjama trousers that were covered in Batman logos. Rory wasn't even going to ask why, how or where he got them. Albie was the same guy who'd turned up to their university graduation wearing a silver suit that looked like something they'd wrap around runners at the end of a marathon. Now he was approaching thirty, but his fashion sense was still stuck somewhere around his 'Marvel / DC Comics, teenage comfy' years.

Albie spoke first. 'My offer to be your bodyguard still stands. I've worked out twice this year and I'm fairly sure I could crack nuts with these biceps.' To demonstrate that fact, Albie held up his arm and flexed, then immediately yelped. 'Fuck, I think I pulled something.'

'I might go for a hard pass on the bodyguard offer,' Rory said, laughing, even though inside, all hilarity had been beaten to death by the prospect of what could be ahead of him today.

Albie was still rubbing his arm. 'Fine. But call me if you need a getaway driver. The Beetle is souped up and ready to go. It'll be like a cross between *The Italian Job* and *Herbie Rides Again*.'

This was the kind of conversation that took place when you were crashing in your best mate's tiny spare room, the same pal who was convinced he was going to be the next stand-up comic to come out of Glasgow. Billy Connolly. Kevin Bridges. Albie Pratt. The name wrote its own jokes.

Albie still lived in this same city-centre flat they'd shared in their student days, although there had been a succession of flatmates and girlfriends since Rory had left six years ago to move in with his then-girlfriend, Julia. Rory would never have believed that he'd ever be back in this bedroom, let alone sharing it with two broken bikes, a skateboard, a wet suit and a snorkel set, but three months ago, five years after they'd married, he'd moved out of the home he'd shared with Julia to give her the space she'd requested. He'd thought it would only be for a couple of weeks. Somehow, that had stretched into months, and he was still here, but hopefully that was about to change today.

'I'll keep that in mind,' Rory replied. 'You're definitely my second-best option. Number one being that my wife agrees to give things another shot, and we leave the hotel together in her Mercedes.'

Albie shrugged. 'I can see why that would be preferential. Shallow, but more conventional.'

Albie wandered off down the hallway, humming 'Don't Look Back In Anger', and Rory got back to the serious business of trying not to cause a shaving injury with his trembling hands. He wasn't prone to nerves, his job as a forensic corporate accountant frequently called for a cool head and the ability to work under pressure, but the jitters had come out of nowhere this morning. The only other time he'd ever felt this anxious about seeing Julia was on his wedding day, five years ago.

On that special morning, he'd woken up in bed at a sumptuous, eye-wateringly expensive five-star hotel on the banks of Loch Lomond, with Albie's feet in his face, after a few drinks at the bar the night before with the attendees of the rehearsal dinner had somehow turned into a late-night pre-celebration. His mum and dad had been on unusually good form that night, chatting and celebrating with Julia's parents, raising toasts and thrilled to be joining the two families. Larry McLenn, Member of Parliament, and Roger Fieldow, founder and CEO of the Fieldow Financial Group, generally regarded as one of the most prestigious financial companies in the country, were both cut from the same Master of the Universe cloth.

Julia had, of course, been gorgeous. The hen holiday at a spa in Marbella the week before had given her a caramel tan and her copper waves fell down the back of the white, knee-length, off-the-shoulder dress that she'd worn for the practice run up the aisle. Rory remembered thinking he'd never been happier.

That feeling was surpassed the next day when, all nerves forgotten, he'd watched her coming down the aisle towards him, with everyone they loved looking on, in a room that was bedecked with white flowers, with the string quartet playing 'Evergreen' by Barbara Streisand.

Turns out they weren't evergreen after all. The leaves fell right off that love tree only a few years later. Back then, though, he hadn't even considered that they might not go the distance, not even when her family had insisted on a prenup. It was par for the course, especially when marrying into a family as financially astute and wealthy as the Fieldows. Julia had no desire to join her father's company, preferring the relaxed hours of a part-time career in interior design, but she and her sister still stood to inherit the business. At that point, back in the summer of 2019, Rory had already been a forensic accountant there for four years, since the day after he'd graduated from university, so marrying the boss's daughter came with an in-depth understanding of the level of assets that were at stake. He'd been happy to sign, because he neither wanted nor needed any stake in Julia's future fortune. He already earned a sizeable salary, so he wasn't dependent on anyone. Changed days from when he and Albie lived on cheap beer and noodles while at uni. And besides, he was absolutely confident that their marriage would last until the 'death do us part' stuff.

It was truly astonishing to him that it had all managed to go to absolute crap in such a short period of time. He'd left the house three months ago, but the derailment had happened long before that, as soon as his family's name and reputation had begun the interminable slide into the gutter. For someone like Julia, who had lived a carefree, privileged life as the apple of her father's eye, the scandal and embarrassment had been unbearable. She'd tried to ignore the shame caused by the downfall of the family she'd married into, but eventually she'd had enough and asked for a break.

He didn't even want to let his mind go back there right now, so he was just going to brush right over that. The reality was that when shit hit the fan, a marriage either forged together or fell apart. They'd fallen apart in spectacular fashion, but he hadn't given up hope that they could glue their lives back together again.

He finished shaving, thankfully injury free, rinsed off his face and then ran some mousse through his thick dark hair, pushing it back off his face the way she liked it. Every little thing helped. Next, he took a quick sip from his lukewarm mug of black coffee, as he flicked through the shirts that were hanging on the curtain pole, his makeshift overflow wardrobe. Sure, he could have checked into a hotel or taken out a short-term rental, but Albie was happy to have him in the spare room and Rory appreciated having a mate around that made him laugh. Suit on, he was adjusting his cuffs as he took his coffee mug into the kitchen and put it in the sink.

Albie was already there, still in a state of semi-dressed super-hero. He rolled his bloodshot eyes in Rory's direction.

'Bloody hell, I forget that you look like something off an advert, and then you walk in here and I think Tom Ford has invaded my kitchen. How come when I wear a suit, I look like I've borrowed if off a grown-up to go to a funeral and you look like David Beckham in his prime? The life lottery is shit, you know that?'

'Yeah, but you got a sparkling personality,' Rory teased him, pulling out a variation of the discussion they'd been having since they met in high school.

'I'd rather have that jaw,' Albie fired back. 'Anyway, want a pep talk before you go? Some kind of emotional support? Maybe a hug?'

'Nope, that would crush my shirt. Right, mate, I'm off. I'll phone you when it's done. Hopefully to tell you that I'll be vacating your spare room tonight.'

Even saying it made his skin prickle. Was that where today was going to go? When Julia had texted him and said she thought it was time they talked, he'd been relieved and hopeful, but now he wasn't so sure. It was complicated. There was a huge part of him that wanted to fix this, but he'd be lying if he denied there was a voice in his head that occasionally whispered his disappointment that she hadn't stood by him in the first place. He wasn't his father.

He'd had nothing to do with the scandal. In fact, he'd been forced to walk away from his own family to protect her. Why wasn't that enough for her?

He shook that thought off as he stepped out into the warm May morning, and decided to walk, leaving his company Audi parked outside the building. The hotel they were meeting in, The St Kentigern, was a twenty-minute stroll away, but with the one-way system in Glasgow, and the morning rush hour, he wouldn't be much off that if he drove from Albie's flat on Miller Street, in Glasgow's Merchant City area.

He'd already let his office know that he was taking the morning off, so there was no rush to get this over with either. His secretary, Mandy, had raised an eyebrow when he'd told her what he was doing. She'd worked with him since he'd started there as a junior accountant and she was a part-time receptionist, and they'd risen through the company together. She'd been the first person who'd noticed that the boss's daughter was dropping by more often than normal and making a point of stopping by his desk to chat. And she'd been the first person to warn him that marrying said boss's daughter could either be a career-boosting or a career-wrecking move. Thankfully, their marital problems had been kept out of the office and Roger, Julia's father, had not so much as mentioned it at work. Inside the company offices it was strictly business and Rory respected that, grateful that there had been no awkwardness or blurring of professional lines. The last thing he needed was to be talking about his personal life between analysing the accounts of major corporations on the hunt for evidence of a serious fraud or embezzlement.

He wasn't sure he believed in all that manifestation stuff, but he did his best to picture the rest of the day. Hopefully, by the end of the morning, he'd be in the office as normal, after resolving everything with Julia, and he'd be moving back into their house tonight, and celebrating their reunion.

The streets were busy, and the temperature was higher than usual for this time of year, so he slipped his jacket off and slung it over his shoulder, then pulled his tie down a little and opened his top button. As he'd done every day for the last year, he thought about calling his mum to see how she was doing, to tell her how much he missed her, to talk about what they could do to fix their situation, but again, as he did every day, he put the thought out of his mind. She'd made her decision to sever all ties perfectly clear and he wasn't going to cause her more grief by challenging it. Not today. One problem at a time.

He'd planned this conversation with Julia out in his head many times over the last twelve weeks. There had been many texts and a few phone calls, but in all of them, Julia had just kept repeating that she needed time. Space. That they'd talk things through properly when she felt ready. Now that time was here, his mind blanked and his preparations for this moment were suddenly gone. He would just have to listen to what she had to say and then wing it.

A tall doorman, about the same height as Rory's six foot four, held the door open for him as he jogged up the steps to the hotel entrance. This had always been their favourite place for lunch on the weekends and drinks after work, so he felt like it was a good omen that she'd asked to meet him here.

'Thank you,' he nodded to the doorman, before turning left in the foyer and heading into the hotel restaurant, his footsteps dull thuds on the black and white marble floors. He scanned the stunning Art Deco room, with its ceiling-height windows and stone walls, and the corners of his mouth turned up when he saw her.

His wife was undeniably beautiful. Her rich, deep red hair was pulled up in a ponytail today, and she was wearing a simple black

T-shirt, with gold jewellery and barely any make-up. He hated to say it, but separation looked good on her. Hopefully she disagreed.

She was staring at something on her phone, so she didn't see him until he was almost at the table.

'Hey,' he said, instinctively leaning down and kissing her lightly on the lips.

'Hi.' She didn't look particularly uncomfortable. Another good sign. But then, Julia Fieldow – she'd dropped her married name off the end of her title as soon as the scandal had broken – had that easy confidence of someone who came from money and who knew exactly where she was going in life. She always had. It was one of the things that had attracted him to her in the first place. That, and her undeniably gorgeous face, her fierce intelligence, her quirky sense of humour and her absolute determination to make the most of every day and have a wonderful life.

The waiter interrupted them and Rory ordered a coffee, to match the one that was already sitting in front of his wife.

'It's good to see you,' he said truthfully. *Okay, ease into this. Take it slow. It's been a while.* 'You look great.'

'Thanks. You too.' Her eyes were the kind of blue that made Caribbean shorelines glisten.

'How have you been?' From him. Small talk. They had to start somewhere.

'I've been...' She stopped, their eyes locked, and he instantly felt that recognition, the connection they'd always had, that invisible pull of attraction. He was sure she must feel it too, and that meant they were going to be okay. Didn't it?

His hopes lasted no longer than a spilt second.

'I'm sorry, Rory, I can't do the small talk. I want a divorce.'

5

VAL

I'd been pacing back and forth on the white granite floor of Carly's huge open-plan kitchen since we'd arrived at her house an hour ago. On the car ride back from Heathrow, I emptied that damn bag ten times, then put everything back in and I even had Carly stop at Heston services on the M4, so I could rake through both my cases, even though I knew, with absolute certainty, that I'd put the rings in the pouch and then put the pouch in my handbag. And, oh dear God, I'd felt sick to my stomach. Tearful. Panicked. And I could barely think straight because all I could hear was thunder inside my head.

Sitting at the breakfast bar, Carly lifted her gaze from the laptop in front of her. 'Okay, so the Glasgow Airport Lost and Found is on a website and I've checked it, but there's nothing there for today yet. According to the British Airways website, if anything is found on a plane, it gets handed in to the arrival airport. I've checked the Heathrow Lost and Found website, but there's no mention of anything there either. I'll keep checking though.'

'Can't I just call someone? Explain to them? Tell them how important these are?' I pleaded. This bloody online world was a nightmare. I missed the days when I could just phone and explain a problem to a human. Now it was all bloody AI and chatbots and I didn't even know or care what those actually were.

Carly shook her head, two little lines of anxiety between her brows. 'I've tried, but there are no contact numbers. It's all done online.'

'Oh, for fuck's sake,' I blurted.

Carly nearly choked on her coffee, then dabbed at a couple of drops of spluttered Nespresso on the white marble of the counter-top. 'Sorry. I don't think I've ever heard you swear before. That used to be Josie's superpower.'

I bit my bottom lip, trying to make it stop quivering at the mention of my dear pal's name. What would Josie say if she were here now to see me being so bloody careless and losing the one physical thing I had to remember her by?

Josie's daughter, Avril, had given the ring to me on the day of her funeral. 'Mum would have wanted you to have this. I mean, she actually wouldn't, because that would mean she was dead, but it's this or her Billy Idol record collection.' Avril had managed the same smile as her mother, but hers was tinged with heartbreak. 'I'm going to go out on a limb and say take the jewellery.'

I'd cried and hugged her and we'd hummed Mr Idol's 'White Wedding' as we poured wine for the other mourners. Josie would have approved. I just hoped she wasn't looking down on me right now, because she would definitely not approve of this.

'I'm sorry, I'm just so bloody mad at myself. How could I have been so stupid? There's a wee zipped compartment in the back of my bag and I always put anything valuable in there and zip it straight away, yet this morning I didn't. I have no explanation. None. Other than I was tired, and stressed, and so bloody wrapped up in my own head that I wasn't concentrating.' I choked on a sob and gulped it back down. 'I mean... you know I'm not materialistic.

I couldn't give a toss about anything like that. But, but...' I couldn't go on. My brain wouldn't let me put into words that it wasn't about the metal and the stones. It was about the people they represented. It was about folding my fingers around something that the people I'd lost had touched, that they'd held, that still had the imprint of their existence on it. And now I'd as good as tossed them away. How could I ever forgive myself for that?

The back door opened, and I felt a rush of warm air as our Carol swept in, dropped her bag at the door and rushed at me, folding me into a bear hug. Although both these women lived in London now, they were Weirbridge born and bred and had never lost touch with their roots. It was one of the many reasons I adored them both. Technically, Carol was my niece-in-law by virtue of her marriage to Carly's brother, Callum, but I'd known this lass since she was Carly's best friend in primary school, so we were every bit as close. Back in the day, Carly had been thrilled when one of her closest pals had got hitched to her brother. We all had. They'd been joined at the hip ever since, and now Carly and her husband, Sam, had bought a house next door to Callum and Carol, so they were all practically cohabitating. It was far less confusing than it sounded. The gist of it was, blood related or not, this lot and a few of Carly and Carol's other lifelong friends were one big family and I auntie'd them all. They'd had their fair share of heartbreak, but they'd also built smashing lives for themselves and raised lovely families. Despite all their success, though, and even though they were now circling fifty, they were both the very same girls who were climbing out of bedroom windows to go to parties when they were teenagers. No airs and graces. No trying to pretend they were something else.

'I got Carly's text about your rings, and I'm gutted for you, Aunt Val. What can I do to help?' Carol asked, and I could see the concern on her perfect face as she released me.

I shook my head. 'I honestly don't know. Nothing. I've phoned Amir next door and asked him to check the path and the walkway down to where the taxi was parked, but he's not phoned back yet.' Amir and his wife, Nish, had moved in a few years ago, when our lovely neighbour, Chrissie, had got married and gone to live with her new husband. Chrissie still popped over most weeks for a cup of tea, so we hadn't lost touch, and Amir and Nish had become firm friends too.

'And I've called the taxi company, but they said they can't contact the driver right now,' Carly added.

The ring of my mobile interrupted us and I snatched it up. 'Hang on, that's Amir. Hello?'

At first, I fell quiet as I listened, but I was sure that the tremble of my chin and the crack in my voice gave away the news when I finally spoke.

'Okay, thanks Amir. I appreciate you doing that, love. No, I'm not sure when I'll be back. I'll knock on the door when I get home and let you know I'm there. And thank you again.'

In reality, I knew it would have been near miraculous for them to have been sitting on the front step just waiting for Amir to come and scoop them up. That would have been too easy, but even so it was crushing to hear him say they weren't there.

A sob escaped my throat as I hung up. Somewhere in my body, I felt a twinge of pain, and I realised my feet were killing me. These mules weren't made for an hour of pacing on a solid stone floor. After pulling out one of the stools at the kitchen island, I sat down, elbows on the marble, my head in my hands.

'This is my fault,' Carly groaned, making me raise my head again. 'If I hadn't talked you in to coming down here, this wouldn't have happened. I know you just wanted to stay home, but we thought the change of scene and the company would help. We just wanted to take care of you for a change, since it's always the other way around.'

Shaking my head, I reached over, put my hand on Carly's. 'I know that, and I appreciate it, my love. This is no one's fault but mine. And maybe on another day, at another time, I would be handling this better but...' My words trailed off as I realised that if I kept on speaking, I was going to dissolve into a tsunami of tears and that wouldn't help anyone.

This wasn't just about the rings. It was about Dee. It was about Josie. It was about Don. It was fifty years of living one way and having absolutely no idea how I was going to go on in a solitary existence without waking up next to the man who'd been my whole heart. Our bed was empty, our house was empty, my entire bloody world felt empty without him. Even in the last few years, as Don had descended further into the grips of Alzheimer's, there were still glimpses of him in there. It had been hard, and it had made my soul ache, but even on his worst day, I would wait until he was asleep in bed, then wrap my arms around him and just for a minute or an hour or a night, I could pretend that he was fine, that he was still the gorgeous, kind, stoic, funny big man he'd always been. That was all I had, but I was grateful to take it, because at least he was there. Now there was no pretence. He was gone. And so was the ring he'd worn every day of our married life.

Arms wrapped around me from behind and I knew it was Carol. 'I feel so helpless. There must be something we can do.'

I was about to say 'nothing' again because I was at a loss and I hated, more than anything, to make a fuss or a demand. It wasn't in my nature, unless it was on behalf of someone I loved, and then I'd fight to the death for them. Something stopped me replying though, because I had an overwhelming feeling that I had to do something about this. I had to take some kind of action. I couldn't stay here and hope they turned up somewhere. I'd just be torturing myself. At least if I went back home, I could search the airport, I could pitch up at the taxi company, I could retrace my steps, I could do something, anything, instead of sitting here, feeling useless, just waiting and praying that I'd get a call with good news.

'I'm really sorry, lassies, and it breaks my heart to say this, but I think I need to go look for myself. I love you both more than words, and I'll come back down when things are better, I promise. But all I want right now is to get back to the airport and go home.'

As soon as it was out, I felt equal amounts of relief and anxiety. I hated to hurt their feelings, but at least I had a plan to actually do something, to take action. Waiting for the world to decide my fate had never been my way.

There was silence for a few seconds, and I saw Carly's gaze go to Carol, and some telepathic conversation taking place. They'd always been able to do that. It had got them out of so much trouble as teenagers, when they'd both been able to come up with the same excuses at the same time.

'I'm coming with you,' Carly blurted, before Carol immediately piped in with, 'And so am I.'

'Absolutely not,' I argued, touched, but adamant that I couldn't let them do that. 'I appreciate the gesture, but I'm not taking you away from your lives and your families here and putting everyone out. Not happening.'

'Only, it is,' Carly argued, with kind but calm certainty. 'We both cleared our schedules this week to be with you, so you're not getting in the way of anything. Kate was only sorry she wasn't here to see you too, but she's in New York on a work trip with Bruce this week.'

Kate was another one of their gang of five lifelong pals from their time at Weirbridge High School. One of them, Jess, now lived in Los Angeles, Sarah had tragically passed away in New York a few years back. Kate, Carly and Carol had all moved to London in their twenties and had made their lives here.

'And as for our families,' Carly went on, 'Sam is on location in some far-flung place I can't even spell...' Carly's husband was a big-time movie producer that she'd dated decades ago when they had nothing, and then they'd got together again and married a few years ago after her divorce.

'And Callum,' Carol added, 'would expect nothing less of us because you're his aunt and his favourite person on earth.'

That statement was almost the undoing of me, but my natural resistance to putting people out on my behalf continued the argument.

'But the kids...'

'The kids are grown adults who are all busy living their own lives,' Carol argued. 'Charlotte and Toni are so tied up with work and friends that I'm lucky if they stop by once a week, and I know that's how it should be, but it still stings. Carly and I are now the mother and aunt who try to guilt them in to coming over for Sunday lunch and invent ailments in the hope that they'll feel sorry for us and drop by.'

'She's had imaginary athlete's foot twice this year,' Carly piped up.

'See! We have no shame.' Carol said, point proven.

Charlotte and Toni were Carol's twenty-four-year-old daughters. Or were they still twenty-three? I lost track of all the young ones' ages these days. Either way, they were smashing young women. Charlotte was training to be a lawyer and Toni worked as a mental health counsellor for youngsters, and if I was a betting woman, I'd put my last pair of mules on them running the country one day. And doing it better than any of those jumped up, chinless career politicians.

'We are completely pathetic,' Carly concurred. 'As for my two,

Mac is away with Sam because he's decided he wants to be the next Brad Pitt and was looking for industry experience. Sam has him making tea and running errands for divas.'

'Just like home,' Carol piped in.

Carly ignored her. 'And Benny has no leave for the next month, so I wasn't expecting him anyway.' Benny was Carly's youngest, who'd joined the Air Force when he left school at seventeen and oh, my heart still swelled every time I saw him in his uniform. 'Have you not listened to our podcast, Aunt Val? Honestly, this empty-nest struggle is real, so you'll be doing the two of us a favour by taking us with you.'

Carol and Carly had a podcast called *Twisted Knickers* where the two of them and their girlfriends discussed anything that was troubling them. Not sure how that was an actual job. I'd been doing that at my kitchen table with my pals for decades. Those Loose Women wouldn't have been able to get a word past our Josie when she was alive. Now, Nancy and Tress were regular visitors to my kitchen and my biscuit tin and there was nothing we didn't talk about.

'Of course I've listened. That one when you talked about Benny leaving home had me and your Uncle Don in floods.' I had to clear my throat to get rid of the lump of grief that was suddenly stuck there, before going on, 'Brought back so many memories. I used to make up all sorts of excuses to drop in on Dee when she flew the nest.'

'Bit more difficult when they're on an air base hundreds of miles away. And, you know, the whole armed guard and barbed wire thing makes it difficult to do any parental stalking.'

I could hear the sadness under the joke and my heart went out to her. I remember what it was like when our Michael and Dee left home. I didn't know what to do with myself. Why does no one prepare us for that? One minute, you're indispensable to their very existence, and the next you're hoping they'll remember your address because you haven't seen them for a week and a half.

Still, much as I appreciated the arguments these two gems were putting up, they had other things going on in their lives that they shouldn't just drop for me.

One final objection. 'But what about your jobs?'

I'd never entirely got to grips with all the different elements of these lassies' careers. There was the podcast thingy, and Carly was an author too. She'd written a couple of novels, but a few years ago she'd switched to ghost-writing celebrity biographies. Carol's job still boggled my mind. In her twenties, she'd travelled all over the world modelling for brands I couldn't spell, no less afford, but now she was one of those folks that had millions of followers on social media websites, and companies gave her huge cheques to plug their products. Huge. You could buy a car with what she earned for one of those adverts. I'd offered to subcontract for Tunnocks and Tetley, but she hadn't taken me up on it yet.

'We can work from anywhere,' Carly countered. 'I just finished the final edits on my next book and I'll bring up the stuff we need for the podcast...'

'And I can create content and livestream from anywhere,' Carol added.

No clue what any of that meant, but I got the big picture. They wanted to come and it wasn't going to inconvenience them. Yet again, I wanted to cry, but this time it was fuelled by gratitude.

'Are you sure?'

'We're sure. Give me two minutes...'

Carol still had her arms around me, as if she was holding me together, while we both watched Carly's fingers fly across the keyboard of her laptop, then switch to her phone and click up a storm.

'Right, done. Three seats on a flight from Heathrow that leaves in two hours, and the Uber will be here in fifteen minutes. If he channels Vin Diesel, he'll get us there in time. Carol, go pack a bag, and I'll do the same. Just hand luggage. We can pick up anything else we need when we're up there.'

'I love it when she bosses me,' Carol quipped, before disappearing out through the back door.

Carly snapped the laptop shut, then nipped round to my side of the island. 'Don't worry, Aunt Val, we're going to find your rings. Uncle Don will find a way to get them back to you. I can feel it.'

I had never hoped more that she was right.

6

SOPHIE

Sophie had only a vague understanding of what had just happened to her. She remembered waking up with a searing pain in her head and her shoulder. And there was noise. So much noise. Beeping horns and shouting. She must have blacked out again, because the next thing she heard was sirens and banging doors and someone thudding on her window, yelling, 'Hello? Can you put the window down? Can you open the door?' More blackness, just for a second, then again, 'The window! Can you put it down? Sarge, she's out of it. We're going to have to break the window and cut her seat belt off.'

That got her attention. Break what window? Her eyes finally managed to focus. She was still in the back seat of the taxi. Okay. That was where she was meant to be. But something was off. The flashing lights. And all the noises had changed now. They were on the motorway, so shouldn't there be the sound of other cars? And wait, how could there be someone banging on the window? This didn't make sense at all.

Focus, Sophie. Try really hard to focus.

Her eyes went to the front now. She was sitting behind the

passenger seat, but she could see that the driver was still there. Something didn't make sense. He wasn't driving any more. He was slumped to the side, his head dangling over the seat in front of her, and he was completely still. Okay, things were clicking. Memories. She'd come to Glasgow to find Ash, and she'd got into a taxi at the airport. They'd been driving and then something had happened and... A bang. A crash. They'd been in a crash. Yep, that was it. Urgh, thinking was making her head hurt.

Neck aching, she managed to turn her face to the side, and she saw a police officer there. He must have been the person who was banging on the window and shouting. There was pain when she turned her head, but she could move her eyes, and when they flicked to the left, she saw that there was another one, two, three police officers behind him. And a police car that seemed to be facing the same direction as the taxi, cutting right across the road. It must be blocking the motorway, because no cars were passing them.

Deep in her mind, she heard her mum's voice. *Come on, Sophie, stay awake. Make this make sense.*

She groaned, as she continued to try to put the pieces together. They'd been in an accident. They were still on the motorway. The police were here. They'd stopped the traffic. A siren was coming from an ambulance that she could see now was approaching them. And the police officer had, from somewhere, produced a metal thing and was staring at the front passenger window as if he was trying to work out the best way to smash through it.

She registered another sound. The car engine. It was still running. She suddenly felt a desperate need to get out of there, but she couldn't work out how. Rewind. The police officer had asked her to put the window down. Surely there was no way the window would work if they'd been in an accident, but... She sent desperate signals from her brain to her hand. Move. Press the button. Try to make it happen.

The police officer hadn't even noticed that she was staring at him again now so she couldn't get his attention.

Her mum's voice again. *Come on, Sophie. Press the button. Make it work.*

Finally, her hand moved, her shoulder ached, her elbow hurt, but her fingers made contact with the button and somehow, by some freaking miracle, the window started to roll down.

Immediately, the cop flinched, then came right up to the window. 'You managed it. Well done. Didn't think you'd heard me. What's your name?'

He was using the same tone she'd heard a million times in episodes of *Casualty*. Calm. Caring. Reassuring. But urgent at the same time.

'S... Sophie.'

'Sophie, I'm Dan. You've been in an accident, but we're going to help, so don't worry. We need to get you out of there first. Can you roll the window down further?'

It was so strange. This was the middle of the day. In the middle of a road. And there were emergency vehicles. A siren blaring. People shouting to each other too. But all she could hear and process was the police officer's voice.

She did as he asked, and the window went down more than halfway. She felt him try to open her door again, but the handle wouldn't do its job. Must still be locked.

'That's great, Sophie. I'm going to reach in and unlock the door, okay?'

She nodded, and ouch, that made her head hurt again. An internal monologue kicked off in her head, desperate to keep a lid on the terror that kept bubbling up in her chest. *I'm okay. I can breathe. I can think. I can move. I'm okay. I can breathe. I can think. I can move. I'm okay.*

His hand came through the window and then snaked around to the front passenger door. He grunted as, blindly, he stretched and felt for the handle. After a few seconds, he found it, pulled at a lever, the central locking system of the car made a noise, the passenger door pinged open – and then all hell broke loose.

Dan opened her door, just a tiny bit, then pushed his hand in to hold her shoulder steady while he opened it the rest of the way. The next thing, a collar was being put around her neck by a paramedic, who was talking to her and asking questions while checking her over, shining a light in her eyes, taking her pulse, doing other tests that she was vaguely aware of.

Before long, a stretcher was beside the car and she was being lifted on to it. Just as she reached it, something fell, and she saw the police officer, reach down and pick up a mobile phone.

'It's mine,' she whispered gratefully. If that hadn't happened, she'd have forgotten all about it and how would she have been able to contact anyone?

He slipped it into the cross-body bag that she was still wearing.

'And the backpack is yours?' he asked her.

'Yes,' she croaked.

'No worries. I'll bring it up to the hospital. We're taking you to Glasgow Central, so when we get this cleared up, we'll follow you. I'll need to check on you and ask you a couple of questions, is that okay?'

Despite the collar, she managed to nod.

The whole time, as the medics dealt with her, she could see another crew working on the driver. A team of police and paramedics took him out of the car through the passenger side and laid him on the tarmac. There were raised voices, shouts, and they were using one of those machines that restart a heart – she couldn't think of the name of it right now. Her head still hurt too much. Someone kept shouting 'clear' and then barking orders. There was more shouting, before he was lifted onto another stretcher and then they were running with him to the second ambulance. He was lifted in, more shouting, doors slammed shut, another bang, and then that ambulance was away, just as she was being lifted into hers.

Still trying to put everything together, she scanned the road and the bashed up taxi she'd just left. Had they crashed into another vehicle? She searched for any other damaged cars, but there were none. No, she could see now that they'd hit the barrier in the central reservation. That must have been what caused the bang. The back of the car behind the driver's seat seemed to have caught the worst of the impact and was crushed like a discarded Cola can. Thank God she hadn't been sitting on that side or... She shuddered, stopping the thought.

As soon as she was in the ambulance, her brain began sending out signals to the rest of her body, checking it out. Okay, she could move her fingers, her arms, her toes, her legs. She clenched all the muscles in her thighs, her pelvis, her torso, and everything felt fine until she got to her shoulder and the side of her head, which were sending back internal howls of pain. Apart from that, everything else seemed to be working though. She could see, hear, speak and think – all of which calmed the tremble of fear that she'd had since she came to in the wreck. It was fine. She was good. Everything was going to be okay. Like the internal monologue from earlier, she just kept repeating that, over and over, until she felt the ambulance stop.

Sophie had no idea how long it took to get to the hospital, but it seemed like no time at all before they were lifting her out of the ambulance and wheeling her into the building. Despite the pain in her head, her brain had cleared enough for her to feel relieved and a bit emotional. She wanted Ash, she wanted her sister, she wanted her dad, she definitely wanted her mum, but she was also aware that right now she couldn't have any of them, so the best thing to do was to stay calm and keep the voice of reassurance in her head going. *Don't be scared. You're fine. You're good. Everything is going to be okay.*

'Hello there,' a nurse, maybe in her fifties or sixties, and clutching an iPad, came through the curtain to the cubicle she'd been wheeled into. 'I'm Brenda. Sounds like you've had quite a morning.'

'It's definitely not how I thought it was going to be,' Sophie croaked, trying to smile as wide as the new pain in the side of her jaw would allow.

'Well, if it's any consolation, we're going to take really good care of you. In case no one has told you, you're in Glasgow Central Hospital. Can you remember how you got here?'

'Ambulance. I was in a taxi that crashed. The police got me out of the car and then I was brought here.'

Nurse Brenda seemed happy with that answer. 'Well done. And how are you feeling now?'

'Like I've been spun around in a tumble drier.' That made Brenda chuckle as she clipped an oxygen monitor on to Sophie's finger. 'But apart from that, I'm okay. Everything still feels like it's working.'

'That's what we like to hear. Right, deep breath...'

She was sounding Sophie's chest now and then she ran through a whole load of other tests.

Sophie had only been in hospital twice in her life that she could remember. The first time was when she was about five, and Erin accidentally hit her on the head with a shovel when they were helping their dad clear snow from their driveway, and the second time was when she broke her nose playing hockey.

Of course, she'd been there plenty of times when Mum was sick too. She and Erin would take turns going to the chemo sessions, and they'd do everything they could to keep Mum amused and make the time go quicker.

'All right there?' Nurse Brenda asked, as if she somehow knew that Sophie was letting her mind go back to a dark place.

Sophie pulled back from the memories, whispering, 'I'm fine. Thank you.'

Brenda picked up the iPad again. 'Okay, now that I know you're in no imminent danger, let me get some details. Your full name?'

'Sophie Smith.'

'Date of birth?'

'The twenty-ninth of March, 1997.'

Brenda paused, grinned. 'Oh my goodness, that's the same day as my youngest daughter, although she's two years older.'

Sophie had absolutely no idea why that made her feel a little better, but it did.

Brenda carried on with more questions.

When Sophie gave her address, the nurse paused. 'Are you just here visiting? Do you have friends or family in the area?'

Sophie winced as she instinctively shook her head. 'No, I'm just on...' She paused. How to explain it? I've come all this way to track down my ex-boyfriend to see if he's still in love with me, because, two years ago, he asked me to marry him and I said no, then left and didn't come back. That just about covered it. Instead, though, she went with: 'I'm on a weekend break. Just being a tourist.'

'Oh, you poor thing,' Brenda seemed genuinely sympathetic. 'Not the best start. Is there anyone from home that you'd like us to contact for you?'

Sophie immediately said no. The last thing she needed was her dad and sister charging all the way up here. The shock and fear would kill her dad and he'd been through enough.

The nurse moved on, taking more details, and then resuming her physical examination, asking a load more questions about the bump to her head. 'So you lost consciousness?' 'Do you know how long for?' 'Any problems with your vision now?' 'Light-headed?' 'Pain?'

And on the questions went until Sophie decided that Nurse Brenda now knew her better than some of her own family.

'Right, that's us for now,' the nurse eventually said. 'I'll have a word with the doctor, and she'll come in to see you and I think we'll probably do a head and shoulder X-ray just to rule out any damage. Since you lost consciousness, even though it wasn't for long, we'll probably keep you in overnight for observation, especially if you don't have anyone up here that you can stay with and that can keep an eye on you.'

Sophie's first thought was that she really wished she hadn't paid upfront for the hotel. Her second was that staying here overnight was going to lose a whole day of trying to track down Ash, but she wasn't exactly in a position to argue.

Brenda pinged off her blue Latex gloves and dropped them in a tall white bin with a foot pedal. 'Right then, Sophie, you sit tight and I'll be back shortly.'

'Brenda, just one more thing...'

The nurse stopped to let her go on. 'Can I ask how the taxi driver is doing?' A memory was niggling at her. Someone shouting 'clear'.

Sophie saw a visible change in the nurse's expression. 'Erm, I'm not sure. I know they were working on him when he came in. I'll check for you and let you know. You just rest up and try not to worry about a thing. You're going to be fine.'

There was something in her tone that told Sophie that the same didn't go for the angry man who'd been driving the taxi.

7

ALICE

The driver that had been sent to collect Alice and take her to the hospital could barely make eye contact with her. Wasn't a surprise, really. Either he didn't know what to say because he wasn't great in difficult situations like this, or he'd met Larry and hated him just as much as most people did these days. In fact, as far as she could surmise, and only based on their earlier conversation, her husband's fan club only had one member and that was Sandra in the taxi office.

Alice remembered being shocked when Larry had got his taxi licence and gone to work on the roads, but the bottom line was that he needed to earn money. He was pretty much unemployable. He'd been stripped of his pension and his earnings. His legal bills had taken every penny of profit from the sale of their house and left them with crippling debts. They were flat broke. Alice had managed to find the two cleaning jobs, but Larry had nothing, except a favour he could call in from the owner of the taxi company he had pulled strings for when he could still get permits granted and contracts awarded.

In some ways, the job made sense. All charges against him had been dropped, so he had no criminal record, something that would have disqualified him from many positions, including driving taxis. It was an occupation where he didn't have a direct boss, so he didn't have to break a habit of a lifetime and bow down to authority. He didn't have to spend all day with judgemental co-workers because he operated alone. And physically he'd changed so much over the last two years, gained more than fifty pounds, grown his hair, stopped shaving, that most people didn't recognise him, so he wasn't faced with customers dragging up his past.

If the driver was expecting her to be in floods of tears and falling apart though, then he should be reassured that she was holding it together, sitting in the back seat, still in her favourite lilac dress and pale pink cardigan, just watching the world pass by as they made their way towards the city centre, then veered off to Glasgow Central Hospital.

She knew this hospital well. It was where both her parents had passed away. It was where her son had been born. And, once upon a time, when her husband was one of the most recognisable politicians in the country, she'd been the head of the fundraising committee, a voluntary team that worked on supplementing the hospital's budgets.

Bygone days.

The lunchtime traffic was relatively light, so they made it there in less than twenty minutes. At the hospital doors, she offered to pay, but the driver, ten out of ten for decorum and manners, told her that there was no charge, then mumbled something about telling Larry that everyone at the company was rooting for him and wishing him a swift recovery. Alice politely thanked him and went on her way.

At the Emergency Department reception, she explained that she was here to see her husband, who had apparently been brought in after a car crash this morning. When she gave her name, and the name of her husband, the receptionist's eyes widened. Obviously someone who watched the news.

Alice didn't flinch, but she recognised the irony. In her previous life as the wife of an esteemed politician, she'd have been treated like a VIP here. Now she was a cleaner from a less than salubrious area of a run-of-the-mill town, and she was far prouder of the person she was now than the person she'd been back then. She refused to let anyone else's energy, judgements or opinions pierce her shell. When you'd been through as much as she had, when you'd reached the lowest point it was possible to go, when you'd been dragged into someone else's disgrace and publicly shamed day after day, none of this stuff mattered.

'I'll just call through and let the team know you're here, Mrs McLenn.'

She took a seat in the waiting room, next to maybe ten people waiting to be seen. A few of their ailments were visible, but most were not, although they all shared similar fed-up, anxious or irritated expressions. In previous days, Alice might have started a conversation, or made eye contact and smiled to make a connection or give some comfort, but not now. She just stared straight ahead until the double doors to her left opened and a tall man in a white coat who she recognised straight away, strode towards her.

'Mrs McLenn? Alice?' He held his hand out towards her, and the gesture was so unexpected that for the first time she felt a chink of emotion dent her armour.

'Hello, Richard.'

Doctor Richard Campbell was the former head of the Emergency Department, back when it was called Accident & Emergency and Alice had helped to raise funds for a children's playroom where little ones could be kept amused while waiting for treatment or consultations for themselves or their family members. It was one of the most rewarding projects she'd been involved in and on the day they'd opened it, Richard had insisted that she cut the ribbon. Alice had enlisted the help of two little boys who were there with their gran, waiting while their mother's head injury was stitched. After the ceremony, Alice had taken the family to the canteen to make sure they ate, then checked on the mum before she left and watched the woman's relief that her children were fine. That was all most mothers really wanted, wasn't it? No matter the age of their children, they just wanted them to be fine. Alice could relate to that all day long.

'Sorry to be meeting again under such awful circumstances,' Richard said. 'Please, come into my office.'

He walked quickly, and Alice kept pace with him, through the double doors, along the main corridor of the department, with cubicles on either side, which Alice was fairly sure would be full. They always were. This was one of the busiest EDs in the city, although it seemed relatively calm today.

He stopped at a white door, with a sign on it that she didn't catch, before he opened it and let her go in first. 'This isn't actually my office. I'm up in the ICU now, but I'm down here covering because the ED chief, Cheska Ayton, has gone to America, and we haven't appointed her replacement yet. Please take a seat.'

'Thank you.'

Alice did as he suggested, then waited for him to speak.

Instead of going behind his desk, he pulled a chair over and sat next to her. 'Okay, let me tell you where we are. Larry was brought in earlier after a road traffic accident on the M8. I believe he drives a taxi now?'

Alice nodded. 'A red Skoda.' She had no idea why she'd felt the need to give that information, but if Richard Campbell was surprised, he didn't show it.

He went on, 'When the paramedics reached the scene, he was unresponsive, and they immediately realised he was in cardiac arrest. The police tell us that an eyewitness in another vehicle saw his head fall forward right before his car went out of control. The paramedics resuscitated him at the scene, but he arrested again on the way here. Thankfully, they were able to resuscitate him a second time. They got him here and they took him straight into surgery. I just called up when reception said you were here, but the team are still working on him. That's as much as I know for now. You're very welcome to wait here, or I can show you to the family room. Here might be a bit more private.'

She appreciated the gesture, and she knew that he meant well. What he was really doing was protecting her from the negative reaction that her name, her husband and her past could evoke, but she didn't want to be an imposition or get special treatment.

'The family room will be fine. In fact, is the prayer room open?'

The renovation of the prayer room had been another of her projects when she was on the fundraising committee. It was a non-denominational room of peace, somewhere that people of all religions could go to connect with whatever god they worshipped. Alice wasn't religious, but she found solace in the peace of a church, a temple, a chapel – anywhere that allowed her to sit in quiet reflection.

'It is. I can show you there and I'll keep you posted just as soon as I know more.'

She nodded gratefully, and wondered if he thought it strange that she wasn't crying, anxious, devastated or begging for reassurance. She couldn't do any of those things – again, not a good enough actress. Hopefully, if he thought her reaction was strange, he'd put it down to shock, or frozen terror. It was neither. She'd trained herself to be numb for so long that she didn't know how to be any other way. And even if she did, none of those reactions would be the ones that came naturally to her. Not where her husband was concerned.

They left the office, and if people in the department – patients or staff – nudged each other or raised an eyebrow because they recognised her as she walked beside him, she didn't see them. Living her life with blinkers on, just staring straight ahead, with no peripheral vision had become her speciality.

The prayer room was empty when she got there. Richard left her at the door, with kind words. 'We very much appreciated everything you did for us here, Alice. I hope you know that.'

Again, his sincerity and his kindness dented her emotional shell, but didn't quite pierce a hole. The last two years had made it impenetrable.

She sat in the closest seat, at the end of the back row, and bowed her head in the calm silence, trying to sort out the tangle of thoughts and memories that were roaring in her brain.

That Alice McLenn, the one who had dedicated her life to public work, was a different person. Back then, the work had made her feel valued, given her purpose and the fulfilment that came from making a genuine difference to other people's lives. That satisfaction and her time with her son were the only bright spots in a life she hated, so she was grateful to be of use, even if it was only as a sidekick to her husband. She already despised him with every fibre of her being, and marriage to him was only bearable because he spent most of his time working in London. She'd thought about leaving him a thousand times, but he'd made it quite clear what he'd do if she tried. He treated her with general disdain, and his son with barely disguised disinterest, except in public, where he played the family man because it won him votes and popularity points. That happy image was crucial to his career and he wasn't going to let her wreck that. He'd threatened to ruin her if she left, to seek custody of their son, to make her life hell and she knew, without a single doubt, that he had the power and the malice to do it.

Alice had never had the courage to test that, because she'd feared he'd win. He was a different person then too. Important. Respected. Charismatic. Successful. He was also volatile, aggressive, dishonest and cruel, but the public didn't see that side of him. He reserved that for colleagues who'd fallen out of favour and for his enemies. That's who Larry McLenn was then. And he'd been that man of importance for over two decades before a covertly filmed video uncovered his true personality, agreeing to take a bribe while boasting that he would bury anyone who got in his way, because he was untouchable.

Turns out he was almost right. The charges hadn't stuck, because the treachery was exposed before he actually accepted the cash, but the disgrace had welded itself to them all.

He'd been fired almost immediately, and the story had run on TV, online and in newspapers for weeks. All the while, the public made two crucial assumptions. The first was that he'd done it before. They were right. A police investigation found unexplained bank transactions going back years. Only the skill and cunning of the highest paid lawyers in the city had managed to keep him out of jail by alleging entrapment, making claims of deep fake recordings and countering with a barrage of appeals over technicalities and errors in the case.

The second assumption was that Alice was either in on it, or at the very least, turned a blind eye. They were wrong on both counts. She'd had no idea. But in the court of public opinion she was guilty as charged.

That Alice, with the fine clothes and the fake life and the superficial friends, had lost everything and gained a whole pile of shame, embarrassment, humiliation and disgrace.

And now?

Now, she was a cleaner who was proud of the fact that she earned an honest wage for an honest day's work.

Now, she spent hours every day wearing a tiny splash of expensive body lotion and living a life of anonymous solitude, putting on nice clothes and eking out joy in the simplest of ways in the hours that she was alone.

Now, she had no contact with her son.

And she was still the wife of Larry McLenn, former MP, who'd disgraced his office, betrayed his family and burned their lives to the ground. They'd gone from a lavish home and a privileged, respected existence, to poverty, isolation and shame. And every single day since then, Larry had lived in rage and petulance, and Alice had lived in quiet determination that she would one day escape from him.

Now, she prayed to any god who would listen that that day had come.

8

RORY

Rory was still trying to process the words that had come out of Julia's mouth. 'I want a divorce.'

That was one way to cut right through the small talk. He actually felt like he'd been punched in the gut and was winded, so it took him a moment to find his words. The whole time, Julia stared at her coffee in front of her, not even giving him the grace of eye contact.

'You honestly mean that?' he asked eventually.

She nodded slowly. 'I do. I'm sorry, Rory.'

'Why now?' was all he could get out.

She shrugged and he could see her discomfort. 'I've been spending a lot of time in London with my sister over the last couple of months...'

Two things struck him about that. First of all, she didn't even particularly like her sister. She'd always said she was overly judgemental and prone to snobbery. And, secondly, he'd been squeezing his six-foot-four frame into the single bed in Albie's spare room for the last few weeks when he could have been stretched out in his own bed, in their Victorian duplex in Park Circus. He'd only stayed away from their home out of respect because she'd said she needed space. Also, if he were honest, because the townhouse had been Roger and Arabella Fieldow's wedding gift to them, so it had always felt more like her place than his.

He realised she was still talking. '...And I remembered what it was like to go out and not have people staring at me. Or, rather, at my husband. I hadn't processed how much I missed the freedom to just be me, and not worry that everything I said and did could end up in a newspaper or online, just because I was the daughter-in-law of a bent politician. Being away from this city made me remember what it felt like to be proud of who I am, to feel the way I did before everything changed...'

'Who you were never changed. Who I was never changed either,' he replied, not from a need to be confrontational, but more of an instinctive desire to reassure her.

'But the way people thought of me did. The way people thought of us.'

He wanted to tell her she was being ridiculous, but he knew she was right.

'Everyone just associates us with your dad now and we can't get away from that. As long as we're married, what your dad did is always going to haunt us. We'll always be linked with him. If we have kids, they'll be thought of as his grandchildren. He's always going to be everywhere, Rory.'

His father. His fucking father.

Years before, when Roger Fieldow had first hired him as a summer intern at Fieldow Financial, Rory had used only his mum's maiden name on the application, because he didn't want to land a job on the strength of his father's name or status. When the internship ended, Fieldow had been impressed enough with him to offer him a junior role on graduation, but even then, Fieldow had no idea that young Rory Brookes was the son of councillor

Larry McLenn. His mum and dad weren't married when he was born, and the smartest thing his mum had ever done was give Rory her surname, because, he had found out later, she had no faith in his father to actually keep his promise to marry her. Even after they made it to the registry office to tie the knot, Alice had never officially changed Rory's name to McLenn, although he'd been known as Rory Brookes McLenn throughout his childhood. It was her one act of rebellion, but it had been an important one that he'd been grateful for many times in his life, especially over the last two years.

When he'd gone to university, they'd automatically used the name on his birth certificate, Rory Brookes, and he hadn't corrected it. He'd had no desire to be connected to the controlling, narcissistic asshole, who was, quite frankly, a shit father but who had somehow convinced the world that he was a decent enough human being and politician to be considered qualified to be a Member of Parliament. On the day he was first elected, teenage Rory had got drunk with Albie, and contemplated emigrating. Years later, their relationship was still non-existent, but Rory didn't care, because by that time, he had his feet under a desk at Fieldow and was already falling in love with the gorgeous, accomplished, sexy daughter of the boss. The one who was now telling him she wanted a divorce. Given the temporary separation, it shouldn't have been a surprise, but yet it still was.

'Don't do this, Julia,' he said calmly. He wasn't going to fall apart, or beg or plead, because he knew that she'd hate that, but at the same time, he had to fight his corner. 'We were so good together.'

'We were,' she agreed. 'But that was when we were joining two well-respected Glasgow families, and the whole world still thought that your dad was a stand-up guy.'

There was no arguing with her point, because even their

wedding photos backed her up. The ceremony had been like a who's who of the city's politicians and important players. Their parents' guest lists had been longer than their own.

'I don't think you realise the shame that my parents felt when your dad was caught,' she went on, 'and I caused that pain for them because although you already worked here, it was me who brought you and your family into our world. It was my fault.'

Wow. Just wow. He couldn't believe that's where she was going with this. She knew how much he detested his dad, and she was well aware of the sacrifices his mum had made for them, but she was still acting like they were a package deal.

His father committed the crimes alone. Just him. They'd only been guilty by association.

Rory didn't even want to let his mind go back there. Two years ago, when his dad's downfall had come about in spectacular fashion, the embarrassment had been huge, but the press had pretty much left Rory and Julia out of it. For a second, they'd exhaled and dealt with the family fallout behind closed doors, but then the inevitable had happened. Months later, when the charges had been dropped against his dad due to his super-sharp lawyers twisting the legal system in his favour, the press had decided Larry would pay, if not with jail time, then at least with public annihilation. When the press had picked the bones of Larry McLenn clean, they'd come for his family, and that meant Rory and Julia. Reporters and photographers began staking out their home and his work. There were completely bogus reports inferring they benefited from Larry's corruption. Skewed articles painting them as free-loading socialites. Blind pieces dissecting their marriage.

Julia had struggled and Rory had been furious, but it was his mother who'd taken action. After a particularly brutal hatchet job in a national newspaper, she had asked to meet with them secretly that night. He and Julia had parked in a street near his parents'

new home and Alice had come to them. Just seeing her and everything she was going through had almost killed him. When she'd
climbed into their car that night, she was pale, lines etched deep in
her face. It had always been her and him against the world, and all
he wanted to do was protect her and to protect his wife too.

His mum had been strong and steady, while Julia was
distraught, her eyes bloodshot, mascara tracks down her beautiful
face.

'I can't deal with any more of this, Alice. I'm sorry. I can't. It's
relentless, and it's killing Rory, tearing my family apart. What are
we going to do?'

That's when his mum had dropped the bombshell, with a plan
that she'd clearly thought through.

'You're going to cut us off. They can't talk about you if there's
nothing to say. They can't report if there's no longer a story. I need
you to disown us, and go live your lives. But, Julia, I want you to
swear you'll stick by my son, that you'll make each other happy.'

Julia had agreed immediately, but Rory had fought his mother,
argued, objected. 'Come with us, Mum. You can live with us. Leave
him to deal with his own shit.'

His mum had cut that one dead. 'I can't. He's already threatened that if I leave him, he'll drag you into this even more, he'll
burn your whole world down, including Julia and her family.'

Rory rarely got angry, and he didn't have a violent bone in his
body, but right then he'd wanted to punch out a window with his
bare hands.

His mum had left no room for arguing. 'The irony is, he can't
even stand me, but he can't stand the thought of not being in
control of me even more. I can handle him. I'll be fine, just as long
as you do this for me. You'll understand when you have children,
Rory. You see, I can deal with this, I can take the abuse and the
shame and the disgrace, but watching them tear you apart is

killing me. If you love me, then you'll do it because I need you to. Please. Please walk away.'

It was an impossible decision and it had smashed his soul, but eventually he'd agreed. It had to be real, she'd insisted. No slip-ups. That was why all contact had ended. No secret meetings. No calls. No texts. Numbers changed, so neither side would be tempted.

The next day, a report had appeared in the paper, and he'd known his mum was the 'anonymous source' behind it. The headline read, SON DISOWNS DISGRACED FORMER MP. It detailed how Rory Brookes, and his wife, Julia, had quite rightly decided that his father, Larry McLenn's dishonesty and violation of trust was abhorrent to the values they stood for. They had terminated all contact and the situation was considered to be permanent.

After that, the attacks in the press had stopped, but they'd been wrong to think they could ever go back to normal. Everywhere they went, there were still stares and whispers and judgements. Even when it had overwhelmed Julia and she'd told him she needed time alone, he'd believed in them too much to contemplate their marriage being over.

Apparently, listening to her now, he'd been wrong about that.

'I don't want to keep saying sorry, because I need to stand in my truth...' She'd clearly had a pep talk from her sister, her therapist, or whoever made up those inspirational quotes on Instagram. 'But my feelings have changed. I can't separate how I feel about you from how I feel about what happened to our lives. It's made me look differently at you, and I know that's not your fault, but I can't change it.'

'I wish you could,' he told her gently, thinking even now that she was stabbing him in the chest, she was still beautiful, still his wife. Damn! But if there was one thing that was unmistakable here, it was that she no longer wanted to be with him.

He tried to let that sink in.

She no longer wanted to be with him.

It was over.

And it wasn't as if this was a rash decision on her part because she'd been thinking about it for months. Planning it maybe.

'Julia, don't do this...' he implored again, hoping there was some way, some tiny chance for them.

'It's already done,' she replied, with a finality that made it clear this wasn't up for negotiation. He considered trying anyway, fighting for her, pleading a case for not giving up, but this wasn't the place to do it. And that was the point. He saw now that she'd asked to meet him here so that he couldn't argue. It was one of her father's tricks for breaking bad news. Public place. Upmarket setting.

He took in the determined set of her exquisite face, and the unwavering gaze. This wasn't his fun-loving, rebellious, sexy wife. This was a different Julia, the Julia Fieldow who grew up getting her own way, who never backed down, who wouldn't be swayed from what she wanted. That Julia had always been part of her personality, but their love had softened her edges. Now they were back and razor sharp.

No, he wasn't going to argue, because he didn't have to be her therapist to understand that she wouldn't change her mind. Instead, for now, he decided to search for the off ramp.

'So where do you want to go from here?' he asked, determined to stay calm and dignified. He, or his family, had clearly embarrassed her enough.

It would seem that, like everything else, she had it all worked out. 'I want to sell the house. Or you can buy me out if you can get the money together, but that's doubtful on your salary.'

She wasn't kidding. He earned a decent package, but nowhere near the income he'd need to rustle up a mortgage on a home that cost almost three quarters of a million quid. That was Fieldow money. Brookes' money could probably extend to a nice two-bedroom executive flat in the city centre.

She took a sip of her drink, then went on, 'The prenup clearly stated that it was bought for us as a wedding present and would revert to me if we separated. Same with my bank accounts and pretty much everything else except the savings you had when we met and anything you've added to that since we married.'

They both knew he'd added nothing, because, all too aware that she was the wealthier of them, he'd put every penny he earned into their lives together to try to even up the balance.

'Good of you to leave me with that.' He hadn't negotiated hard on the terms of the prenup, because he hadn't thought for a heartbeat that they'd ever divorce.

'Don't make it difficult, Rory.' For the first time, he saw a flash of her judgemental sister and her ruthless father and wondered if she'd always been that way and he'd just fallen for a façade.

A silence fell between them, and he wasn't sure what else there was to say. If he stayed, there was the possibility that the conversation could degenerate into insults and blame, so he decided the best thing to do was to leave.

He took twenty quid out of his wallet and placed it on the table.

'It's okay, I'll get it,' she said immediately.

'It's fine. By the sounds of things, you'd get it in the divorce anyway.' A low blow, but he couldn't stop himself. He was gutted. Devastated. And so disappointed, he could barely breathe. This woman that he hardly recognised was tearing his life apart, so he felt that one barbed dig was allowed.

'Take care, Julia. Tell your lawyers to send the paperwork. I'll sign whatever you want.'

With that, and as much dignity as he could muster, he got up,

walked away from the table, through the lobby and out into the
May sunshine.

And he had absolutely no clue what to do next.

His first instinct was to call his mum, but that was off the table.
He didn't even have a number for her now. Instead, he texted
Albie.

She wants a divorce.

The reply was almost instant.

Is the correct response to sympathise or to throw random insults in your
defence?

Both.

Ah, I'm sorry, mate. And her eyes are too close together (it's the best I
could come up with at short notice). Come home and we'll drink until
we come up with something better.

Need to go to work. Can I reserve a spot in your spare room for the
foreseeable future?

Only if you pay me in Friday night kebabs.

Even in the depths of hell that made him smile.

Done.

Rory put his phone in his pocket and started walking the mile
or so across town to the office, replaying the conversation with
Julia over and over, looking for threads he could pull on to unravel

the arguments she used for breaking up. He wanted to remind her how great they'd been. How much they'd loved each other. He wanted to reassure her that despite everything, they could still have the future that they'd planned. But for any of that to land, he'd need someone who was prepared to listen, and today, her cold hard gaze had made it clear that she wasn't. Right now, her mind was set. He saw that. Maybe time would change... He stopped that train of thought dead. No. Julia wasn't one for changing course on anything. Her stubbornness had been one of the things he'd found sexy when they'd met. That was now biting him on the arse of his best suit trousers.

As he approached the headquarters of Fieldow Finance, he felt a tiny glimmer of comfort. At least he still had his job. He'd had his career before Julia, and he'd have it long after. He wasn't even sure that Roger would be aware of Julia's decision but even if he was, then Rory was confident that they'd maintain the invisible line between work and personal life.

When he got there, he took the stairs instead of the lift, as he'd done every working day for almost ten years. The enthusiasm he'd had on his first day here had never diminished. Although, back then, if anyone had told him that he'd marry the boss's daughter, he'd have been resolutely against it. Growing up, he'd seen so much cronyism and political climbing in his father's life and that had made him want to succeed entirely on his own merit. Meeting Julia had changed his mind. For better and now for worse.

As he entered the office, he thought he caught a couple of strange glances from the receptionists, but he just gave them his usual grin and walked on by. Just because his personal life was now going to shit, didn't mean that he had to ruin everyone else's day.

He went through the glass doors, into the ultra-modern, polished offices. Now that he was a senior member of the team, he had a private office, directly across the other side of the open-plan expanse that housed the junior teams, the assistants and the secretaries.

As he crossed the room, he was still deep in thought about the conversation with Julia, so it was only when he got close to the glass floor-to-ceiling partition in front of his office that he noticed there were people already in there. Strange. He had no meetings in the diary for this morning.

When the hammer dropped, it came with a sinking feeling in his gut.

The men in his office were security. And they were emptying his desk.

'Rory, I'm so sorry. I couldn't stop them. They wouldn't listen to me.'

He saw the distraught expression on his secretary, Mandy's face, and he understood even before she said it. They both knew what was happening here.

'Mr Fieldow wants to see you in his office as soon as you get in,' she blurted. 'And, Rory, I don't think you're getting a promotion.'

9

VAL

I still couldn't quite believe we'd made it, but only a few hours after I'd arrived at Carly's house in Chiswick, I was back in Glasgow, this time, with Carly and Carol in tow. Today had consisted of two flights, a devastating loss, a heart-stopping panic, many frantic phone calls, a London taxi driver who drove like he was in a high-speed chase, and an act of generosity so great it made me well up and thank the stars that I had these two wonderful women in my life – and it wasn't even dinnertime yet.

Before we got on the plane at Heathrow, we'd returned to the area Carly had parked in earlier, and, eyes down, scrutinised the ground all the way back to the terminal. We did the same thing at Glasgow. As soon as we'd got off the flight, at the same cluster of gates where I'd boarded this morning, I'd gone into bloodhound mode, retracing my steps, searching every corner and under every seat, even asking at the coffee bar and the passenger services desk if anything had been handed in. It hadn't.

We'd taken our time walking up the long corridor towards the baggage reclaim, all three of us scanning the floor, to the irritation of blokes in suits with sour expressions who were having to break their very important strides by going around us. I couldn't remember if I'd popped into the toilets halfway up the walkway on my way to my first flight, but I checked anyway. No joy.

'Look, there's a cleaner,' Carly announced, striding off in the direction of a lady in a yellow jacket pushing a cleaning cart.

The clicks of my heels sounded like a ticking clock as I raced to join her.

'I'm sorry to bother you, but I was here this morning and...' I went into the whole story, with Carly taking over when I suddenly teared up and lost my words. Between the two of us, we eventually got all the details out.

'Och, sweet Jesus, that's awful,' the woman sympathised. 'It's just me and my pal, Caz, that have been on today, but I haven't come across anything. She's on her tea break, but hang on, let me see if she's found them.' She pulled a walkie-talkie out of her pocket and summoned the crackly voice of her friend. 'Caz, are you there?'

'Aye, Jenny. But I hope you're no' going to tell me that Gerry Butler is in the lounge. I fell for that yesterday when I was on with Bobby and near pulled a muscle racing back there. Bugger was pulling my leg.'

Jenny flushed and rolled her eyes. 'What have I told you? Don't believe a word that comes out of that man's mouth. Anyway, you can stay where you are, I just need to know if...'

She explained what she was looking for, and we all waited with bated breath for the response, then deflated when it came.

'Nope, I didn't find anything. That would break your heart, so it would. Say to the woman to ask at the customer services desk downstairs. They can maybe check with security too.'

As advised by Caz, after I picked up my case at the baggage reclaim, we went to the customer services desk in the main terminal and explained the situation. The very helpful lady did her best, made some calls, checked something on her computer system, but ultimately come up blank.

Undeterred, I searched the escalators, retraced my path to the security gates, then went back downstairs and scoured the area around the check-in desks. Still nothing. Eventually, I conceded defeat, but only temporarily.

There was barely a queue at the taxi rank when we came out of the terminal building, but we went right around it and crossed over the road to the car park, and then turned left to the drop-off zones where I'd been deposited by that grumpy arse of a driver this morning, all three of us still scanning the ground like missile lasers trying to lock on a target. It was busy now, so we had to navigate groups of passengers getting in and out of cars, greeting each other, and in one case, alighting from a minibus with twelve chums singing, 'We're leaving on a jet plane', while wearing the West Of Scotland's full stock of pink Stetsons and T-shirts declaring they were on 'Demi's Hen Weekend 2024 – Hoes Before Bros'.

I guided Carly and Carol to the point where I'd pulled my bag out of the car, my heart in my mouth, silent prayers being shot up like they were messages on a ticker tape. Again, we scoured the area. Nothing.

'The driver that dropped me off was a rude git, so I didn't linger here long.'

'What about the taxi?' Carol asked. 'What company did you use?'

'Lochside. They cover all the villages out our way, and they're always the most reliable.'

Carly was first to whip her phone out and start searching for the details. 'Right, their office is actually not far from here. We could stop in on the way.'

I nodded, approving of that idea, and we headed back to the official airport taxi rank to get one of their trademark white cabs.

The urge to cry was gone now, replaced with hope, determination, the relief of knowing I was at least taking action to fix this and just a tiny, tiny sliver of optimism and positivity. A sliver that got even smaller when we reached the taxi office.

We asked the airport cab to wait for us, and then we all piled in, to see a stout bloke in maybe his fifties or sixties sitting at his desk, ignoring two ringing phones and barking orders into another. He put his hand over the mouthpiece of the phone he was using.

'Ladies, I've no cars right now, so you'll need to wait and I'll help you just as soon as I can.'

'We don't need a taxi,' I told him, trying my hardest not to sound like a woman on the edge. Which wasn't easy, because, well, I was a woman teetering as close to the bloody edge as I could get. 'We need some help, pal. It's important.'

There must have been something in my tone that registered with him, because he went back to his call with, 'Angus, I'll pay you double time. Just get your arse in here and give us a hand.'

He hung up and gave us his full attention, still ignoring the other two ringing phones.

'Sorry, ladies, it's my worst nightmare today. We're short on drivers and Sandra, who works the phones, downed tools and went off sick at lunchtime. There was no one to cover, so it's just me, doing ten bloody jobs and all of them badly.'

'I'll get straight to the point then and not take up your time,' I replied. 'I was in one of your taxis this morning, from Weirbridge to the airport, 8 a.m. booking. I think I might have left something really important in the car. I lost my hairbrush, not that I care about that, but I think it might have fallen out of my bag and taken a wee pouch of jewellery with it. It's my late husband's... it's my...' I stopped. Couldn't say it.

'The pouch has four rings in it,' Carly finished for me once again. Dear God, why couldn't I relay simple information without the words failing me? Exhaustion, both physical and mental, were shutting down my ability to function. 'And they're really important to us. They belong to family members that are no longer with us.'

A look of sympathy passed across the man's face, rapidly followed by irritation as the phone he'd just hung up began to ring again.

He opened the top drawer on his left and rummaged through it. 'If anything valuable had been handed in today, Sandra would have put it in here, but there's nothing. Just more mobile phones than a Vodafone shop.' He pulled out a book from the front of the drawer, flicked it open at a page and ran his finger down the paper. 'And there's nothing in the lost property log for today either.'

My stomach began to churn again as he went on, 'What kind of car was it, love? Did you get the name of the driver?'

'No, but it was a red Skoda. And he was a heavy guy, long hair, not exactly chipper.'

As soon as I said that, the taxi boss put the book back in the drawer and I noticed a sudden change in his posture. A glance to Carly and Carol told me they saw it too.

'I'm afraid I can't check with that driver at the moment.'

'Look, I wouldn't ask you to do this if it wasn't so important to me,' I pleaded.

The bloke put his hands up. 'Missus, it's not that I *won't* check, it's that I *can't*. That driver... erm... well... He went off sick today and I've got no way of contacting him. Look, all I can tell you is that if he found anything, he'd have radioed in straight away, and according to this logbook, there was nothing recorded. So I'm sorry.'

If he thought I was giving up, he had another think coming. 'Do you know when he'll be back? Can you ask him then?'

The change in his attitude was strange. My crack CID interrogation skills, developed while bringing up two kids in the eighties, could absolutely sense that something was amiss. Had the driver been fired? Arrested? Punched in the face for being an arrogant arse? None of those options would surprise me.

'I will, love. If and when he comes back, I'll definitely ask the question. Leave me your number and I'll call you if there's anything to tell.'

There was no point pushing it any further, because he obviously wasn't going to budge, so I did as I was asked, then the three of us trudged back out and into the airport taxi that had been waiting there the whole time.

* * *

It was dusk by the time we got into my kitchen and pulled out chairs at the same table I'd sat at this morning, before my whole world had been turned upside down. I'd already searched my bedroom, the stairs, the hall... nothing. Now I was just desperate for a cup of tea and a cry, but I didn't want to upset the girls. They'd done so much for me today already.

'Carol, are you going to stay at your mum's, pet?' Carol's parents still lived in Weirbridge, and they were the best of folks. They'd both come to Don's funeral, and they'd popped around a few days later to check how I was doing.

'No, I'm going to stay here, if that's okay. Mum and Dad turned my bedroom into a gym. I'm trying not to be offended.'

Despite the fraught circumstances, that made me smile.

'Don't be, love. Rumour has it that Elsie Cannon in Turner Road has turned her spare room into a sex dungeon. I don't think it's true, but I really hope it is.'

I didn't have to ask Carly the same question about her sleeping arrangements. Carly's dad, my Don's older brother, passed away years ago and her mother had long since retired to Spain with the latest in a string of men that had too white teeth, too dark tans, too much money and too little sense to see that she was one of the most self-obsessed creatures that ever lived. Carly barely heard from her, feckless woman that she was.

'Carly, you take Dee's room, and Carol, you take Michael's.' Neither Michael nor Dee had lived in this house for over a decade, but that was still how I thought of the bedrooms, and I always would. 'Let's get something to eat, and then we can call everyone and check those websites again tomorrow. I'm not giving up.'

'We're not either. In fact, I've got an idea,' Carly said, with the kind of conviction that she used to have when she was a lass, and was coming up with another of her daft plans that ultimately ended in disaster. This was the same woman who'd once decided to travel the world, hunting down all her ex-boyfriends to see if she'd missed out on 'the One'. Actually, as bonkers as it seemed at the time, that particular escapade had somehow ended with her marrying the man she spent the next twenty years with, so maybe it hadn't been completely crazy, but still. Now she was older, wiser, but just as unpredictable. 'I think it's our best shot of finding them, but you're going to absolutely hate it.'

As Carly started to outline the plan, I knew my niece was right. I hated the idea. It made my toes curl inside my tights. But I also knew that I'd caused this mess myself. And there was nothing I wouldn't do to fix it.

10

SOPHIE

Sophie must have nodded off because when she woke up, Dan, the nice police officer, was walking into her cubicle. 'How's the head?' he asked, making Sophie instinctively put her hand to the lump on the left side of her crown.

'Still there, so that's a bonus,' she replied.

'Ah, sense of humour is restored. Always a good sign.' He held up her black backpack. 'Can you confirm again that it's yours? Actually, the travel tag on it with your name and number gives it away, but I need to check.'

'Definitely mine. Thank you.' Sophie reached over and took a sip of the water that had been placed on the table beside her bed.

'The nurses tell me all your tests were fine and your X-ray was clear, so they're just keeping you in overnight to be on the safe side.'

Sophie nodded. 'Yes, the doctor said I've got a mild concussion, but everything else looks okay. I think if I lived here or had someone with me, they might let me out, but they don't want me alone in a hotel.'

'Makes sense. Do you feel up to answering some questions?'

'Of course, but I don't know how much help I'll be. I have no idea what happened. The whole journey is a bit hazy.'

He pulled a blue plastic chair over from the corner, and then took his notepad out. 'Fair enough, but let's see how you get on. Let's start with the personal details.'

At his prompting, she ran through her name, address, date of birth and the flight details for her arrival this morning.

'Business or pleasure?' he asked.

She wasn't sure how to answer that. Definitely not business. Not much pleasure so far either and maybe not at all.

'Maybe the second one. I used to date a guy from Glasgow, and I was coming up to see him.'

'Was he expecting you? That isn't an official question. Just an offer to contact him for you if you want me to.'

Sophie was about to shake her head, when she remembered that it hurt, so instead she just explained, 'No, he didn't know I was coming. I haven't seen him in a long time. Two years. And when I tried to get back in touch, his number had changed, so I'm just going to go to his flat and see him there.'

'You can't contact him through social media?'

Sophie sighed. 'If only I could. He's a teacher like me, and they have strict policies about that stuff, so he decided it was easier just not to bother with it. It was never his thing.' The fact that Ash wasn't interested in social media and didn't feel the need to put his whole life out there for some kind of validation was something that she'd loved about him. Not so handy when she was trying everything she could to track him down though.

'No arguments from me on that. You wouldn't believe the trouble all that online stuff causes now, all the cyber bullying and stalking shenanigans. We're dealing with it every day. Anyway, okay then, so this morning. Can you run me through what happened after you arrived?'

'I went to the airport drop-off zone because the queue at the taxi rank was long and I thought I might be able to pick up a taxi over there. I know that's not allowed. The driver told me that. I'm sorry.'

The policeman shrugged. 'Least of our worries today. Go on.'

'He wasn't very nice. Sorry, I shouldn't say that, but he was pretty rude. Said no at first, but then agreed to take me into Glasgow to the hotel.'

She remembered that bit clearly, but was struggling to piece together what came next. 'Then we were in the car, on the motorway and we were talking...' Saying that gave her chills and she couldn't work out why. What had they been speaking about? It was as if it was right on the tip of her tongue, yet she just couldn't remember. She tried to think what happened next, but nothing was computing. 'I think the next thing I remember is the car swerving and then you being at the car door asking me to put the window down. I honestly don't know what happened in between. Is that normal? To forget stuff?'

He nodded, then spoke to her with a bit of humour in his voice that she found reassuring. 'I'm no medical expert, but I'd think a clatter on the side of the head can do that to you. Okay, then, I'll get out of the way and let you rest. I've got your number if we have any more questions, but if you remember anything else, can you give me a call at the station? I'll put my card with the number right here.'

'I will do. And thank you. You've been really nice.'

He placed a business card down next to her drink. 'I hope the rest of your trip is way less eventful. You take care of yourself.'

'I will. Thanks again. And, Officer, I asked the nurse about the driver, but she couldn't tell me anything. Do you know how he's doing?'

Unlike Nurse Brenda, his face gave nothing away. 'I'm afraid I can't say either. Patient confidentiality. So many rules and regulations these days.'

'I understand,' she said, truthfully, although that didn't mean she had to like it. 'But there were no other cars involved? No one else was hurt?'

'Nope, quite miraculous really. The road was fairly busy, but somehow the other vehicles managed to bypass the taxi or stop safely. Your car hit the central reservation, but it was the only one affected. Someone up there was definitely looking out for you,' he raised his eyes heavenwards. 'Get some rest and if you think of any other details, please let us know.' With that, and a kind smile, he was off, leaving her staring at the door.

She had no doubt at all that someone had been looking out for her. 'Thanks, Mum,' she whispered, swallowing a lump of emotion and relief in her throat. Her mum had been looking over her and everyone else on that road today, but she might have taken her eye off the driver though. Sophie really wished she knew what had happened to him. She had such a feeling that if he was fine, then they'd hint at that, so all this secret stuff was just making her think the worst.

Her stomach suddenly lurched as a realisation hit her. The driver was only there, on that motorway, because she'd asked him to give her a lift. If it wasn't for her, he'd probably be going about his day, living his life quite happily. That thought made her head hurt again. Was this her fault? Was this poor man badly injured or worse because of her?

Just at that, Nurse Brenda opened the door and came in again. 'Ah, you're alone. I popped my head in earlier but you were chatting to the police. We've got a bed for you up on the admissions ward, so the porters will be along shortly to take you up there. As the doctor told you earlier, all the tests have come back fine, but we just want to keep an eye on you overnight. Have you got any questions?'

Sophie felt her eyes well up and tried to hold back the tears, but the nurse spotted it.

'Don't worry. This happens sometimes when the adrenaline wears off. It's the shock. It can hit you afterwards and it can be quite upsetting.'

'No, it's not that, it's just... Nothing. It's fine. I know you're busy.'

The nurse continued chatting as she smoothed the bedspread. 'I was actually just about to take my break, so don't you worry about me. I'll just take it right here and you can talk to me for a few minutes. For once, it's not like the January sales out there, so we can take a breather anyway. It'll be a different story tonight when the city-centre rush gets going. So tell me, love, what's upsetting you?'

'I'm just worried that the taxi driver is dead because of me,' Sophie blurted. 'I mean, if I hadn't got in his cab, this would never have happened.' The tears were unstoppable now.

Brenda reached over and put her hand on hers, hesitated, then spoke, choosing her words wisely. 'I can't tell you anything about another patient's confidential health situation,' she began, and Sophie could see her mind whirring. 'But all I can say, in general terms, is that a gentleman was brought in this afternoon after a *non-fatal* accident.'

Sophie immediately understood what she was saying. He wasn't dead. Thank God. She felt better for a second, before more doubts kicked her relief out of the park. Maybe he was really badly injured. Critical. That was still down to her.

'And the other thing I'd say is that...' Sophie watched Brenda frown with concentration. 'The gentleman's current condition is not related to the accident and it's likely that he would have required medical attention even if he had not been driving that car.'

It took Sophie a moment to work that out. Her brain was definitely not as sharp as usual. So if she was getting it right, something happened to him that had nothing to do with the crash. Okay. The guilt lifted just a little bit more. That meant it wasn't her fault.

She wiped away her tears with the palms of her hands, before Nurse Brenda pulled some sheets off a blue roll on the wall and handed them to her.

'Thank you for making me feel better.'

'Not at all. Now, let me check again – are you sure you don't want me to notify anyone that you're here? Maybe your mum or dad?'

Sophie shook her head. 'My mum died just over a year ago... pancreatic cancer.'

'Och, I'm sorry, love.'

'Thank you. It's just that, since she died, my dad has become anxious about me and my sister. I think he's terrified that he'll lose us too. So I don't want him to know I'm in hospital, because it'll put him into a complete panic and he'll kill himself trying to get here. I even lied to him about why I was coming. I know that's pathetic at my age...'

Nurse Brenda didn't seem to agree. 'Not at all,' she said, smiling. 'I've got two daughters. The older one, Zara, and Millie, the one that shares your birthday. I'm pretty sure they don't tell me the half of it. You're allowed to live your own life.'

'I know, but the thing is, I came up to see my ex, but I didn't want to tell my dad that because I know he'll just start worrying that I might get back together with him and move up here. Like I said, he's become a bit... overprotective.'

'So hang on – your ex lives in Glasgow? Do you want me to phone and tell him you're here then? I'm sure he'd want to know.'

Sophie sighed, decided to go with the pamphlet edition of the story. 'That's the thing – I don't have any way to contact him. I last saw him two years ago... It's a long story. I broke things off and we ended up losing touch.'

At first, after she'd returned home, she'd speak to Ash every day... then every second day... then once a week. He'd said all the right supportive things, tried to cheer her up, to be there for her, but she couldn't shake the feeling that he wanted something from her that she just didn't have to give when all her focus was on being there for her mum. He wanted the carefree girlfriend he'd fallen in love with, but then, right at that moment in time, she was just a struggling daughter trying to cope with a sick mum and a dad who was worrying himself to death right next to her. It was too much.

After a few months, she'd begged Ash to give her some space. She'd stopped taking his calls. Ignored his texts. Lost herself in caring for her mum, her dad, herself. As her mum got sicker, that space had stretched... and stretched... After Mum had died, it had taken everything she had just to get out of bed in the morning. Her new job helped, another thing to fill her time, to stop her from crumbling, but she'd put Ash to the back of her mind, not ready to tap into her feelings again. In her black fog of grief and confusion, she'd cut him off completely, feeling that she had no right to be happy or in love when her mum was dead.

It was months later that she found a message he'd sent just a few days after her mum's funeral. It had come in the midst of a flurry of sympathy messages that she hadn't had the strength to read. It was a WhatsApp message, a single photo, a year to the day since his first proposal. It was an image of her ring, placed on the ground in George Square, in the exact place he'd proposed. By the time she'd called him back, she'd got a message saying the number was no longer in service. She'd thought about coming up then, but she still couldn't bring herself to leave her dad, even for a weekend.

Or maybe that was an excuse. Maybe her heart was just still too broken to think about loving again. It had taken time, healing and a whole lot of prodding from Erin, but she was here now. She just hoped he was too, because a huge piece of her mended heart was terrified that she'd let the love of her life go without a fight.

'This is the first time I've come back to see him, but I'll have to let him know in person because his old number has been disconnected. Anyway, thanks for listening. And sorry. I didn't mean to pour my heart out there.'

'You're very welcome,' Brenda said, gently. 'There's rarely enough time to stop for two minutes on this ward, so it was good to take a load off these feet of mine. The nurses up on the admissions ward you're going to are a lovely bunch, so just let them know if you change your mind and want to call someone.'

'I will do. And thanks again.'

'Anyone around here looking for transport to the executive suites?' A booming voice interrupted them before Brenda had even got to her feet.

'You can keep saying that, Hamish, but it doesn't make it true,' Brenda fired back, laughing. 'Sophie, this is Hamish. He always wanted to work in a flash hotel, so he just pretends this is it.'

'A man's got to dream, Brenda,' he bantered back, before getting to the important stuff. He and Brenda conferred, checked they had all the right details of who Sophie was and where she was going, then he put all of her belongings on a shelf under her bed, flipped the brake off and with another grateful thanks to Brenda she was out of the door and on her way.

Hamish kept up the chirpy chat all the way down the corridor, into the lift, and up to the second floor. The doors pinged open and he took a right, went through another set of double doors and into a ward.

A friendly faced nurse was at the desk and seemed to know she was coming.

'I hear you've been through the wars today,' she said lightly, making Sophie immediately feel a little bit better. 'Let's get you along to your room and get you settled. You've missed dinner...' Sophie hadn't even thought about food all day, but the minute the nurse said that, it was as if her stomach sprung to attention and demanded sustenance. '...But I'll phone along and see what we can rustle up for you. Room 2, Hamish, thanks very much.'

She was on the move again, as the porter steered her into a room on the opposite side of the corridor. She'd expected to be put on a ward with lots of other people, but there was just one other woman, maybe in her early thirties, who appeared to be fast asleep. That was fine with her. The last thing she felt like was making small talk.

Hamish said his goodbyes and went on his way, just as the nurse came in and ran through all her details, then told her food would be along shortly, and that she'd check in on her regularly.

She'd just left when Sophie heard her phone buzz.

A text from Erin.

FaceTime?

A brief panic as she tried to come up with something that was as plausible as possible. If she told Erin she was in hospital, her sister would freak out and demand she come home. Or pitch up here with their dad in tow. Sophie couldn't bear the thought of causing fuss or drama. They'd all been through enough. 'Sorry about the white lies, Mum,' she whispered skywards as she began to type.

I'm in the hotel restaurant having dinner.

With Ash?

Nope, not found him yet. Knackered so going to have an early night and hunt tomorrow.

You're a lightweight. I'm going out with the girls for drinks, but if you need me, call me IMMEDIATELY. Love you. Xx

Phew.

You go enjoy yourself and I'll call you in the morning. Love you too.

Sophie put the phone down, then realised her sister wasn't done. Another ping.

Tomorrow is going to be a good day. I can feel it in my water. By this time tomorrow night, you'll have found him.

Sophie had never hoped more that her sister was right.

11

ALICE

On the ground floor of the hospital, Alice had no idea how long she'd been sitting in the prayer room. Hours perhaps. Once or twice, she'd got up, walked around the room just to keep her circulation going, then sat back down again, stared straight ahead. It struck her that most people in this situation would have people to call, family to notify or friends to summon for support. It was without a whiff of self-pity that Alice acknowledged she had neither. That was the thing with sinking ships – everyone jumped off. As soon as the scandal broke, all those friends who'd been delighted to be seen with her when she was an MP's wife scattered. Not a single call. Not one. All the people she'd helped along the way? Amnesia. And she didn't blame them one bit.

And as for family? Her parents were gone now, and she was an only child, so there were no siblings to lean on. And Rory... she'd done the only thing that she could do to protect him. She'd let him go.

'Mrs McLenn?'

She raised her gaze to see a policeman standing in the doorway. 'Yes.'

'I'm Officer Dan Reiss. I wonder if we could speak?'

Police officers asking questions. She'd been here before, but two years ago it had been detectives and investigators from the fraud squad, who'd relished the fact that they were dealing with a case that could potentially make their careers. There had been a lot of crushed people, including her, when Larry had escaped justice.

'Of course. Let me come outside.'

Even though she was there by herself, the prayer room didn't feel like the right place to have that kind of conversation.

There was a row of four empty seats against the wall in the corridor outside, so Alice sat on the nearest one.

The police officer left one seat between them, so that he could turn to face her. The first thing he did was hand her a shopping-sized blue plastic bag. 'I believe these are your husband's belongings, Mrs McLenn – the traffic officers retrieved them before the car was removed from the scene of the accident.'

Alice didn't care to look inside.

'Can I just take a few details please, for our records?'

'Of course.'

He ran through a few basic questions: address, telephone numbers, her husband's employment details, when he'd joined the taxi company, et cetera. She could see in his face that he didn't have to ask what Larry had done before that. He knew. Everyone knew.

He closed his notepad and gave her a sympathetic smile. 'Thank you, Mrs McLenn. If we have any further questions, we'll be in touch.'

'Is my husband going to be charged with anything?'

That seemed to surprise him. 'No. We are awaiting the results of a blood test to check for any alcohol or chemical substances, but at the moment there are no grounds for an arrest.'

Alcohol hadn't even crossed her mind. When she'd come in from her cleaning shift last night, he'd still been up, sitting in his usual chair, with his usual bitter expression, watching his usual news channel on TV and there had been his usual glass in his hand. She'd taken no notice, just gone straight upstairs, showered and then gone to bed to catch a few hours' sleep before getting up for her morning shift.

A thought struck her. 'One other thing, was anyone else hurt?'

'There was a passenger in the back seat of your husband's car. She was brought into this hospital after the accident, but her injuries weren't serious, and we expect her to be discharged tomorrow.'

Alice exhaled, relieved. Poor woman. She was probably just going about her day and then everything changed because she had the misfortune to get into Larry's taxi. 'Can I speak to her? I'd just like to apologise and pass on my best wishes for her recovery.'

'I'm afraid we can't reveal her identity as that would breach her privacy,' he said regretfully.

Alice understood. If Larry was in any way at fault, the last thing the police would want to do is facilitate contact with anyone else involved.

The officer left and she considered going back into the prayer room, but decided to stay put for now, lowering her gaze to the floor when a young couple walked by, holding hands. They were maybe in their twenties, and the gent's hand that wasn't holding hers was in plaster and secured against his chest in a sling.

'I mean, seriously, what were you thinking?' she was chiding him, but Alice could hear the affection in her voice. 'Arm wrestling. You're a grown man. And I tell you, if you'd won those football tickets, you wouldn't have been going anyway because it's my mum's birthday that day and we're taking her out for lunch. And no, a broken wrist doesn't get you out of it.'

Alice didn't catch his reply, but she heard him groan, then laughter as they disappeared around the corner.

Had she and Larry ever been like that? Playful? Affectionate? In love?

Maybe at the start. They'd met when Alice was a receptionist at a legal firm and he'd come in to talk to one of the solicitors in her office about speeding charges he was trying to evade. It was the early nineties and Alice had just split up with her boyfriend of six months, a Premier League football player who had transferred to a club down south and also transferred his affections to a Page Three girl who'd offered to go with him.

After the break up, Alice knew she should be heartbroken, but she wasn't. It sounded arrogant, and she didn't mean it to, but she had the kind of looks and confidence that would ensure there would be others. Or maybe not, she'd pondered. Perhaps she should swear off men for a while and concentrate on her career, maybe even go back and finish the teaching degree that she'd bailed on after her second year, because she'd been desperate to get out into the world and experience life. Those thoughts had all been discarded the minute Larry McLenn had walked into her office. His physical impact was instant. In his early thirties, he was well over six feet tall, with the broad shoulders of a rugby player and the cheeky grin of a man who knew that he could charm his way in and out of anything. That included the speeding charges, which would be waived after a judge heard how he was rushing to an emergency – all fabricated, of course. Not that Alice knew that at the time.

God, she'd been besotted by him. In those days, he owned a trendy, hugely popular bar in the city centre. That's how his interest in politics had started. He'd challenged the council over their rejection of his application to extend his alcohol licence for special events, and he'd won. The victory had given him a taste of power that had only grown over the years to become the insatiable desire that would destroy them.

Again, though, she hadn't known that back then. When the exceptionally pretty, gregarious twenty-five-year-old Alice Brookes had smiled at him and watched as he sat on the edge of her desk and asked to take her out for a drink, all she'd seen was a handsome, charismatic, successful businessman who'd made her feel butterflies in her stomach. She'd gone for that drink, then dinner, and by the time he'd dropped her home in his flash Porsche, at the flat she shared with a couple of friends, she was in love. Or maybe in lust, but she'd been too damn young, stupid and swept away by this suave, charming man to know the difference.

The next six months had been a whirlwind of romance, of wining and dining, of showing her a good time. Of course, her parents had been completely unimpressed. Sean and Andrea Brookes were older than most of her friends' parents. Alice had been a surprise late baby, born when Andrea was almost forty and long after they'd resigned themselves to believe that God's plan for them didn't include parenthood. They'd also had been working-class people who'd given their daughter the core values of kindness, decency and the merits of a hard day's work, a savings account and church on a Sunday. They'd expected her to marry someone just like them, to settle nearby and to live a contented life. Alice had adored her parents, but their view of her future hadn't matched hers. She'd wanted excitement and glamour, and she'd seen all of it in the force of energy and revelry that had been Larry McLenn. He'd treated her like a princess and he'd promised her the moon and the stars, and she'd truly believed he could deliver.

Then everything had changed.

On their six-month anniversary, she'd realised she was pregnant. Her quiet, conformist, religious parents were horrified and demanded that they marry. Larry stalled on making it official, even after their son was born, and her mum and dad had never forgiven him.

In the end, they'd married three months after Rory came into the world. Looking back, the red flags were all there, but she'd still been in love with him then, and she'd been so desperate to make things work and so eager to show her parents that she hadn't made a huge mistake. Perhaps that was why she'd never turned to them when the problems started.

Slowly, day by day, week by week, month by month, Larry had changed. The chase was gone. He had her. More than that, she'd come to rely on him and he veered between revelling in that and resenting it.

It was small stuff at first. A cruel word. A sneer. After Rory had been born, he'd shown complete disinterest in their child, staying out late, claiming work events that never seemed to end before dawn. He'd insisted that she stop working, and to begin with, she'd thought it was because he wanted to make her life easier, but later, she would come to understand that it was all about control. Just as he'd got a taste for power and politics, he'd come to relish the kick of controlling another human being. She'd become his toy to play with or to discard depending on his mood. Over time, her friends had drifted away after too many invitations were refused, or because they couldn't stand the arrogant way Larry spoke to them. She avoided her parents because she didn't want to see the sadness on their faces or for them to see the reality of her trapped existence. And Larry just got more and more disdainful and disinterested.

It had come to a head in the middle of the night, when Rory was barely a year old. He was teething and had kept her awake for what felt like days. Larry's bar closed at one o'clock, but, as always by then, he had rolled in at 5 a.m., a little drunk, dishevelled, but still with that cocky swagger of someone who was living his best life.

She'd been sitting in the dark, on the couch, too exhausted to move but too angry to sleep.

'Where have you been?' she'd asked him, calmly, flicking on the lamp beside her.

After he'd got over the surprise of seeing her there, he'd taken a bottle of whisky from the top of the dressing table, opened it and taken a swig, before flopping down on one of the black leather armchairs. He'd refused to let her change a single thing when she'd moved into the house, so it still looked like the bachelor pad it had always been.

'We had a lock-in. A celebration. Because after months of working on it...' He paused to knock back another swig. 'Your. Brilliant. Husband.' He said the words separately, leaving a pause between them that he filled with a smug leer. 'Has just been asked to run for city council, and told, by a collective of very distinguished gentlemen,' he milked that by adding clipped, posh vowels, and a dramatic flourish, 'that should he do so, he'd be guaranteed the win.'

Of course he would. She'd come to realise that Larry McLenn didn't do anything unless he knew he would win.

'Congratulations,' she'd said, her words absolutely dead.

'I tell you something though – you're going to have to smarten up. My wife will be expected to look and act the part. Look at the state of you. You're an embarrassment.'

Something inside her had snapped. 'Because I've been up all night with our son! The one you pay absolutely no fucking attention to. Why did you marry me, Larry? Why?'

If he'd been surprised by her challenge, he hadn't shown it. Or maybe he just didn't care. He'd just shrugged. 'Because you and that kid were a loose end. And people like me, with the kind of future that's ahead of me, need to look the part. I can't have loose ends that could come back and bite me.'

So that was it. She'd been a political decision. Marry the woman that got knocked up with your kid, because politicians don't need those kinds of skeletons in their closet.

Of course, she should have left him, but with what? She'd painted herself into the corner of a gilded cage and there was no way out.

As he'd predicted, he became a councillor, but that wasn't enough for him. Over the next decade, he'd manoeuvred, schemed and schmoozed his way up in power, his career rising to heights that even he couldn't have anticipated. Westminster. The Houses of Parliament. Larry McLenn, Labour MP.

Alice had been thrilled when he'd been elected, not because she was happy for him, but because the job, mercifully, came with a flat in London that got him away from her and Rory for several months of the year, leaving her to find happiness in the kind of work that made a difference. Fundraising. Volunteering. Mentoring. But her greatest and most important role had been as a mother to her son.

She'd protected Rory as a child and she'd protected him as an adult, when she cut off all ties. After that, Rory's life had gone on. And as long as she knew that he'd escaped the sins of his father, that he'd managed to preserve his marriage, his career, his prospects for a happy future, she could sleep at night.

Two nurses in scrubs walked past her, snapping her out of the past.

She was still sitting in the corridor. Still staring at the opposite wall. The only movement was the hands of her watch, but she'd stopped checking the time. The news would come soon enough and nothing she could do would make it any quicker. She thought about going to find a café or even a vending machine, to get a cup of tea, but decided against it. All it would take was for one person to spot who she was, and the situation would become unpredictable. Here, in an empty corridor, she was invisible, and that was how she preferred to be.

Endless minutes later, she jumped when footsteps came around the corner, raised her eyes to see the serious expression on Dr Richard Campbell's handsome face.

'Alice, I've just heard from my colleagues on the surgical team.' He gestured to the prayer room door. 'Let's go back in here so that we can speak in private.'

12

RORY

'So, let me get this right.' Albie held up the hand that wasn't clutching a beer, and then leaned forward so that the other drinkers in the pub wouldn't overhear their conversation. 'They've fired you...'

'Correct.'

'But they're giving you two years' salary up front?'

'Also correct.'

'Piss off. Last time I got fired, all I got was my P45 and a dose of food poisoning from the salmonella chicken I'd swiped from the restaurant kitchen.'

Before Albie had begun to make a meagre but sustainable living from being a stand-up comic (available for stage shows, corporate events, weddings, birthdays, retirement dinners and funerals), he'd had an endless stream of jobs in bars, restaurants and nightclubs, all of which he'd been fired from for offences covering the entirety of a disciplinary action handbook. Drinking on the job. Socialising on the job. Being late to the job. Forgetting to turn up for the job. Arguing on the job. Swearing on the job. Pilfering food or drink on the job. Refusing to do the job. And even, once, although he almost lost his bollocks in the process, having sex in the walk-in freezer. On the job.

Rory nodded ruefully, realising it could be worse. But not much.

That afternoon, Roger Fieldow had kept him waiting outside his office for fifteen minutes before finally granting him an audience. The whole time, Rory had sat outside the door, trying to analyse the situation from all angles. If security was clearing out his office, it was a pretty safe bet he was getting fired, but he'd done nothing to warrant that, so that gave him options. He had run through his memory of employment laws and procedures, wishing he'd paid more attention in that Business Law & Ethics module at uni.

When he'd eventually been shown through, Roger hadn't made one of his usual gestures of shaking his hand or slapping his back or greeting him with a cheery hello. Stern-faced, he'd just gestured to the chair in front of his desk.

'Take a seat, Rory.'

Rory had done as he'd asked, then waited, putting the ball firmly in Roger's court. If he was getting the chop, he wasn't going to go first in the procession to his execution.

'I believe you met with Julia this morning,' Roger had opened, his tone all business, as if he was speaking to a client, not his son in law.

'I did.'

'She's divorcing you.'

'She is.'

Roger had sat back, fingers crossed, sighed. 'Look, Rory, there's no painless, easy way to say this, but it's clear that your position with the company has become untenable.'

'Clear to who?'

He'd never, in almost ten years of working with this man, and five years of being married to his daughter, spoken to him in this way. But then, he'd never been fired either.

'To me. To my family. To the board.' Roger's eyebrows had risen, probably shocked at Rory's audacity. Not many people challenged the boss around here.

'Not to me. Is there anything wrong with my work? Have there been any complaints?' Rory had asked calmly, confident of the answer.

'No, of course not.'

'And am I still your highest billing member of the team?'

He had seen that Roger was beginning to realise that he wasn't going to be a pushover. Rory had known it wouldn't get him anywhere, but if he'd learned anything from being the son of an omnipotent narcissist, it was that you had to stand your ground and put up a challenge to get even a sliver of respect or recognition, especially in a negotiation. And Rory had a feeling that's what the discussion was about to be.

'You are.'

'Okay. Then I don't see the problem. I've worked here my entire career. I don't see the need to cut ties because of personal situations. I am more than prepared to carry on doing my job to the highest standard and the best of my abilities.' Rory had been aware that he sounded like he was giving some kind of oath of allegiance, but keeping it formal and straight to the point was the only way to play this because it would force Roger to spell it out. And that's exactly what he'd done.

Roger had leaned forward, elbows on the desk, his whole posture changed as he abandoned the game plan. 'Look, Rory, there's no way round this, so I'm just going to be frank. Julia wants you out of our lives altogether and she's my daughter, so I'm going to give her that. We stuck by you when your father disgraced the whole fucking lot of us...'

'He did nothing to you.'

Roger's laugh had been low and cold. 'You don't think we were stained by association? We'd given him a seat on the board because of the connections between our families.'

A seat that he was promptly fired from when the scandal broke, Rory had noted silently.

'You gave him a seat on the board because he was important and he had connections that you wanted to exploit for the benefit of your company.'

Roger had dropped all pretence of the higher moral ground. 'You're right. And it backfired spectacularly. But we kept you on, hoped we could get past this. Now, with the divorce in the works, the only way forward is a clean break.'

Rory had held it together, stayed perfectly calm, even though his stomach was churning and he was fairly certain that if he stood up, he may collapse at the knees.

'And what does that way forward look like?'

'You don't contest the divorce or the prenup. You leave the house permanently. You tender your resignation and sign an agreement not to pursue any kind of legal action against our company on any grounds. In return, we'll make it clear you left of your own volition, and we're offering six months' salary, all due bonuses, and the guarantee of an excellent reference if we are contacted by a future employer.'

'No.' It was out before he'd even processed every aspect of it. What Rory did recognise, however, was that he had the upper hand. They couldn't actually fire him. Not without a valid reason and even then, only after following the correct process as laid down by law. Those classes were coming back to him. So what they were, in fact, doing here, was bribing him to leave.

Roger's eyes had narrowed. 'No?'

'No.'

Roger paused and Rory knew him well enough to detect the irritation under his calm facade as his boss and mentor went on. 'So lay it out. What do you want?'

Rory had to think on his feet. If he was going to go, he had to make sure there was at least a tiny cushion of protection.

'All the contingencies that you mentioned. I won't contest the personal stuff and I'll agree to no future legal action. But I want two years' gross salary, the removal of any non-compete clause, full pension, my company car and reasonable relocation expenses of six months' rental on the apartment of my choice, upfront, tax-free and paid directly into the account of my choice.'

It had felt like a lot saying it out loud, but Rory knew it was probably less than Roger dropped in golf fees at his private clubs in Scotland, Marbella and Florida every year.

His boss had made a pretence of thinking it over, but they both knew he would accept. There was nothing he wouldn't do for his darling daughter and in terms of the Fieldow wealth, this was nothing. But Roger Fieldow also hated to lose a negotiation, so it was through gritted teeth that he'd eventually said, 'I'll have the paperwork drawn up.'

Rory had nodded, stood up. There had been nothing else to say.

He was almost at the door, when Roger had surprised him by saying, 'Rory, you know it's nothing personal.'

Rory had smiled, kept his voice calm and steady as he'd turned back. 'Really, Roger? Because it feels very fucking personal to me. Give my regards to the family.'

With that he'd turned, walked out and hadn't looked back. When he was in the lift, with trembling hands, he'd sent two texts. The first one was to Mandy, asking her to forward his things to Albie's address.

Mandy had replied immediately.

Of course. Can't believe this is happening to you, my friend. I'm so sorry. I would quit in solidarity, but I've booked to go to the Maldives next week and I need the money. But you know I love you.

I do. And right back at you, Mands. If they cause any problems for you, let me know. I haven't signed the leaving deal yet so I still have some leverage. Give me a shout for a beer when you get back from the beach.

She'd replied with an emoji of a beach, a thumbs up and a blue heart.

He'd understood. She had a life, commitments and responsibilities – if she'd genuinely wanted to quit as a show of support, he'd have talked her out of it. The last thing he needed was anyone else being affected by this shitshow, or any more damage on his conscience.

The truth was, he couldn't even blame Roger. He was looking out for his profit margins, his family and his employees. And Julia? Well, she'd signed up for something that had disappeared. She'd thought she was marrying a respected politician's son and that they'd have a glittering life among her peers and the social elite. Instead, she'd had her name dragged through the mud and been connected to one of the biggest political scandals to rock the city in decades.

His second text had been to Albie, who had replied in a more succinct manner.

Beer?

Hell yes.

So now, they were sitting in a city-centre bar, on a Friday afternoon, contemplating the rest of his life.

'What are you going to do next then?'

Rory shrugged. 'I've got absolutely no idea. I can't see any other accounting companies in the city wanting to touch me with a bargepole. Even with a different name from my dad, they'll still make the connection. And there isn't anyone in the industry who won't know that Roger Fieldow's daughter has divorced me, and I've been pushed out. No matter how gleaming my reference is, they'll read between the lines. Public scandal. Corruption. Fired from establishment corporation. Not exactly the top three things that employers look for when they're hiring.'

'Do you know what kind of company won't care about any of that shit?'

Rory held his beer bottle mid-air. 'Can't wait for you to tell me.'

'Male strippers. You're never out of that gym. You should at least put all that graft to good use.'

'I'll get on to my careers advisor straight away and set that up,' Rory agreed, realising that this wasn't going anywhere serious. Albie's understanding of the finance industry was up there with his in-depth knowledge of, say, quantum physics. Or global warming. Or how to have deep, profound emotional conversations when your best mate was having an existential crisis and had just watched his life turn into a train wreck.

'Or we could set up one of those micro-breweries. Two birds with one stone. Gives you a job and you can get so pissed that you'll forget your missus dumped you. Too soon?'

Case in point.

'I think I'd be better putting the money to good use buying new mates,' Rory suggested.

'Right, well, don't say I didn't try. In the meantime, you'll always

have a home in my spare room, and if you fancy a bit of a distraction, Belinda behind the bar at the Comedy Den has been totally
besotted with you for years and has been praying to the gods of very
strong tequila that you'll one day be single and notice her. Talking
of which...' He checked his watch. 'Shit, the soundcheck for my gig
tonight is in half an hour, so I have to boost. Are you coming along?'

'I'm not sure. I'll see where I'm at.'

Even as he was saying it, he knew that there was only one place
that he wanted to go. Over a year ago, he'd made an agreement
with his mother that he would keep his distance, cut off all ties and
eradicate his parents from his life. Every part of him had resisted it.
He'd wanted to stand by her, but the stress of watching him under
fire was only adding to the pain she was going through, so, against
every instinct and value he possessed, he'd reluctantly agreed. It
was the most selfless thing she could ever have done, cutting him
loose while staying to deal with his vile cretin of a father. Rory
couldn't have loved her more for it, but now he considered that
deal null and void. He wanted to see her.

The worst had already happened. He'd lost his wife. He'd lost
his job. He'd lost the life that they'd built together.

What more did he have to lose?

SATURDAY

13

VAL

'I still can't believe that you're making me do this. I'm not built for it. I'll crumble and then I'll be mortified and won't be able to show my face in these streets again. I'll have to leave the country,' I chattered on, wholeheartedly believing every word I was saying. Centre of attention was never somewhere I was comfortable being, because I was way too prone to blurting out the first thing that came to my mind. As Josie often said, I needed a lifetime supply of gaffer tape for my gob.

Carly was sorting out the microphone. 'Aunt Val, enough. It's not like you're going jogging in your knickers. All you're doing is talking. Telling your story. And we'll be right here, so if you feel yourself starting to get upset, just give us the nod and we'll jump in and rescue you. It'll be fine. And it might just work, so it'll all be worth it. Hang on to that.'

I blew out a breath so strong that my cheeks puffed out and my hair, despite being fortified by about half a can of Elnett, was forced to quiver.

What a morning I'd had, and it was only nine o'clock. After a sleepless night of tossing, turning and replaying every second of yesterday, I'd got up at the crack of dawn, as soon as it was light. The sick feeling in my stomach was still there, right beside the knot of absolute devastation that I'd lost the most important possessions in my life. I'd let them down. Don. Dee. Josie. I'd been careless with their memories and I couldn't look myself in the mirror.

The first thing I'd done was empty out all my bins, just in case, by some powers of osmosis, my rings had somehow found their way in there. It was mad, I knew. I had a vivid recollection of exactly what I'd done with them, and yet, I was doubting myself. But then, I'd been so tired, stressed and overwrought yesterday. What if it was one of those situations like I'd had when I was pregnant, or just after the babies were born, or in the grips of the bastard menopause, when I'd find my tights in the freezer and my fish fingers in the washing machine?

After putting everything back in the bins, and disinfecting my arms from the tips of my fingers to my elbows, I'd gone out of the front door, and with the slow, steady focus of a police search team on a murder enquiry on every episode of *Taggart*, I'd once again scoured the path, the front garden, the walkway down the front of our terraced row of houses to the car park. Nothing. I'd continued round all the cars and Willie from number 16's camper van, where he went at night to hide his secret smoking habit from his wife. Still nothing.

On the way back, my gaze had fallen on the bloody Neighbourhood Watch sign and I'd been tempted to punch it. If I hadn't seen that yesterday, then I wouldn't have been gripped by the fear of having my rings burgled while I was away, I wouldn't have gone back in for them and they wouldn't be lost. I'd had to take several deep breaths to compose myself, at which point Nish from next door had dangled out of her window.

'Val, love, are you okay? Are you having one of those panic

attacks? Someone was talking about them on *Loose Women* the other day.'

I'd shaken my head, tried to smile. 'No, I'm fine. Just a bit out of puff.'

'Ah okay. Did you find your rings? Amir told me about what happened. He was out there with his metal detector yesterday looking for them on your lawn.'

'He's a gem,' I'd said, meaning it. 'Would you thank him for me? I haven't found them yet, but I'm not giving up. I'll let you know what happens and thanks again.'

Nish had disappeared back inside the window and I'd come back through my front door. When I'd got to the kitchen, Carly and Carol were out of their beds and they'd both been sitting at the table, drinking coffee out of my oversized mugs, staring at me like I was deranged.

'Aunt Val, were you just having a conversation with Uncle Don?' Carly had asked warily.

I was confused. 'What are you talking about? Why would you think that?'

Carol had taken over. 'We looked out of the window and you were shouting at the sky.'

Despite everything that had happened, despite the heartbreak, the tears and the devastating loss, I'd found that hilarious. 'I was talking to Nish next door. She was hanging out of her bedroom window.'

'Oh thank God for that. We thought you'd lost it,' Carol had blurted.

Next jobs on the list had been to call the taxi office again. This time, we'd got someone different, who'd informed us that, no, nothing had been handed in, no, they still hadn't managed to speak to the driver, and no, Sandra didn't work weekends so she couldn't be contacted either. I'd said I would call back tomorrow and hung up.

Carly had checked the Lost Property websites for both Glasgow Airport and Heathrow. Nothing.

'Have you called the police yet? Maybe something has been handed in there?' Carol had suggested and I could have kicked myself for not doing that last night.

I'd phoned the local police office, based in the next village, and reported the loss, gave descriptions and asked them to keep an eye out. The very nice female officer on duty had obliged and I'd heard her tapping away on a keyboard, before she came back and said that nothing matching that description had been handed in.

So here we now were, all sitting at our kitchen table again, preparing to participate in the idea that Carly had come up with yesterday. I still thought of it as 'our' table. Mine and Don's. I knew I always would.

'Tell me again what it's called – an Instant Live?' I wittered, trying to fix my hair again and straightening my good pink blouse, worn specially for the occasion.

'An Instagram Live,' Carol corrected.

The girls – yes, in my mind, I still called them 'the girls' even though they were in their fifties – had made a go of explaining it all to me last night so I had a grasp of it now. Carol's job promoting things on social media apparently had quite the following – 5.5 million to be exact.

'What?' I'd gasped when I'd heard that. 'Five and a half million people follow you on the socials now?'

'That's just Instagram,' Carol had nodded. 'I've stopped using Twitter and Facebook because I didn't feel they had the same impact.'

I was aware of the overall principles of social media and my niece's job. We'd all gone to New York a few years ago – me, Carol,

Carly, their pal, Jess, and Carol's daughter, Toni – and Carol had been taking pictures the whole time and clicking away on her phone like a demon uploading them. She'd explained that advertisers paid her to promote their brands, and I got that – it was not much different from the modelling that Carol had done since she was a teenager, but she'd explained how it was changed days now that women still got smashing modelling jobs well into their fifties and beyond. Just last year, she'd even been on *This Morning* twice – modelling handbags the first time and wedding hats the second. I'd beamed all day and told everyone I met. Carol had said a shoot the next day for Valentino had been more impressive, but I was sticking to my opinion that morning telly had to be the high point of the week.

The whole social media thing though?

I was very well aware that many women my age were completely savvy in these technologically advanced times, but I just had zero interest. I preferred to have my conversations with my pals in person over a cuppa and a Tunnock's caramel log. This Instagram Live thing was just like that, they'd explained to me – only Carol's followers could tune in and watch us. I'd never wanted gaffer tape more.

'Okay, are you ready?' Carol asked me, flicking her long, poker-straight blonde hair off her perfect face, with its high cheekbones and those huge eyes.

I wasn't. Stomach churning. Hands shaking. Chest tight. Terrified. But if it helped… 'I'm ready,' I whispered.

Over at the other side of the table, Carly added some advice. 'Okay, remember, just act like you're speaking to Carol. If you need me, I'm over here, but I'm staying out of shot because my hair looks like a fight between two sheepdogs.'

'Right, one, two, three…' Carol said, then immediately started speaking into the camera on her mobile phone, which was balanced on some kind of hook in the middle of a big round white light on the table in front of us. 'Hi, gang, how are we all doing this morning? Thank you so much for tuning in. I've been flagging up this "live" all morning because it's one that's really personal to me, to my family and to one of my favourite people in the world – my Aunt Val.'

She did a zoomie-out thing on the phone, and suddenly I could see myself on the screen. I aimed for a smile, but it probably came out somewhere between 'in pain' and 'serial killer'. Five and a half million people. Okay, so they wouldn't all be watching this, but Carol had said something about loading it up to her story so that anyone looking at her page all day could see it. My knees began to shake and this time I did have a conversation with Don. *Help me out here, love. Help me do this.*

'So, the reason for coming on this morning is because Val has lost something extremely precious, and we want to put it out there in case someone, somewhere, comes across it. It's a little black pouch like this...' Carol held up a picture of an identical little velvet bag. 'And in it are four rings that mean the world to her. They're irreplaceable. We'll tell you about them all throughout the day today, both here on this Insta Live and later, on *Twisted Knickers*, the podcast I do with my sexy sister-in-law, Carly Morton.'

Off camera, Carly made a daft face, but I caught it out of the corner of my eye and it de-escalated my anxiety just enough to make my knees stop trembling.

Carol went on to give all the details about the route I had taken and the places it could have been lost.

'What we thought we'd do is tell you a little bit about each ring, so you'll understand how important they are.' She turned to me.

'Aunt Val, which one do you want to talk about first?'

She'd told me she was going to ask that, so I was prepared. I took a deep breath and sent up another SOS. *Don, love, I need you...* And then I began to speak.

'I think maybe we start at the beginning. You know, I started dating Don when you and our Carly were just wee pals in school. Lord, we weren't much more than kids ourselves. We'd been class-mates from our very first year, but we didn't start dating until we were teenagers. It was all very angelic then. Some kissing. A lot of cuddling. Mostly we were just best pals that were a special kind of happy when we were together...'

I felt myself getting lost in the memory, and suddenly it was as if there were just the three of us there, and we were reminiscing about some of the happiest days of my life.

'I don't know that I remember a time when I didn't think I'd marry him one day. It wasn't a question of whether, just a question of when... It wasn't just that he was the most handsome big bugger I'd ever seen...' My hand flew to my mouth. 'Sorry! Can I say bugger on the Instants?'

Carol nodded, with a reassuring smile, and said softly, 'You can. Go on.'

'Okay. I just don't want to get you into trouble. So, anyway, it wasn't just that he was a handsome big b... bloke, but, oh my, his heart. He cared about people. He wasn't soft on the outside – he'd stand up to anyone that was going after someone he loved – but that was because on the inside he had the most caring soul of anyone I've ever known. He was... what is it they say nowadays?' I paused to think. 'He was my person. That was it. Don Murray was my person. And I was his.'

I heard a sniff and realised that Carly was wiping away tears with the wristband of her jumper. I really hoped I was doing this right. Carol had told me not just to talk about the ring, but to share a bit about why it mattered, because that way it would catch people's hearts and perhaps they'd talk about it and spread the word.

I took another deep breath and went on, 'Sorry, I got a bit lost thinking about him there. Anyway, so after we left school, Don got a job with the council as an apprentice draughtsman and oh, we were so excited. A real job. And money at the end of it! On the first Friday that he got a pay packet, he burst through my door with a box of chocolates, all beaming and so happy. I was so proud of him, and thrilled to bits about the chocolates if I'm being honest. Turns out that wasn't the only surprise. A song came on the radio that we loved – Gladys Knight and the Pips sang it and it was called "Midnight Train to Georgia", when he pulled me up for a dance. We did that a lot in the kitchen. There were only three TV channels, so dancing in the kitchen was one of our favourite ways to pass the time. His big arms went around me and we were swaying, until he suddenly stopped, pulled out a little box from the pocket of his good work trousers. Next thing, he was down on one knee, the box was open and inside was the most beautiful ring I'd ever seen. Gold. With three little stones in a row. "They're not real diamonds, Val, but I promise that one day, when I've made something of myself, I'll get you a real one. Will you marry me and stick around for that?"'

Now, sitting in my kitchen, it was my turn to wipe away tears, but unlike Carly, I used the back of my hand, because there was no way I was spoiling my good blouse. I thought I'd be embarrassed, with all those people watching, but, weirdly, I didn't care. I just went on with the story...

'"I'll marry you and you never need to buy me another thing, Don Murray," I told him. I meant it as well. Every word. All I cared about was that we would spend our lives together. But turned out he never forgot his promise. It took decades for us to have two extra pennies to rub together, but when we did, well, turns out

Don had been saving those pennies for a long time. On our thirtieth wedding anniversary, he bought me a new ring with real diamonds this time...' I rubbed at that ring, on my wedding finger now, where it had been since the day he gave it to me. 'It's gorgeous, but if I'm being honest, the original one means so much more and I'd have been happy with that one forever. It was the one that was on my finger for over thirty years, and it was the one that represented us loving each other when we had nothing, and for every year afterwards, until...' I choked and Carly forgot about avoiding the camera and flew over to take my hand and held it tight until I could speak again. 'Until he died just a few weeks ago. So you see, now he's gone and I've lost the most special thing he ever gave me.' I had to pause again for a moment, because the guilt was fighting with the grief inside me. How could I have lost it? How could I have been so bloody careless?

'Can we see what it looks like, Aunt Val?' Carol prodded gently and I was grateful that she brought me back to the present.

'Of course, love.' I held up a picture of that night, of Don and me when we were barely seventeen, joy splitting my face, holding my hand up to show off the ring my boyfriend had just given me.

'Here it is. So if you, or someone you know, finds a ring that looks just like the one in this photo, then please let our Carol know. I can't tell you how grateful I'd be to have that part of him back with me.'

Carol took over again, finishing off with all the details, while I sent a silent message up to someone who definitely didn't have Wi-Fi or access to social media.

I'd just have to wait and see if my darling Don received it.

14

SOPHIE

Sophie woke up to the sound of a trolley trundling along the corridor outside the room and the cheery woman who was pushing it greeting everyone with a sing-song, 'Good morning!'

She wondered if the lady was like that all day long, or if she left work and slumped into a trance to conserve her energy until it was time to come back in and be relentlessly chipper again the next morning.

Sophie yawned, still tired after a night of broken sleep. She'd been sleeping so lightly that she'd instantly woken up when the lovely nurses had come around to check on her every couple of hours.

Before she stretched, or pushed herself up, she did an internal check of her body parts. Okay, so everything was still there. She moved her legs and was relieved that there was no pain. She wiggled her fingers. All fine there too. Next came a gentle twist of her body, so that she was lying on her back. So far so good. And finally she pushed herself up and felt like the tea lady had just dropped the happy act and punched her in the face. Okay, so still some residual pain then. Her head hurt, mostly on the side where she must have banged it on the window, and her neck and shoulder were aching too. Pulling her hospital robe away from her body, she peered down under it and saw a massive blue black bruise mapping out the exact spot where her seat belt had been. It wasn't pretty, but having the belt on had no doubt saved her from so much worse.

There were two of them in the ward, and Jasmine, the woman in the other bed, was rousing herself up to a sitting position too. Last night wasn't how Sophie had expected to spend her first night in Glasgow, but it wasn't all bad. Jasmine had been brought in with a cyst on her ovaries, and they were scheduling her for surgery today. There had been something quite liberating for both of them, being able to chat to a complete stranger about what had happened to them.

'How are you feeling this morning, Sophie?' Jasmine murmured as she stretched gently, not putting her arms too far above her head. Understandable. Jasmine's biggest worry last night had been that the cyst would burst, and it would become an emergency situation.

'Sore head, sore shoulder, feel like I've been in a car crash, still can't believe that happened to me, but happy I'm still in one piece.' That just about summed it up.

'Still planning on doing the *Sleepless in Seattle* thing today then?' Jasmine teased and Sophie couldn't help but laugh. Last night, she'd explained why she'd come to Glasgow, and even as she was saying it, she knew she sounded bonkers. And it wasn't down to the concussion.

Jasmine had put her hands up to stop her at one point. 'I need to get this right, because I'm going to have to repeat this to all my mates and I don't want to miss anything out. Two years ago, he proposed to you in the middle of George Square. And you said no.'

'Correct,' Sophie had confirmed, making her jaw ache because she couldn't help but laugh at Jasmine's incredulous reaction. Not that it had been a surprise. If it was the other way round, Sophie would have been thinking Jasmine was nuts too. 'But not because I didn't love him because I did, even though we'd only been together for a few months. But I needed to go home because my mum was sick.'

'It's just not fair. She was way too young to have cancer,' Jasmine had said, and Sophie had seen a flicker of worry go across the other woman's face. Earlier, when Sophie had told Jasmine about her mum's cancer, she'd shared that she been told that the cyst on her ovaries was likely to be benign, but she was terrified that they were wrong. Sophie had tried to reassure her, and hoped that she'd made her feel a little better.

There had been a pause, and Sophie had seen that Jasmine's worried expression was back, so she had tried to distract her with, 'So then what happened? Come on, this is a test to check if you were listening.'

Jasmine had chuckled, pressing her hand against her lower right stomach, as if trying to make sure it was protected. 'So you told him to ask you again a year later, but then you dingied him...'

Sophie hadn't understood. 'Dingied him?'

'It's Glasgow-speak for stood him up. Ignored him. Swerved him. Dodged him.'

'Yep, I guess I dingied him then,' Sophie had agreed, voice full of regret.

'Exactly,' Jasmine had gone on. 'So you dingied him, but then, last year, exactly a year after the poor bloke proposed the first time, he sent you a message with a picture of the ring, sitting on the ground in George Square. That might be the most romantic thing I've ever heard. Apart from when my Travis asked me to marry him by putting a ring in my prawn chow mein. If I hadn't seen it, I could have choked, but he said he wasn't worried because he's done First Aid.'

Sophie couldn't help giggle. Jasmine had already told her a couple of stories about her boyfriend and he sounded hilarious. She'd kept the conversation on track though. 'You're right about the message. But I didn't see it until about a month later. It was on WhatsApp, and I'd missed the notification altogether. When I eventually replied, I got a message saying it couldn't be delivered.'

Jasmine had eased up on to one elbow. 'So tomorrow night is the second anniversary of the date he proposed and you want to find him again to see if he's the one for you. Jesus. It sounds like the kind of romcom I watch when I've got PMT and I've demolished all the Dairy Milk.'

'That's what my sister says too. She thinks I've lost the plot. She might be right.'

They'd both fallen asleep at that point, but now, with the sun streaming in and the hospital stirring, Jasmine rolled over on her side, so that she was facing Sophie. 'I woke up during the night with a question.'

'I'm afraid,' Sophie joked, as Jasmine got straight to the point. 'The whole lost boyfriend thing. I get that his phone is no longer connected and he's not on Insta or Snapchat, but what I don't understand is why didn't you come up before now? You said you know where he lives and it's not like you were a million miles away. Or in jail. Although, that happened to my pal, Britney, and she managed to get messages out on a dodgy phone.'

Sophie didn't feel it was right to pry into Britney's criminal history, so she let that go. She thought about the answer for a moment. There was no simple way to explain, other than the truth. 'Because after my mum died, I just... fell apart, I suppose. I was sad for a long time and I kind of threw myself into my job and I guess other things just took over. I think I wasn't ready to be happy again.

But now, I'm much better, and this date was coming around and I just thought, stuff it. I've absolutely no idea what I'm hoping for, but I just couldn't let it go without trying to find out if he still loves me.'

'If you don't text me and tell me what happens I'll never forgive you. It'll be one of the great unanswered questions of my life.'

That made Sophie giggle, as the nurse who'd checked on her throughout the night came around and took all her vitals again. She seemed satisfied with what she saw, but she had the weirdest request Sophie had ever heard.

'Okay, go with me here because I just want to check your short-term memory. I'm going to give you three words to remember and I want you to repeat them back to me when I come back later. Trumpet. Balls. Custard.'

Sophie raised her eyebrows and said, deadpan, 'This is the strangest place I've ever been.'

'I'll take that as a compliment,' the nurse laughed. 'I'll ask you to repeat them to me when I come with the doctor on his rounds in half an hour or so.'

Trumpet. Balls. Custard. She was still saying that to herself when the cheery tea lady came in with breakfast. Sophie accepted gratefully, much to the disgust of Jasmine, who'd been informed that she was nil by mouth before her surgery today.

They chatted as Sophie tried to discreetly eat her food and she was grateful for the company. Although, right now the thing she'd be most grateful for was a shower and a change of clothes. Oh, and somewhere to charge her phone because it had died, and she wanted to send her sister another check-in text. She'd forgotten to bring a charger with her, and hadn't wanted to ask the nurse for one the night before. Hopefully Erin would be so wiped out from her big night out last night that she'd be in bed with a hangover until noon, and it would totally escape her that anything was wrong. Sophie had two choices – tell her sister what had happened and swear her to secrecy, or tell her nothing about the accident until she got home. As always, she hated the thought of causing anyone worry, so she'd probably go with the second option.

Actually, the thing she was most thankful for right now, and probably until the end of time, was that someone had been looking out for her yesterday. She wasn't sure if she believed in higher powers or spirits or guardian angels, but she was going to trust that it was her mum who'd had an eye on her and saved her yesterday. She'd even overheard one of the police officers saying that there weren't many people who had a high-speed crash on the M8 and walked away from it practically unscathed.

The thought took her mind to the taxi driver. Hopefully he was fine. Although she definitely wasn't nominating him for Scottish tourist ambassador of the month. She couldn't quite remember all their conversations, but she had an overwhelming sense that he'd been a complete arse to her.

'Good morning. I'm Doctor Choudry. Pleased to meet you... Sophie,' she finished, as she checked the name on her iPad. 'I'm just going to run a few tests with you while we speak, is that okay?'

'Yes. Thank you,' Sophie answered, appreciating again how nice everyone had been to her.

The doctor came right up to her side and used a small torch to check her pupils and Sophie couldn't help notice how stunning she was. No make-up, no false lashes, just a beautiful face. 'How are you feeling today?'

'I actually feel okay. My shoulder is a bit sore and there's a bruise, and my head hurts where I banged it, but nothing unbearable.'

The doctor raised her finger and told her to follow it with her eyes. Then ran through a load of other tests, squeezing her hands, pressing against her palms, sticking her tongue out, and so it went on for about five minutes.

'Okay and your memory? What do you remember about yesterday?'

'I can remember everything almost up to the crash, more or less. I'm a bit fuzzy about the conversation I was having right before it, but everything else is there. I remember being taken out of the car and brought here and everything after that.'

A few more questions, a few more tests, and Dr Choudry seemed happy with everything that she saw. 'Finally, nurse gave you three words to remember before I came here. Can you tell me what they were?'

'Trumpet. Balls. Custard.'

Smiling, Dr Choudry shook her head, turned to the nurse beside her. 'You do that deliberately, don't you?'

'Can't help myself,' the nurse replied, with a shame-faced, but mischievous, shrug.

Dr Choudry returned her attention to Sophie. 'The reason we do the three-word test is to make sure your short-term memory is functioning perfectly, not just to amuse Nurse Barker.' She threw an amused purse of the lips in her colleague's direction.

'Okay, Sophie, the good news is that I'm happy to discharge you. I'll write up a prescription for some painkillers to take if you need them. It goes without saying that anything out of the ordinary – acute pain, nausea, vomiting, dizziness, vision or hearing issues, numbness or tingling in your face – come straight back to us. Do you have any questions?'

'No, but thank you. Everyone has been so kind.'

Dr Choudry smiled and Sophie thought again how gorgeous she was, so calm, together and clearly successful. This wasn't a woman who went tearing up to the other side of the country to see if a man who once proposed to her was still kicking around and interested.

'You're very welcome. I hope that the rest of your weekend is much better than it's been so far. It can only get better.'

As she swung her legs round, and climbed out of her hospital bed, Sophie sent up a silent prayer to her mum that the doctor was right.

15

ALICE

The irony didn't escape Alice. Only yesterday morning, she was tucking away twenty-pound notes because it was all she had to show for her existence in this world. She'd spoken to no one. She'd been anonymous. Faceless. Invisible. Yet, now, she was being told that there were still press at the reception of the hospital, trying to speak to her, to get information on her life. Or, more accurately, trying to find out if she was here. If her husband was here. If he was alive. Or dead. And only to herself would she admit the option that she would prefer.

'He made it through surgery,' Richard Campbell had told her, when he'd found her sitting outside the prayer room. It went without saying that he probably thought she was beseeching some higher power to save her husband's life and bring him back to her. She hadn't told him otherwise.

'But I'm just going to be honest with you, Alice, he's not out of the woods yet and it's going to be a waiting game for the next few hours. Tell me what you want to know, because I don't want to overload you. Do you want the details, or shall I stop at that for now?'

'Details. Tell me everything you know, please,' she'd said.

He'd nodded thoughtfully, 'We're sure now that Larry had a heart attack in the car and that was what caused the accident. All signs pointed to that, and when they scanned him, they found a blockage in one of the main arteries feeding his heart. The surgical team performed a coronary angioplasty to clear the blockage and they've inserted a stent to keep the artery open, but it's impossible to say what damage has already been done. We don't know how long he was down before the team got to him at the scene, and we don't know the scope of any resultant damage to his brain or his other organs. He's out of recovery, but he hasn't come round yet, so we're bringing him down to intensive care. Unfortunately, I can't let you stay with him, because ICU visiting is restricted to specific slots, but I can let you see him for a few minutes.'

'Thank you.' If he'd detected her reluctance, he'd had the good grace not to question it.

'Normally, I'd tell you to go home at this point, or at least to go to the hospital café and take a break, give it some time to see how things develop in the next few hours, but I don't think that's wise. Reception and security have reported a couple of journalists have been in asking questions, so the options are that we can get you safely to your car...' He obviously hadn't known that she no longer possessed her own vehicle. 'Or you can stay here for now.'

She'd pondered over those options. She could go home to the place that she hated, where every single thing reminded her of Larry: the ridiculously oversized furniture, the sag on the couch where he sat every night, the razors that he left lying around the bloody bathroom. Although, if she did that, maybe she could make a good cup of coffee, put her feet up, read a novel and escape into the kind of fictional world that allowed her to forget the reality of her day-to-day torment. Or she could stay here, protected, but around real people, who were kind and who spoke to her like a human being.

'I'd like to stay please.' She had felt like she should qualify that, explain it as if she was a normal, loving wife, so she'd lied. 'I'd like to be here when he wakes up.'

Richard had nodded. 'Okay.' There was a slight pause and she'd thought he was done, until he'd carried on, his words caring and sympathetic. 'But, Alice, I need you to know that might not be today. Or tomorrow. We have no way of predicting when his situation will change.'

'I understand. I'd still like to stay for now. I'll wait in the family room if that's okay?'

She knew exactly where the family room was because she'd been there on the day that it had re-opened, after her fundraising committee had raised the finance for its renovation. She knew there were two sofas there, and a television and a coffee machine. It wasn't lavish, but it was comfortable and that was all she'd needed.

'But can you take me to see him first?'

Richard had led the way, down the mire of corridors that led to the ICU unit. When they'd got there, he'd taken her in, but two of the medical staff were by Larry's bed, so she'd stopped at the nursing station, from where she could see her husband lying perfectly still a few metres away. It was a strange sight. It was Larry, but at the same time it wasn't. That man was in a hospital gown and he was surrounded by machines and tubes. His skin was grey and his cheeks were sunken, like the sand pits on the kind of golf courses he used to swagger around in his heyday. But the most remarkable difference was that Larry's huge presence, his hulking physicality was gone and that man, there, lying in that bed was... small. Unimposing. Non-threatening.

'As I said, it's a waiting game now, Alice,' Richard had said, with a gentleness in his voice that had no doubt been developed over decades of doing this job. Alice had heard him speak to patients and their families like this before, but she'd never considered that one day it would be her.

'Thank you, Richard. For everything. If you don't mind, I'd like to go to the family room now. If there is any news, will you let me know, please?'

'Of course. I'll be leaving for the day shortly, but I'll make sure that the consultant in charge knows where you are and notifies you if there's any change. I'll be back in first thing in the morning though, and I've asked the charge nurse tonight to call me at home if there's any change and I'll come straight back in.'

'You don't need to do that,' she'd assured him, wondering why it irked her that even now, Larry was getting special treatment. Bastard deserved none of it. 'I'm sure your team will take very good care of him.'

'Alice, it's not just for Larry, because you're right – the team here is the best. I'll come back in so that you have a familiar face if anything changes. I'd do the same for any friend.'

Tears had shot to Alice's eyes and she'd had to blink them back. Over a lifetime with Larry, she'd trained herself to shut down her emotional responses, to stay strong, to hold her defences around her like a brick wall that protected her from feeling pain, or hurt, or heartbreak, but the kindness in Richard's words had almost slayed her. It had been a long time since anyone had called her a friend.

As soon as she'd got to the family room, Alice had called the supervisors at both her cleaning jobs and let them know that she wouldn't be in until further notice, because of an illness in the family. She didn't give any more information than that, but no doubt her supervisors would soon hear news of Larry's accident through the internet or the newspapers.

Calls made, Alice had laid down on the sofa, and a wave of exhaustion had hit her like a train, forcing her to close her eyes. The next thing she knew, Richard was knocking on the door and her watch was telling her that it was morning.

He'd arrived with two coffees, making her stomach growl as she'd realised she'd had nothing to eat since yesterday morning. Not that she ever had much of an appetite these days, but still. She could probably have gone out to one of the shops in the foyer last night, or even just found a vending machine with snacks or drinks, but she'd had this room to herself all night, and she hadn't wanted to leave the cocoon of privacy and comfort. She'd stretched herself up from where she'd been lying on the couch, and pushed her hair back, embarrassed because she knew that she must look like an absolute riot. Same clothes as yesterday. Dishevelled after a night on a couch. Hair that hadn't seen a brush for a whole day.

'Is... Is he...?' She'd stopped, rephrased, 'Has there been any change?' That sounded better.

Richard had shaken his head as he handed her one of the coffees, then produced a muffin from the pocket of his white coat. He'd sat down on the couch opposite her. 'No, none, I'm afraid. It's not unusual, Alice, and please don't read anything into it. We're still cautiously hopeful.' She'd had a strong suspicion that they were hoping for different things.

The coffee had been hot and the warmth felt good against her lips as she took a sip.

'Listen, it's completely up to you, and you're welcome to stay here, but I would suggest that you go home, even for a little while. Just take a break, sleep, eat. You have to take care of yourself too.'

He was right, but still, she'd felt no desire to face the outside world. 'I will, but perhaps not yet. I'll wait for a while longer, if that's okay.'

'Of course. I'll pop back in later, but if you decide to leave in the meantime, just let reception know. Is there anything else you need?'

The answer to that question was way too long and way too complicated. She needed friends. Family. Happiness. Joy. Love. A new life. An escape from the bastard who was lying through in that bed.

'No, I'm fine. And, Richard, thank you again for your kindness. It's been such a comfort.'

'You're welcome. Just be aware, though, that there are still journalists hanging around outside. We've asked them to leave, but they're pretty relentless and keep coming back. I think I know the answer, but do you want to give them any comment? I can get the hospital spokesperson to give them something short and vague, but that might just be enough to get them to go.'

'No. No comment. I've got nothing to say to them.'

There was the irony. Yesterday, she was nobody. Today, the press were desperate to know about her life. These were the same people who had relentlessly pursued her, vilified her family, made unsubstantiated claims and sensationalised every single detail of the scandal. Larry had been the architect of their ruin, but the media had relished and exploited it.

Now, as she sat on the sofa she'd slept on all night, grateful for every small kindness, she knew that she'd never give them another second of her life.

Richard closed the door behind him, and Alice immediately ripped open the muffin, took a small piece and popped it in her mouth. She switched on the television with the volume turned down, just feeling the need to see that the world was still turning, still existing out there. The first programme that came on was a property show, so she pressed another button. The next channel had some tall, leggy brunette in a bikini top and sarong, walking along a beach on a travel show. Alice fixed her gaze on the screen, took in the crystal turquoise seas, the golden sands, the wooden bungalows on stilts that stretched over the water. They'd once taken a holiday to a place like that. Larry had ordered fine wines and smoked huge cigars, but he'd had no interest in joining her and Rory as they'd paddled on canoes near the shore.

She remembered thinking that one day she'd go back there without him and she'd breath in warm air, feel the heat on her skin and she would be free.

There was no way that she could ever afford a trip like that now, but she didn't care about the sun or the sand. Until yesterday, she'd trained herself to be patient until that twenty pounds she tucked away every week could buy her freedom.

Now, she wasn't sure she could wait that long.

16

RORY

Rory's first reaction when he woke was to wonder if a transit van had run over his head during the night. His second reaction was to swear that he would never drink again. Never.

He waited for the wave of nausea to pass before even trying to move. It was just as well, because when he tried to push himself up off Albie's impossibly fricking uncomfortable sofa, he realised that the transit van had stopped, turned around and then run right over his body as well.

Shit, what a state he was in. He managed to get himself to sitting, and squinted open one eye, to find that the world was still there, and he seemed to be alive and sitting in the middle of it, in Calvin Klein boxers, next to an empty tequila bottle and the remnants of a kebab.

He heard a noise behind him, realised it was a female voice, grabbed at the grey furry throw he'd been using as a blanket and pulled it across him to protect his modesty until he could work out what the hell was going on.

'Bye, sweetie,' he heard next, then the sound of blowing kisses, before Belinda from the Comedy Den bar appeared from the direction of Albie's room and walked right past Rory on the way to the door, wearing her usual kaleidoscope of primary colours that belonged on a kids' TV presenter from the nineties. 'Sorry, Rory,' she said with a breezy shrug as she passed him. 'One day you'll be crushed that I've chosen Albie, but I couldn't wait forever for you. You'll never know what you missed.' And with an uproarious cackle, she opened the front door and was gone, leaving Rory wondering if he'd just imagined that.

The sight of an unkempt and crumpled Albie shuffling out of his room next, in just pants, hair pointing in a hundred directions, accessorised with an unlit cigarette dangling from his mouth, told him that it had probably been real.

'I think she broke me,' he croaked, before slumping down on the other sofa.

It took Rory a minute to react, because he was still trying to rewind the hours to work out what had happened. Yesterday, after Albie had left him in the pub, he'd made the decision to go see his mother. It hadn't been an easy one. The prospect of seeing his dad had no appeal, but just before contact with his parents had been broken off, he'd learned that Larry had started working as a taxi driver, so he was banking on him being out at work.

Decision made, he'd grabbed his jacket and hailed a taxi outside the bar. The streets had been busy, probably a mixture of tourists and the Glasgow locals whose Scottish DNA insisted that at the first glimpse of sunshine, you had to get outside because you didn't know how long it would last or when it would reappear.

On the journey, he'd changed his mind a dozen times. The address had been imprinted on his brain, because it was only one street away from where his mum had met him and Julia in their car that night, when they'd made the deal that had forced him to cut off all ties with her. It had devastated him. He'd pleaded with her to let him help, to allow him to pay for somewhere else for them to live, or even to move in with him and Julia. His mother had refused. Now he wondered how Julia would have reacted if she'd said yes. Would she have called it quits back then, pulled the Band Aid off quickly, instead of waiting another year for the infected, seeping wound to kill them?

He'd asked the taxi to wait when he'd pulled up at the house, only a few miles but a world away from the mansion he'd grown up in. It was a row of five houses in a terrace, and theirs was at the end. As he'd gone up the path, the only sign of life had been the music thumping from the house next door.

He'd rung the doorbell, waited, but there was no answer. He'd rung it again. Still nothing.

He'd peered in the front window, but it was difficult to see anything through the net curtains.

After trying the door a couple more times, he'd given up, defeated. Disappointed. All he'd wanted was to see his mum, to check on her, to tell her what had happened, and call quits on the separation she'd forced on them.

Crushed, he'd jumped back in the taxi, then come back to Albie's place, because he wasn't really sure where else he wanted to go. What did a bloke who'd just been dumped and fired usually do with his days?

Apparently, the answer was day-drink with his mate, then go out for burgers and beers, while contemplating the meaning of life and uncertain futures, before going with Albie to his comedy set, then having an after-party at the flat that only ended when their downstairs neighbour banged on the ceiling.

In the midst of the revelry, he did remember Belinda declaring her undying love in the kitchen. He recalled telling her as gently as possible that he wasn't ready for a new relationship, and then trying to make up for it by calling Uber Eats and requesting the delivery of a dozen kebabs. It had made sense at the time. He'd also stopped drinking at that point, because he had a deathly fear that if his fingers fell under the control of Budweiser, they might decide it was smart to text his wife and tell her that... Actually, now that he was sober, albeit hungover, he had no idea what he'd have said, which is probably why it had been a good idea to switch to water at that point. His next memory was of everyone leaving and him crashing out on the couch from pure exhaustion, and that was it until he'd been woken by the dulcet tones of Belinda's heartfelt departure.

'Hope you don't mind me surrendering to Belinda. I've always had a thing for her, to be honest. I like a woman that can pull off purple, green, yellow, red and blue all at the same time,' Albie was telling him now.

Rory shook his head, and even though it hurt to grin, he went for it. 'I think I'll cope. I like her though. She's a good contrast to your deep dark cynicism and general disdain for the world.'

Albie scratched at the crazy mass of ginger spikes on his bedhead. 'You might be right. I almost feel cheery this morning. I'll go lie down until it passes. What's your plans?'

Rory took a slug from a bottle of water he'd found under the blanket, not sure of the answer. There were so many things that should really be on the list. First, check his emails to see if the terms he'd agreed with Roger yesterday had been sent in writing. He was almost certain they'd be there. It had been made perfectly clear that Rory was a boil on the arse of the Fieldows' existence, so now that they had a way to cut him off, they'd want to get it done quickly. He had a couple of mates that were lawyers and he'd already decided to appoint one of them to deal with Fieldow going forward, until everything was settled. He could quite happily live without seeing his father-in-law's face ever again. He'd add their fee to his termination package.

Next? Just trifling issues like retrieving his personal belongings from his marital home, then finding a place to live, a new job and a new purpose for his entire future. Oh, and coffee and a shower were on the list too. Probably at the top.

However, the unsuccessful trip to see his mum was really bugging him, so the big stuff was going to have to wait until he'd gone back to her house to see if she was there now.

After Albie shuffled back off to bed to restore his dark soul, Rory put a mug in the coffee machine and pressed 'pour'. While his large black extra-strong Americano was brewing, he jumped in the shower, washed his hair, brushed his teeth and then dried off. Back in the kitchen, he retrieved his coffee and drank it while he was getting dressed, pulling a black T-shirt from a hanger on the curtain rod, and a pair of black jeans from another. He found one of his Nike Low Dunks under the couch, but it took him a few minutes to locate the other, which was, bizarrely, behind the living-room curtain.

His final task was to blow on the breathalyser he'd bought a few years ago, when Scotland's new drink-driving limits had come into force and there were stories in the press day after day about people being stopped, breathalysed and arrested for drunk driving the morning after a night out because there was still too much alcohol in their system. That was before his father and the scandal had become the daily headlines in the papers.

Thankfully, switching to water last night had paid off, and the breathalyser told him he was now good to go, so he grabbed his wallet and his keys and headed out to the company car that had been included in yesterday's negotiation. He made a mental note to make sure all the paperwork was sent to the DVLA next week to make it official.

It took thirty minutes to get back to the same door he'd knocked on yesterday. Today being Saturday, the street was busier, with a few kids out playing football on the communal grass area, and an elderly man cutting his lawn a couple of doors along.

Rory parked up the Audi, and paused, staring straight ahead, taking a minute to prepare himself for the possibility that his father would answer the door. Every time he'd imagined this moment, he'd wondered how he would react to coming face to face with the man who'd barely acknowledged him his whole life, except if they were in public, when he played at being dad of the year. Now he knew how he'd handle it – the same way his dad had treated him when they'd lived in the same house for eighteen years and he'd rarely looked in his direction – he'd ignore him. He was here to see his mum, that was it. He had zero interest in any dialogue with Larry McLenn.

Psyched up, Rory got out of the car and retraced his steps down the path, nodding a hello to the fellow who was cutting his grass while now watching Rory's every move. Rory knocked on the door again and waited, surprised to feel a swirl of anxiety in his stomach. Or maybe that was just the after-effects of last night's tequila.

He knocked again. Waited. Still nothing.

The lawnmower stopped. 'They're not in,' the elderly man shouted from his garden. 'When he's there, he parks his red Skoda behind next door's transit.'

Rory gave him a wave of thanks. 'Cheers, pal. I'll try again later.'

He started to walk back down the path, but he wasn't getting away that easily. 'Are you polis, son?' The neighbour shouted, using the Glaswegian colloquialism for police.

Rory stopped at the gate. 'No. Just a friend.'

He was about to go through the gate and get back in the car, when something stopped him.

'What made you think I would be police?' he shouted back

over, curious about the assumption, wondering if it meant his dad was in trouble again.

The old man took a sharp intake of breath, shook his head, his face twisted with disapproval. 'Because that's a bad yin that lives in there. And I wouldnae be scared to tell him that to his face either. Real arsehole. I wisnae happy when he moved in here either. This is a decent street and we don't want the likes of him here lowering the tone.'

Two thoughts immediately collided in Rory's head. The first one was that the old man was right. That was swiftly followed by a sweet sense of justice that his dad's former elite circles weren't the only people who now shunned him as scum.

'I don't disagree with you.'

'Aye, when I'm right, I'm right. Mortifying it is, when I see that arse's name in the papers. I tell folk I don't know him and he disnae live here. I said the very same thing to ma pal in the bookies this morning.'

Again, Rory was about to move and then stopped. 'Hang on, was he in the papers this morning?'

'Aye. Totalled his motor. It was on the front page of the *Glasgow Chronicle* this morning. Couldnae happen to a nicer guy.' The sarcasm was dripping off his words, before he leaned over, restarted his lawnmower, making it clear that the conversation was over.

Rory's anxiety got a new layer of urgency as he rushed back to the car, not for his father, but for his mum. Was she in the accident too? He jumped in, pulled out his phone and googled his dad's name, then scrolled down to the website of the *Glasgow Chronicle*. The headline was the first thing he saw:

DISGRACED MP IN HORROR CRASH

Right below it was a grainy photo of a red Skoda in the middle of a motorway. It had obviously hit the central barrier because it was crumpled on one side.

Rory's eyes speed-scanned down the rest of the article, taking in flashes of information. Male driver. Reported to be Larry McLenn. Resuscitated at scene. Why had his mum not called? They'd broken off all communication, but she knew where to find him in an emergency. She could have phoned the office and got a message to him. He kept on scanning and it felt like his heart stopped. Female passenger. Injured at scene. Taken to Glasgow Central Hospital. No further information on her condition.

Fuck. Fuck. Fuck. That had to be his mum. Was she hurt? Worse? He didn't give a toss about his dad, but his mum was a different story. It had always been her and him against the world, even when that fight meant they'd had to cut off contact for a while to get the press off his and Julia's backs. Now the reasons for that, his mum's insistence on protecting his marriage and career were no longer in play, had he... He could barely finish the thought. Had he left it too late to see her?

Thunder pounding in his head, hands trembling, he pressed the ignition button on his car and pulled off. This morning he hadn't been sure where he should go today.

Now he knew the only place he had to be was Glasgow Central Hospital.

17

VAL

I'd never heard or seen anything like it. Carol's phone had been pinging all day long, and she'd spent hours on it, filtering through all the messages and checking all the comments that had come in since our live chat this morning.

'I've uploaded it to my Stories and to YouTube, and we've had over fifty thousand views, more than ten thousand comments and around the same number of shares. I've had messages from two newspapers, wanting to share your story – I've told them I'll get back to them on Monday if your rings still haven't been found, Aunt Val.'

'Thank you, ma love. Have I said how much everything you two are doing for me means to me? I love you both with all the bits that are left of my heart.'

Carly leaned down, draped her arms over my shoulders and hugged me.

'It's because we're so loveable. Although my kids seem to have forgotten that. I haven't heard from Mac or Benny since yesterday morning when I texted to say I was coming up here.'

Carol glanced up from her phone. 'I've had three calls from

Charlotte, but only about borrowing clothes and warning me there's a photo online of her snogging some random bloke who looks like Harry Styles. Apparently it's not him, but I'm holding out hope.'

My cloak of guilt about taking them away from their normal lives and their families got just a tiny bit lighter.

It wasn't just the help and support that these girls were giving me that was holding me together and allowing little glimmers of optimism to flutter through my brain for the first time since Don's mahogany casket had been lowered into the ground. It was just having them here, chatting about the normal stuff, about kids, and jobs, and marriages and life. I'd missed the feeling of having people living in the house with me. I saw that now. For the happiest part of my life, we'd been a busy, chaotic, family of four, bursting with love and laughs. But then Dee was taken away and our Michael got married and moved out. And the last few years... Well, I'd tried my best to put a smile on my face every day while Don had been in the grips of his disease. I'd had smashing support too. There had been a stream of lovely carers in and out doing their best for him, and our pals Nancy and Johnny, and Tress and Noah were here at least once a week. Our Michael had been a godsend, spending all his days off with his dad to give me a break. But all of that had been centred around Don's illness, the invasive, evil lodger that had come to destroy our lives. Now, having Carol and Carly here – despite the absolute bloody heartbreak of the situation – felt like real life. Like the way it used to be when Don was well, and the kids were around, and there was an endless stream of pals and family coming in and out the door for food, encouragement, a shoulder to share their woes and some chat and laughs at this table.

'Right, Aunt Val, are we ready to do this?' Carly asked, as she slipped into a chair and began fiddling with some buttons on a box on the table. Apparently, the microphones in front of us were all linked and this was how they broadcasted their live podcast. In my day, we just called it a radio show and I would never have believed I'd ever be doing something like this from my kitchen. Although, when I thought about it, I got so nervous I wanted to put my head between my knees in case I fainted, so I was just going to block out the fact that there would be thousands of listeners.

'We don't usually video the podcast, but we're going to do that today and then upload it to YouTube and we'll send traffic there later.'

I had no inclination to decipher what that meant, so I just nodded in agreement.

'How's my hair?'

'As Josie would say, it's the size of a motorcycle helmet and you could smash a shop window with it,' Carly replied.

'Excellent. We're good to go then,' I quipped, thinking how Carly's comment was absolutely the right thing to say at this very second. I needed a bit of Josie with me right now. She'd left part of her DNA on my soul and it was time to channel it.

Carly pressed another button, then reached over and gave my hand a squeeze while she was speaking.

'My fellow Twisted Knickers out there, welcome to this week's podcast. This is Carly Morton, and, as always, I'm joined by my far more successful sister-in-law – model, influencer, social media superstar and all-round babe, Carol Cooper.'

'That was some introduction,' Carol piped in. 'You're either after money or something in my wardrobe, so what is it?'

'Neither,' Carly chirped. 'I want you to do Christmas dinner this year and I'm starting early with the coercion. Anyway, folks, as you know, this show is dedicated every week to whatever subject is twisting your knickers, getting you in a flux-with-an-L, bringing you down or heating you up, but today is a bit different because we're also joined by our very favourite relative – don't tell our kids we said that – our Aunt Val. Now, if you caught Carol's Instagram Live post this morning, you'll know why Val is here, but for those who have no idea what I'm talking about, let me fill you in.'

I took a sip of my tea, as Carly went on to explain the whole story, and mentioned that all the details and pictures could be found on their social media posts and YouTube channels. I had no idea what YouTube channels were, so I made a mental note to get them to show me later. There had been me thinking I was making a ground-breaking technological leap when I got Netflix.

'Aunt Val, I'd give you a drum roll, but you'll only chide me for banging on your table, so I'll just say hello and tell you we love you.'

'That's much better than a drum roll, pet,' I replied, smiling, still blocking out the thought of all those listeners.

Carly was speaking again. 'This morning on Carol's Instagram Live, you told us about the engagement ring that Uncle Don bought you when you were still too young to drink in pubs.'

'I had to snap him up before anyone else got the chance,' I retorted, grinning at the thought of that memory again. 'And I never regretted it for a second. He was one of a kind, my Don. I never stopped feeling lucky that he chose me and I chose him. We slow danced in the kitchen that night and we were still dancing in this kitchen over forty years later.' A flashback to that more recent night hit me like a kick to the chest. Don. Me. Swaying to an old Otis Redding song just a few weeks before he passed. I'm not sure that he knew who I was that day, but he held me tight and I let myself pretend that we were just us, that everything was fine, that his mind was still here. Those were the kind of moments that had kept me going and I ached for more of them.

Throat suddenly tight again, I pushed the memory away for

now. When I was in bed later, I'd let myself think about it, but right now, I had to concentrate on what we were doing.

'Carol and I have danced many a night in this kitchen too,' Carly added, her own memories making her smile. 'I remember you and your pal, Josie, teaching us all to jive during a Hogmanay party. We broke three of your best glasses, knocked over a cheese and pineapple hedgehog and Josie said she pulled a hamstring spinning me round.'

Oh Jesus, another kick to the throat with that one. We'd laughed until we cried that night. I lost my words for a second, but thankfully, Carly nudged everything back on track.

'And that actually brings us to the subject of this podcast today. Because another of the rings that you lost held special significance to Josie, didn't it?'

I caught Carly's nod and knew it was my cue to start telling her about Josie's ring. *Right Val*, I told myself. *Just act like your pals are here. It's just another chat.*

'It did. You know, I listen to this podcast because I like to hear what you and Carol are talking about, and I think you two are smashing. I mean, obviously I'm biased, but I'll stand by that.'

Carly grinned and gave a thumbs up.

'But I also listen because, to me, hearing you speak is like a million conversations I've had with my pals at this table over the years. I'm sure everyone out there knows that you two are related, but the thing is, you were pals first, and you still are, through all the ups and downs and disasters and dramas that have come your way. You're in your fifties now...'

'Hush your mouth,' Carol joked.

'And you're still the same daft lassies that you were when you were fifteen and climbing out the window to go to discos. And the reason I say all this is that sometimes it's hard to keep the laughs and the enthusiasm alive when life has given you a kicking, like it does to us all. I have a few pals that make me feel that way, even at my age, but I lost one of those a few years ago, and believe me when I tell you that the world is a less colourful place without Josie Cairney. She smoked like a train, she swore like a sailor, she had a laugh that sounded like a generator booting up in a power cut, and anyone who got on the wrong side of her had better be a fast runner, but she was someone who made every single person she loved better. She made us stronger. She made us laugh harder. She made us die with embarrassment and she made us feel like we could do any bloody thing that we set our minds to. The night she died, her and I had been at a wedding in a posh hotel, and we were dancing our shoes off, having the best of times.'

As I began sharing my story with anyone who was listening, every moment of that night played like a movie in my mind.

Josie had appointed herself wedding planner for our friends Cammy and Caro, and later that night, after the celebrations were over, the two of us, joined at the elbow, had strolled along the hotel corridor, holding our shoes in our free hands, a bottle of champagne tucked under Josie's arm.

When we'd reached Josie's room, she'd swayed slightly as she put the key card in the lock.

'Are you coming in for a nightcap?'

I'd winced as I'd pulled at the waistband under my best frock. 'Only if I can take these knickers off.'

'Best offer I've had in a long time,' Josie had said, making the two of us hoot with laughter.

In the room, she'd handed the bottle to me, but then, as she'd flopped onto the bed, a coughing fit had consumed her. That had been happening more and more over the previous few months, but Josie had repeatedly brushed it off as a chest infection, a mild dose of the flu, a touch of bronchitis.

I was pouring the champagne into two mugs on the tea tray,

when I'd chided her, as I'd done many times before. 'For feck's sake, Josie, will you get that seen to? You sound like you're on your last legs there.'

What I didn't know then was that I was right. My best pal, the bloody magnificent Josie Cairney had been told that morning by a specialist that she had terminal lung cancer. That would have been the time to tell me, but, God love her, she didn't. Instead, she did something that should have alerted me that something was wrong – she got sentimental.

'You know,' she'd said flippantly, 'that was a brilliant night. It really was. If I popped my clogs right now, I'd go a happy woman.'

Laughing, I'd chucked her over a packet of shortbread fingers. 'Och, don't be daft. I know you're lying. You won't die happy until you've shagged Pierce Brosnan.'

'You've got a point,' Josie had shrugged, with that mischievous glint in her eye. 'Although, I do worry that he's getting on in years and at his age I'd be a bit too much for him.'

Before I could point out yet again that Josie was several years older than Mr Shaken, Not Stirred, she'd blurted, 'Val Murray, I bloody love you, do you know that?'

'That's completely understandable. I'd love me too,' I'd fired back, joking as usual.

That's when I'd held my glass up to celebrate her. 'Congratulations, Josie, you pulled off the wedding of the year today. It was brilliant, it really was. If my Don trades me in for a supermodel, you can do my next one too.'

'No problem. I'll even give you a discount on my fee. So it'll be a large bottle of gin and five boxes of Tunnock's tea cakes.'

I'd plonked down on the chair next to the bed, and for the next few minutes, we chatted about the day, until we'd both drained our glasses. That's when I'd forced my groaning joints back out of the chair. 'Right, I'm going to love you and leave you. I need to get back to my room and get these knickers off. My feet are turning blue.'

She had got up from the bed and that's when she'd done something else unusual – she'd hugged me. And Josie, as she would tell anyone, 'hated all that touchy-feely pish'.

'Goodnight, love. You're the best pal a woman could have, Val,' she'd said.

'And you're a class act, Josie Cairney.' I'd tightened my hug. 'Och, we're getting soppy in our old age. Love you, Josie. See you for breakfast in the morning?'

'Love you too, pet, and yep, I'll be there.'

'Aye, well, don't scoff all the sausages if you get there before me.'

And with that, I'd waddled out of the room, and the door had closed behind me.

Josie didn't make it to breakfast. That night, sometime after I'd left her, she'd died in her bed, and to this day, I told myself she was asleep and never knew it was coming. I also told myself it was how she would have wanted to go: happy, a little tipsy, after a raucous night of dancing and laughter, surrounded by the people she loved.

Now, at my kitchen table, I must have paused, because I saw that Carol and Carly were both staring at me, tears dripping down their cheeks.

I rewound to where I'd been in my story and then carried on, 'I had no idea that there would be no more of those great times with her. But what I do have is the memory of an incredible friend. So the way I see it, this podcast is all about women sticking together and holding each other up. Josie Cairney did that every day of her life. After she died, her daughter, Avril, gave me one of her rings. She told me that it was the ring, or Josie's collection of Billy Idol records. No offence to Billy, but I took the ring. It was a large rectangular emerald on a gold band. I've no idea if the stone is real, so I don't have a clue if the ring is valuable, but to me, it's priceless. Because to me it's Josie. And when I'm finding things tough, I put that ring on, and it's like she's here. The world is more colourful and I can hear her voice telling me I can do anything. You two do that for each other, and I hope everyone has at least one pal like that. And if they do, go dance yer heels off, because life's too short to act your age.'

There was a pause, and I began to panic that I'd gone too far or said something wrong, but as I looked from one niece to another, I saw that Carol's eyes were still streaming and Carly was biting her bottom lip, just like she'd done since she was a kid.

'Sorry for missing a beat there, but we've been doing this show for more than two years now, and I'm just very aware that that my auntie is way more life-smart than I could ever be,' Carly said, sniffing loudly.

I wanted to say that if I were that smart I wouldn't have lost the rings, but Carly was already wrapping things up.

'So, friends, family, and even any ex-boyfriends who listen in to our podcast so that they can reassure themselves that they had a lucky escape, now you understand how much Val's rings mean to her, and to us, please help us find them.'

Like a verbal tag team, Carol took over. 'As we said at the start, pictures are on our social media sites and our YouTube channel, and our comments and messages are open.'

Carly again. 'And if you want to start a petition to permanently replace us with Val and her words of wisdom, we'll totally understand and approve. We know when we're beat. So, goodbye for now, go love your friends, and keep your eye on our socials because we may be doing a couple of bonus episodes over the weekend. Thank you for listening and for being part of the *Twisted Knickers* family. Mic drop from me...'

'And from me,' Carol added, before music began to play and Carly started pressing all kinds of buttons.

This time, it was Carol who puffed out her cheeks and stretched so high her T-shirt flashed her stomach. 'Aunt Val, I adore you, and I wouldn't change being here for the world. I'm so glad we're with you...'

'But?' I knew something was coming and I wasn't wrong.

'But, bugger me, this is the most emotionally exhausting weekend I've had since Callum went missing on that shoot in Amsterdam, and I was convinced he'd overdosed on dodgy Brownies and taken a header into a canal.'

'Technically, you weren't far off. If you swap the header into a canal for sleeping it off in the presidential suite at the Grand Hotel Krasnapolsky,' Carly added.

'The point is,' Carol went on, 'my heart is being shredded here. Any more of this and I'm going to have to ask my doc to increase my HRT.'

'I'm sorry, love.' I felt terrible for dragging them into this.

'No, please don't apologise! I just mean if I'm feeling this way, you must be in pieces inside.'

I thought about that. I still had that sick, swirling feeling in the bottom of my stomach. I wanted to cry. My head was banging and I wanted to punch a wall because I was still so damn furious with myself. But apart from that... 'I just need to keep believing that this will work,' I said. 'What do we do next?'

Carly pulled a bottle of white wine from the rack on the counter behind her and then a bottle of soda from the fridge. 'We wait. We hope. We day-drink. And if it doesn't work, we'll do it all again tonight.'

18

SOPHIE

Standing under the powerful jets of the hotel shower felt like it was the most incredible ten minutes of Sophie's life – until she turned the other way and the drumming liquid hit the seatbelt bruise that remained after her near-death experience yesterday.

It still blew her mind that a day ago she was spinning around in an out-of-control car and now, relatively unscathed, if you didn't count the bruising and a few lingering aches, she was standing in the shower in a luxury hotel. Although, she had cried for a full five minutes when she'd first got here and collapsed on the bed. She'd stared at the ceiling, replayed everything that had happened, right up until she woke up this morning in hospital. She'd whispered, 'Thanks, Mum,' to give credit to the angel who'd been looking out for her, and before she knew it, she was sobbing her heart out into the pillow of a king-size bed. And that was the second teary episode of the day. The receptionist had felt so sorry for her when she'd explained why she'd showed up a day late for her booking that she'd cancelled the charge for the previous night and upgraded her to an executive room.

'Fifth floor, view of George Square. I hope it makes up a little bit for the nightmare you've had since you got here.'

Sophie had spluttered out her thanks through wobbling lips.

Now, though, she was feeling better. She'd had a good long think about whether she should just give this up and go home, but she'd decided that she'd gone through so much that she had to see if there was a pay-off at the end. And if there wasn't... well, sod it, at least she was still in one piece.

Drying off with a luxurious, thick white fluffy towel, she formulated a plan. Get dressed, find the nearest coffee place, grab a cappuccino to go, and then take the underground to Ash's apartment in the West End of the city. She could still remember how to get there, so hopefully it wouldn't take too long. If he was in, fantastic. If he wasn't... well, she would just have to hope that he would send her a picture of the ring tonight, just as he'd done last year. Or maybe he'd just have a nostalgic stroll in the square late in the afternoon, around the same time as he'd proposed two years ago today.

Her phone, sitting on the bedside table and plugged into the charger she'd borrowed from reception, beeped with an incoming text. She knew it wouldn't be Erin, because before her shower, as soon as she'd had power, she'd texted her sister, still debating whether to tell her about the accident.

Hey! Are you alive? Up? Busy?

Sophie had messaged.

Hangover. Dying.

Had been the reply.

That had made the decision for her. Now wasn't the time to

throw a life-threatening incident into her sister's day, especially as the whole trip had been Erin's idea in the first place. A couple of weeks ago, after several failed Tinder dates, including a bloke who asked her if she'd be prepared to put her feet in a bucket of baked beans for him because he got off on that (she'd excused herself to go to the loo and was on the train home before he would have realised she was gone), Erin had lost patience and challenged her. 'Sophie, who is the only guy that you've fallen in love with in your entire adult life?'

'Does Channing Tatum count?'

'No. And stop trying to deflect the question.' Sophie could see there was no way she was getting away with a glib brush off.

'Then okay, it's Ash.' Her heart had thudded just saying his name aloud.

'Exactly. You should go and see him. School is off for the long weekend at the beginning of next month, you could go then.'

'It would never work,' Sophie had objected. 'He lives in Glasgow, I'd only actually known him for four crazy brilliant months when I said no to his proposal, ghosted him and then didn't show up a year later like I'd promised. No wonder he changed his number. I think that tells me something.' The truth was, in the last few months, since she'd started to come out of the brutal depths of her grief, she'd thought about going back up to see him a hundred times, but she was embarrassed by the way she'd treated him and absolutely terrified that he'd reject her. It was more than her wounded heart could take and somehow it was easier not to try. Better just to consign the whole thing to a mad, crazy, holiday episode from the past.

Erin was undeterred. 'It tells me that you might have to put in a bit of effort, but I think you need to woman up and do this. Come on, Soph, no matter what happens, it can't be any worse than what we've already been through.'

The truth of that began to sway her. Nothing could be worse than losing Mum in such a brutal, painful way.

'Plus, not to pull the emotional blackmail card, but Mum would have wanted you to do this. You know she would.'

Erin was right. Their mum had been a 'live for the moment, chase your dreams' type of personality who'd have been pushing her to face her fears and go for it.

Erin went on. 'It can't be worse than a guy that wants you to put your feet in beans.'

She had a point and the beans had been the clincher.

Over the next few days, she'd thought about it, summoned the courage from somewhere deep inside, and then went for it, throwing herself into a whirlwind of flight and hotel bookings, and then packing and preening to prepare to come here. She'd even shaved her legs for the first time in months and taken herself to the hairdresser.

Now she shook out her wet, freshly highlighted hair as she reached for the phone.

If it wasn't Erin texting, that meant it could only be...

She checked the screen. Dad.

Hello sweetheart, how are you today? How's Glasgow? What time are you heading to the concert?

Her mum had been the 'live for today' personality, but her dad was the opposite. Especially now. Since Mum died, he'd checked in on her at least once or twice every day and he always needed to know where she was going and when. The fact that she'd managed to get into an accident and spend the night in hospital without him knowing was utterly miraculous. She'd half expected a SWAT team to arrive at any second. Thank goodness that Erin had put her foot down when he'd suggested that they all install Find My Family on their phones.

She texted him back straight away, because she knew that if she didn't, he'd only worry and she didn't want to cause him a second of panic.

All great, Dad. In lovely hotel and going to do a bit of sightseeing today before I go to the concert. Hope you're having a smashing day. Love you xx

That's good to hear! Will pick you up from the airport tomorrow night as promised. Love you too.

It felt terrible lying to him, but again, she didn't want to add to his stress by telling him the truth. Which was a total copout, but it was still true.

Two years ago, she'd hadn't told her parents about Ash's proposal, because she knew her mum would be outraged that she'd given up her happiness to come home and look after her. Instead, she'd sworn Erin to secrecy, and played it down to Mum and Dad, telling them it was just a holiday romance. Their curiosity about Ash had soon got lost among the treatments and the surgeries and the chemo sessions and then the grief.

It must have been on her dad's mind last week though, because when she said she was coming to Scotland for a gig, he'd visibly paled, while trying his best to act casual.

'That sounds nice, love. And erm... will you be meeting up with that lad you went out with up there?'

She'd heard the anxiety in his tone though, saw the worry across his forehead. He'd lost stones in weight since Mum died and sometimes it seemed like he was living on a balanced diet of fake chirpiness and worry.

'Ah no, Dad...' Which was technically true. 'You know we lost touch a long time ago. He's probably forgotten all about me by now.'

Some of the lines on his face had relaxed, as he'd taken that in. 'You know, pet, I'll never stand in the way of your happiness, but if I'm honest, it would be tough to have you move away.'

'Don't worry, Dad, I'm not going anywhere,' she'd told him, guilt stricken even though she wasn't actually being untruthful. The thought of potentially adding to his sadness almost made her cancel her flight right there and then, but Erin's words kept replaying in her mind. Woman up. Mum would have wanted this. He's the only man you've ever loved. And those beans...

Today she would find out if the subterfuge, the trip, the expense and the near-death experience was all for nothing.

Eager to get going, she chose a simple white vest top, tight and sleeveless, that showed off just an inch of her belly, while concealing her bruises, and on the bottom went for pale blue linen cargo pants. White trainers on her feet, some silver bangles and a bit of pink lip gloss and she was good to go.

There was a queue at Greggs, directly across the square from the hotel, but she waited because she'd decided to treat herself to a sausage roll, then walked in the sunshine down to the Underground station on Argyle Street. She bought a ticket with her credit card, then got onto the first train that came along.

Ash had told her that Glaswegians called it the Clockwork Orange because of the colour of the trains and the fact that it was a circular service. The memory of him made her smile, which was the effect he'd had on her since the first moment they'd met on that beach in Bali. They'd talked all night and, by dawn, they'd both changed their plans and spent the next eleven weeks travelling, talking, laughing and falling in love.

There were only five stops to Hillhead station, five stops for the butterflies in her stomach to breed, ingest steroids and go on a rampage. By the time she came out on to Byres Road, she seriously believed her cardiovascular system was shutting down.

She crossed the road, weaving through the standstill of West End traffic. When Ash had brought her here, she'd immediately fallen in love with the area. It was completely eclectic, teeming with students from Glasgow and Strathclyde Universities, heaving with tourists visiting the Botanic Gardens at the end of the road, and peppered with fancy big cars and women in expensive jewellery from the upmarket crescents and tree-lined streets of Dowanhill and Kelvinside.

On the other side of the road, she turned left into Ruthven Street, then followed that road around to the gorgeous crescent where she'd spent one giddy month all those years ago. She saw the house immediately. It was a tall, beautiful Victorian townhouse in the middle of the terraced curve, opposite the kind of communal garden she'd seen in her favourite romcom, *Notting Hill*.

Legs shaking, hands trembling, she climbed the ten stone stairs to the front door and stared at the silver door entry pad. Number 1B. There it was. She pressed it and held her breath until she was close to fainting, then almost hit the deck when a male voice said, 'Hello?'

It wasn't him. Must be one of his flatmates. There had been two others living here with him.

'Hi. I'm looking for Ash. Can you tell him it's Sophie, please?'

'I can't...'

Oh. He wasn't in.

She opened her mouth to ask if she could leave her number, when the voice at the other end carried on.

'He moved out of here a year ago.'

Crash. That was the butterflies in her stomach hitting a brick wall.

'Do you have a forwarding address for him? Or a number. I'm a friend and I've lost touch. I can show you a photo of us together so you can see that I'm not a random weirdo.'

'It wouldn't do any good, because I don't have any contact details for him. Like I said, he left about a year ago, and then someone else lived here, then we came here a month ago. I only know the name because we get the occasional letter for him, but we just bin them because he's long gone. Sorry.'

Sophie's brain was both exploding and trying to think of any other possible productive question that she could ask, but all that came out was, 'Okay, thanks. Sorry to bother you.'

'No worries.'

That was it. With a beep, the intercom went dead.

She stood there staring at it for a few seconds, trying to come up with something useful, but it was hopeless. He wasn't there.

She turned around and started walking back to the station, thinking so hard it made the large bump on her head hurt again. What else could she try? She had no idea where he worked, because he was starting a new job after she left. That was why he'd taken a year out to backpack, because he knew that after his career in teaching began, he wouldn't have another chance to escape for months on end.

Along the crescent, back down the other street, across the road and into the station she'd only come out of ten minutes ago.

As soon as she sat down on the train, she opened Instagram and put his name in. She'd done it many times over the last two years, but always with the same result. Nothing. She tried every variation of 'Ash Aitken' she could think of, even though he said he couldn't be bothered with any of it, but maybe he'd changed his mind. She kept searching, getting more and more obtuse. Nope, still nothing.

She glanced up and saw a sign saying that the trains had 4G, so she made a WhatsApp call to her favourite person.

Erin answered on the first ring with a croaky, 'Hello.'

'How's the hangover? Have you recovered yet?' Sophie asked, trying her best to sound upbeat.

'Nope, I'm still in bed. I'm having a self-care day. I'm three romcoms in and I'm convinced I'll never find love like that. Tell me you've found Ash.'

'No,' she said, sighing. 'I went to his house, but he's moved.'

'Ah, bollocks. So what's the plan?'

'I'm going to stake out George Square and hope he goes back there tonight, just like he did last year. It's all I've got.' Even as she said it, she felt the hopelessness of the plan.

'I wish I'd come with you – that way, if he doesn't show, I could take you to a karaoke bar and we could sing Spice Girls songs until we feel better.'

'That's where your mind goes in times of heartbreak?' Sophie teased.

'It is. Don't judge me. Oh, wait until I tell you... I thought about you this morning when something made me cry.'

'Because you were missing me madly?'

'Yep, definitely that. Absolutely. Okay, no. I was listening to that podcast I love, you know, the one about knickers...'

'Stop!' Sophie demanded, before going for clarification. 'You listen to a podcast about knickers? Why do I not know that?'

Erin sighed. 'You do. It's not actually about knickers. You never listen. I told you about it before when we did that social media collab with Carol Cooper. She has a podcast called *Twisted Knickers* and I work for a knicker company – it's like the fates have destined that we join together.'

'I think you still have alcohol in your system from last night,' Sophie chuckled, before spotting that the lady across from her was listening intently to her conversation. It was probably all the underwear chat. 'Anyway, why did that make you think about me?'

Sophie carried on half listening as the train pulled into the station and she got up to get off.

'Ugh, it was the saddest story. Her mum... or maybe it was her aunt... I got too distraught to remember the details. Anyway, someone she loves came to visit her and flew down from Glasgow yesterday. You were going in the opposite direction so that's why I thought of you. But on the way this lady lost her bag... or maybe it was her suitcase... like I said, the details are fuzzy.'

Sophie stepped down onto the platform and started walking in the middle of a hoard of passengers along to the ticket barriers. 'Aw, that's a shame. I hope it turns up. You must have been really hungover if that made you cry though.'

The call dropped out as Sophie went through the ticket barrier and climbed the stairs. She'd just made it out on to the busy concourse when Erin rang back.

'I wasn't finished! What made me cry was that in her bag, or her case, or whatever it was, there was a jewellery pouch and in it were four rings...'

A flash of something in her mind made Sophie stop dead. Three people behind her crashed into each other in a human pile-up, then wandered off in a flurry of swear words and dirty looks.

A pouch. Four rings. Her brain could picture it, but why? How?

'And she started telling the story of them, about how one was the ring her husband proposed with and another was her friend's ring who is dead now – that one was a gorgeous emerald... And oh my God, I was shredded and...'

The picture was clearing. A pouch. Rings inside it. It had been in the taxi.

'Erin, stop.'

Sophie said it so quietly that Erin didn't hear and carried on...

'So, of course, then I I went down a rabbit hole and had to go onto her socials and look at all the pictures and...'

'Erin, STOP.' She said it so forcefully this time that a nearby bloke in a yellow high-vis vest eyed her with suspicion.

Snapshots started flicking around her mind like they were attached to one of those old-fashioned Rolodexes.

Yesterday. Taxi. Pouch. Floor. Brush. Rings. The argument with the taxi driver. Spinning. Crash. Pain. Blackness.

'Okay, fine! No need to shout. I mean—'

'Erin, listen to me. The rings. Did one of them have little stones, like diamonds, in the shape of a D.'

'Oh my God, how did you know that? You looked, didn't you? Don't freak me out with all that psychic bullshit.'

'Erin, tell me again, what was the name of the woman on the podcast? The influencer?'

'Carol Cooper. She's like Mollie-Mae, but about thirty years older. I love her.'

'Erin, I have to go.'

'But I haven't told you the rest of the story!'

'I think I know how it ends. I'll call you back. I love you. Bye!'

And there, standing at the entrance to a Glasgow Underground station, Sophie went onto Instagram, found Carol Cooper's page, and typed out a message about four rings to a woman she'd never met.

19

ALICE

Alice had a fleeting moment of curiosity about how long it would take for the world to find her here if she never left. She was still sitting in the family room, in complete silence, and it was through choice, not necessity, because the truth was that the hospital felt like a safe cocoon that she never wanted to leave. In here, in this room, she was protected. She was alone, yet not isolated, because she could hear the bustle of people going up and down the corridor outside, and occasionally someone would pop their head in and ask if she wanted a cuppa. She had a feeling that was Richard Campbell's doing.

She'd even had some company for a while earlier. One of the nurses she'd seen in the ICU yesterday had knocked and come into the room. In a soft, warm voice, she'd introduced herself as Bernadette Manson, and Alice had immediately thought she was probably around the same age as her. They'd no doubt had very different lives though. Bernadette had the easy smile and the relaxed disposition of someone who exuded happiness.

'There's been no change, Mrs McLenn. I just wanted to let you know that I'm coming back onto shift shortly, so I'll be on the ward all day if you need anything. How are you holding up?'

Alice had been grateful for the question. 'I'm fine. I mean, as fine I can be.' It was difficult to know what she should say. *I can't stand my husband, and I'm only here because I can't face going home to a house that I hate? I want to stay, because I want to know if he dies? Or if he lives? Because this is the first time I've felt truly safe and insulated from him in thirty years and I don't want to be in a horrible house where I see him and the consequences of his actions everywhere?*

To her surprise, Bernadette had sat down on the chair opposite the sofa Alice had been on since yesterday.

'Is there anything I can get you? Or anyone you want me to call for you? Can't be easy being here on your own.'

'No, I'm...' To her surprise, Alice's voice had cracked very slightly, and she'd paused, cleared her throat, hoped the other woman hadn't noticed. She'd spent so many years behind her wall of protection, holding it together, detaching herself from real life and acting like she could cope with everything that came her way, that she had no ability or desire to show vulnerability to anyone, least of all a well-meaning stranger. 'I'm fine. I'm happy to wait by myself.'

At that point, Alice had thought Bernadette would get up and go, and it seemed that she was about to, but then she changed her mind. 'I apologise if this is overstepping, but I just want you to know that I used to watch you on TV, and read about you in the newspapers when all that business was going on with your husband, and I thought you were very brave to deal with all that day in and day out. You clearly still are. I just wanted to tell you that.'

The kindness had almost wiped out the last of Alice's defences. All she wanted to do was to collapse, to cry, to run or to hide and right now she was taking the fourth option, the one most familiar to her. Hiding. Yet it felt like this woman could see every bit of her, peer right into her soul. Years of conditioning to stay quiet stopped her from revealing that it wasn't bravery that made her endure the scandal – it was absolute fear of what Larry would do to her and Rory if she defied him and left him to deal with it all on his own. But of course, an outsider looking in, wouldn't see that. Countless articles and opinion pieces in newspapers proclaimed that the fact she stood by Larry made her either mad, bad or complicit in the corruption. None of them ever called her brave.

'Are you married, Bernadette?'

The nurse had shaken her head. 'No. But I was. For thirty years. To a heart surgeon. And I don't say that with pride. The happiest day of my life was the day I left him.'

Alice had flinched with surprise. It had definitely been an unexpected piece of information. 'Really?'

Bernadette clearly didn't share Alice's pathological need to protect the details of her life. 'Yes. Everyone thought he was a wonderful man, but, by God, he was not. He was controlling, abusive and he made my life hell.'

'Yet you stayed for so long?' Alice had blurted the same question that she'd asked herself a million times.

Bernadette had given a sad shrug. 'It's not that simple, is it?'

Alice hadn't been able to tell if that was a hypothetical question, or if Bernadette could sense some kind of kindred spirit in her. And she hadn't had the courage to ask. So much for her being brave.

Bernadette had continued speaking. 'For some of us, it's a trade-off and there's too much to lose. He had more power than me and I was scared of what he'd do to my family. So I waited until the kids were grown. I was lucky. I had a good job and I could support myself. What I've learned is that women like me go when the time is right. Sometimes that's after the first cruel word. Sometimes it's after a lifetime. But one way or another, we leave. And life is so much better when we do.'

The room had fallen silent for a few seconds, but as their eyes met, Alice had felt sure that this was so much more than just a chatty woman who liked to tell people her life story. But still, she'd given away nothing.

After a few beats of her heart, the loaded atmosphere had been lightened by Bernadette, who'd broken into a wide smile as she'd patted her thighs. 'Would you listen to me rambling on?' she'd said, as if they'd been talking about the weather. 'I do it all the time. I swear there isn't a woman who's come in to this hospital that I haven't told that story to. All those years I kept quiet and now I can't stop talking about it.'

Alice had wondered if she'd imagined that there was anything personal in this at all. She'd almost convinced herself that there wasn't, when Bernadette had stood up, and said cheerily, 'Anyway, Alice, I'll leave you be. You know where I am if you need me. For anything at all. Even if you just feel you'd like a chat.'

Again, nothing too loaded in the words, but there was something in the way they were said. Just a feeling. Alice pondered if she'd ever live up to Bernadette's words, and be brave enough to tell her story.

Before she could answer that question, she'd been distracted by a new arrival in the room, this time, an elderly lady who'd come in to have a seat while her husband was having his foot plastered. He'd taken a tumble in the garden while he was trying to prune their roses, she'd told her. They'd had a perfectly lovely chat about gardens and the weather, and it struck Alice that after years of retreat and seclusion, this was the second time she'd had an actual conversation with a stranger today. Despite the circumstances, there was something in the normality of it that felt good and lifted just a little weight off her stooped shoulders.

'And what about you, then?' the woman had asked kindly. 'Nothing too serious, I hope?'

Alice had shaken her head. This wasn't the time to introduce reality or, worse, honesty, into this conversation. She didn't want to risk spoiling the moment or being a topic of conversation for gossip later. 'My husband. Just a routine operation. I'm sure all will be well,' she'd said breezily.

'It was so lovely to meet you,' the lady had said, sweetly, when her son had arrived and told her that her husband was ready to go. As she'd got up to leave, she'd added, 'I'll keep you in my prayers.'

Alice wasn't religious, but she would take any good thoughts that were going. Seeing the woman's son, who must have been in his fifties, guide his mother out gave her a lump in her throat. She'd give anything to have that too.

She was snapped out of her moment of self-pity when the door opened and Richard Campbell came in. Once upon a time, she would have made a mental note to send a letter to the hospital board, expressing her gratitude for the outstanding care that Richard had shown to her husband and to her. Now, she knew that a letter of commendation from the McLenns was more likely to be viewed as a negative reflection on someone's work or character.

As always, she searched his face for some hint of good or bad news, but she saw neither.

Once again, he took a seat on the opposite sofa. 'I'm heading upstairs for a meeting shortly and I'll probably be there for the rest of the day, but I just wanted to check in and see how you were doing.'

Alice managed a grateful smile. 'I know you suggested going home, but I've just not felt ready to leave yet. I'll go shortly.' She was very aware that she was now over twenty-four hours in the same clothes and without a shower. One of the nurses had handed her a little kit with soap, a toothbrush, toothpaste and a comb, so at least she was hygienic, but she must look awful. Thankfully, there were no mirrors in here, so she'd decided that oblivion was her friend.

'I take it there's been no change?' she asked.

He sighed, and a frown crossed his chiselled face. Whoever was married to this man was lucky to have him. Handsome, smart and caring. Once upon a time, back in her naïve youth, she'd thought Larry was all those things too, but she'd learned the hard way how deluded she had been.

'I'm afraid not. We have visiting in the ICU today from 5 to 7 p.m. though, so you're welcome to go and sit by his bed if you'd like to do that.'

She couldn't think of anything worse, but the need to say what would be expected of her kicked in with, 'I'd like that, thank you.'

This would be the time to go home. To shower. To change her clothes. If there were still journalists hanging around here, hopefully by now, they'd have given up and decided that she wouldn't make an appearance.

'I'll get off then. I've let the staff in ICU know to text me if there are any developments. I know it's hard, Alice, but try to stay positive.'

There was a question that had been floating in her mind, and she decided to ask it. 'Richard, how often have you seen people in this situation go on to make a full recovery?'

Of course, everyone was different and there were exceptions and outliers to every norm, but she just wanted to know the likelihood of the best and worst-case situation.

He thought before he answered. 'Many times. I know it's a cliché, but the body really is a pretty amazing thing. I've seen people with very serious damage come back and live a normal life again. But I've also seen it go the other way.' He didn't have to spell out what he meant. 'We don't know exactly why he hasn't come around yet. It could be due to damage caused to the brain when he arrested, or it could be a reaction to the anaesthetic. That's why I'm wary of making promises or being unrealistic, because much as we have to stay optimistic, I also need to be careful not to raise expectations. It's a difficult balance. Cautious optimism – I think we should go with that.'

'I can go with that,' she agreed. Hadn't that been what had got her through the last few years? Cautious optimism that she would find a way to escape from Larry McLenn and that she would spend every day of what was left of her life without having to clap eyes on that cruel, miserable face.

As he got up to go, she spoke again. 'Richard, I feel that no thanks could be enough for your kindness, but I just want to say thank you again.'

'There's really no need. I'll let the nurses know you're planning on coming in to visit later.' With that, he was out of the door and she was alone again. Blissfully alone.

She sat back on the sofa and cast her glance up to the TV. Football. Of course. It was Saturday afternoon. She'd lost track of time. Now she knew why prisoners carved numbers on their cell walls. Her eyes stayed fixed on the screen, without actually watching it. She had absolutely no interest in sport, but she had spent every single weekend of Rory's childhood on the touchline of a football pitch, cheering him on as he played his heart out. Just her. Never Larry.

One morning when he was five or six, he'd been upset that his dad never came to his games, and Alice had broached it with Larry that night. 'He'd really like you to come,' she'd told him, her feelings mixed. On the one hand, her heart broke that it upset her boy, but on the other hand, she had no desire to stand next to Larry for an extra two hours every week. She needn't have worried.

'Fuck, that boy is soft. You've made him that way, you know

that?' It was classic Larry – step one, lead right in with abuse. 'Let me think, let me think,' he'd said, holding his temples dramatically. Step two – follow up with sarcasm. 'What would be the best use of my time this weekend? Meet with industry leaders to discuss plans for the enhancement of the city or come and watch a bunch of fucking kids who can't lace their football boots up without their mothers yet? It may take me a while to decide,' he'd sneered.

She'd turned and walked away, just as step three was kicking in. Self-importance and grandiosity.

'Honest to God, sometimes I think you have no fucking clue how much it takes to move the fucking mountains I shift on a daily basis.'

The following Saturday, she'd knelt by Rory's side and told him that Daddy loved him very much and was devastated he couldn't be with them, but he had to help all the other people who needed him. It was a refrain that got trotted out again and again over the next few years, but, of course, the gullibility of youth hadn't lasted.

Rory had been about twelve or thirteen when he'd realised that the reality was that his dad wasn't out helping other people, he just couldn't be arsed taking an interest in anything his son was doing. Larry gave him nothing. No love. No validation. No interest whatsoever. Just the occasional outburst of irritation if Rory got in the way, if he played music too loud when Larry was on the phone, or had friends over when Larry was working in his home office. Nothing was ever good enough and everything that wasn't about Larry didn't matter.

If she could have gone back and given her twenty-five-year-old self one piece of advice, it would have been to go to a library, take out a medical textbook and look up malignant narcissism, so that she'd know the signs and then run a mile when she encountered them.

Meanwhile, her and Rory were this tight, unbreakable team, who, without ever really discussing it, constructed a family life comprising of just the two of them. Most of the time, Larry was away, so it wasn't too big a leap. Several of Rory's pals at high school were the sons of single mums who did incredible jobs being both mum and dad to their kids and Alice tried to do the same. And Larry never knew that every single week at Rory's football game, she was cheering on her son on the outside, but on the inside she was making plans for the day she would leave the husband she hated.

Now, as she gazed unseeingly at the footballers on the TV screen, her ever-present self-recrimination that she hadn't left him when Rory was a boy swooped in again, followed by the tiny voice that reminded her time and time again why she'd felt there was no way out.

Step four in the Larry McLenn playbook – cruel threats. He'd told her he'd cut her off, he'd sue her for custody, he'd blacken her name and he'd win. They both knew that it wasn't that he couldn't bear to lose them, it was because the dutiful wife and the happy family were crucial to his public image. If she left him, he wouldn't hesitate to tear her apart, to malign her, accuse her of God knows what, because it would be the only way to salvage the optics.

She'd decided that she couldn't put Rory through the trauma of that. Or maybe that was an excuse, because she didn't have the guts for the fight. Until the day she died, she would never know if staying with him made her a coward or a warrior. Maybe both. But at least she'd had her son. A reason to live. Her greatest accomplishment. One that she'd taken the decision to cut out of her life when the fallout of the scandal had threatened his happiness, even though the pain of missing him made her heart ache.

The train of thought was interrupted when she heard footsteps outside and then the door swung open again and Richard Campbell returned.

'I was on my way to my meeting when I came across someone who was looking for you, so I thought it best to bring him back here,' he told her.

Alice's brow dipped into a frown. There was no one she wanted to see, so whoever it was would be unwelcome. Maybe a journalist, who had duped Richard into thinking he was a friend? Or some guy from Larry's taxi office? Her next thought was that maybe Richard felt a priest or a minister would be helpful, so she mentally prepared to put on her public face of polite appreciation, while getting ready to contain her irritation.

She soon realised that she didn't have to. Because Richard stood to one side, and the next words she heard changed everything.

'Hello, Mum.'

20

RORY

When he'd reached the hospital, the first thing Rory had seen as he'd driven into the car park was that there was a press pack hanging about over at the main entrance to the building. It didn't take a genius to work out why they were there. Nothing sold newspapers like scandal, corruption, public humiliation and the spectacular downfall of a titan, and the Larry McLenn story had all of those things. Part of Rory understood why Julia wanted to escape, because even now, years later, the press and public backlash was brutal. He'd just hoped she loved him enough to survive it. Apparently not.

Keeping his head down as he drove past them, he'd retreated to a space in the furthest away corner of the busy car park, then fished over onto the back seat for the baseball cap he'd worn when he was playing golf last weekend. Into the glove compartment next, where he found his sunglasses and slipped them on. He wasn't exactly Brad Pitt or Matt Damon-level paparazzi fodder, but when the Larry McLenn scandal was headline news, Rory had been photographed many times, so his face would be recognisable to anyone in the media. If they were looking for a new image to run with a story about the accident, then one of the villain's son entering the hospital would be the one they'd go with.

He'd ducked out of the car, with a clear plan of where he was going. He'd been at this hospital a few times over the years with his mum, at openings of new facilities (and once, when he was twelve, with a broken ankle after a fourteen-year-old the size of a shed tackled him on the pitch), and on the official occasions, they'd come in through the staff entrance at the side of the building. That was where he'd headed, baseball cap down, skirting the perimeter of the car park so that he wouldn't be noticed. At the staff door, he'd got lucky – someone was coming out as he was going in, so he didn't need to swipe a pass. He'd stepped two feet inside the entrance and was just about to breathe a sigh of relief when he'd heard, 'Excuse me, sir – can I see your ID?'

Busted. A security guard with a very serious demeanour and one raised, menacing eyebrow, had stopped him in his tracks. Shit. He wasn't very good at this undercover entry stuff. If he could never get another job in finance, a career in MI6 obviously wasn't within his skill set.

The only option had been to come clean.

'I don't actually have one, but please don't eject me until I explain.'

He'd pulled his hat and specs off, and saw absolutely no recognition in the man's face. Clearly not a news junkie.

'My father is Larry McLenn and I believe he's been brought in here after a car crash.'

'If you go out to your left, and round to the front of the building, you'll find the main entrance there.'

Dammit, he was going to sound like a completely entitled dick, but there was no option.

'I can't do that. You see, there are photographers there and I don't want them to see me. Like I said, my dad is Larry McLenn.'

Still no recognition. Damn. He should have gone with Billy Connolly or Ewan McGregor.

'Out to the left, and round to the front of the building.'

He'd been getting nowhere, so he'd had to think fast. The last time he was here was about five years ago and he was with his mother at the opening of a children's play area in the Emergency Department. There had been a doctor who had made a speech, and damn, shit, bugger, what was his name?

The security guard was starting to puff up his chest in a blatant power move, when Rory had blurted, 'But Doctor Campbell told me to come to this entrance and ask for him.'

Two eyebrows now raised. Cynical expression, but chest depuffed. Rory wasn't sure if this was a win or just a stay of execution.

'Dr Campbell?'

A quizzical tone.

'Yes... Dr...' Think. Think. Think. 'Dr... Richard!' Yassss. 'Dr. Richard. Campbell.'

He'd sent up a silent prayer that it was the correct name, that the doctor would be here today, and that he'd give Rory the time of day to explain why he'd just told a blatant lie and used him to gain entry to the building.

Five minutes later, he'd got the answer. After a phone call from the security guard, Dr Richard Campbell had marched through the set of double doors to the left, and – thank you, universe – he'd immediately recognised Rory's face. A second thanks went up when Richard didn't turn him away. Rory wouldn't have blamed him, given his family's reputation now. 'Thanks, Eric, I'll sign Mr McLenn in. Come on through, Rory.'

After receiving a pass on a lanyard, and thanking the guard profusely, the doctor had escorted him along into the warren of corridors in the staff area of the hospital.

'You just got lucky – I was on my way to a meeting when I got the call. Two minutes later and you'd have missed me. I'm guessing you didn't want to go past the waiting committee at the front door?'

'I'm camera-shy,' Rory had joked nervously, as they walked. 'Thanks for doing this. I saw the reports about my dad, and I couldn't get a hold of my mum. Is she... is she...'

He hadn't been able to say the words. Hurt. Dead.

The doctor had read his fear.

'She's fine. I was just speaking to her. She's up in the family room, so I'll take you there now.'

It had taken a few moments for him to remember that he should enquire about his dad too. 'And my father, how is he?'

Dr Campbell had given him the rundown. Heart attack. Surgery. Now in ICU. Hadn't come round yet. Cautiously optimistic. Rory barely heard any of it, because all he could focus on was that his mum was fine. She was okay.

Two minutes later, he'd opened the door to a small, windowless room.

'Hello, Mum.'

If he'd wondered what kind of reaction he'd get, he now knew. His mum burst into tears, jumped up and threw her arms around him.

'I'll leave you two alone,' Richard said, backing out of the door.

Rory didn't move, relishing the relief, holding on to his mum until she was ready to let go. When she eventually pulled back, she was still crying, and Rory had another internal twist of panic. He had never seen his mother cry. Not ever. In all the years he was growing up, she'd never shed a tear in front of him. In times of upset or pain, he would watch her jaw clench, but she always remained steady. Even in the midst of the chaos, even when people were saying and writing the most awful things about her, she didn't break down. As a kid, Rory had thought she was indestructible. As an adult, he could look back and see that it was her way of staying strong for his sake.

'It's okay, Mum. It's all going to be okay.' He had no idea if that was true, but he just desperately wanted to reassure her. 'I'm so sorry I wasn't here with you.'

'You shouldn't have come,' she said, when she finally managed to speak.

It had been over a year since he'd been with her and it should probably feel strange to be here, but it didn't at all. He hugged her again. 'Yes, I should. I'm so sorry I wasn't here before now.' And he was. Sorry for not being here this weekend. Last week. Last month. For all of the last year. Since the day she'd told him to go. Their agreement was now null and void. He was here and he was staying with her.

'I had to come. I thought you were dead and I'm top beneficiary in the will.' Her coping mechanism was strength, his was humour and ridiculously stupid comments. 'Sorry, that was a completely inappropriate joke given the surroundings.' But at least it changed her sobs to laughter.

They both sat down on the nearest sofa, but she hung on to his hand.

'I saw a news report and it said a woman in the car was hurt,' he explained.

'It was a passenger in his taxi. Poor woman. I don't know anything about her because they couldn't tell me, but one of the nurses said that she'd been discharged, so I think she's okay.'

Rory sat back and absent-mindedly ran his fingers through his hair as he sighed. 'He just leaves carnage in his wake everywhere he goes, doesn't he?'

His mum didn't need to answer.

'The doctor says he's still not come round after the surgery?' he went on, then listened as she explained, step by step, everything that had happened in the last two days. The gist of it was that his father was alive, but it was a 'wait and see' as to if, when and how he would recover. The strangeness of the situation didn't escape him. Most sons would feel something: sympathy, worry, concern, care, even anger or malice. But he felt... nothing.

As a kid, he'd longed for his father's approval, and when that didn't come, and he'd got older, that longing had transitioned through many other stages. Fear. Dislike. Resentment. Then, as he reached adulthood, indifference and forced tolerance. He'd had no care, feelings or respect for Larry at all. He'd just kept the waters still and declined to rock the boat. But when the scandal broke, the pendulum of his emotions had swung right over to hatred and disgust. Rory honestly didn't care if he never set eyes on the old bastard again.

His mum, however...

It pained him to see that she looked like a very different woman from the one he'd grown up with. Just over a year ago, they'd said goodbye, but she had somehow aged by a decade. Her eyes were bloodshot and heavy with exhaustion, her cheeks were sunken, and her skin was pale and dry. There was no jewellery, no make-up, and her blonde hair had been colonised by grey. If he saw her walking past him now, he'd think that she was someone who'd had a hard life. The contrast, and the reality of it, made him want to hug her again.

'Mum, how long have you been here?'

'Since yesterday, about lunchtime. Feels like so much longer though.'

'Why didn't you go home? Why wait in here? Did you sleep here last night?'

When she nodded, a massive crash of guilt smacked him right in the face. Last night, he'd been drowning his sorrows and his self-pity in a vat of beer and tequila, partying to forget his troubles, and all the time his mum was here on the couch.

'I didn't want to go home in case the press were there. I didn't want to deal with cameras in my face, and the questions and just being the subject of people's conversations again, so it was easier to just stay here and hide. I suppose I need to go at some point though, I want to shower, to change out of these clothes.'

His reaction was instant. 'Then how about we get out of here now? I'll come with you and make sure none of the crap stuff happens.'

He'd thought she'd agree immediately, but she hesitated. 'I still don't want to go back home, son, and I want to be near here in case anything happens. And...'

She paused, so he prompted her to go on. 'And?'

'It's just not a good idea to go to your place. Julia made it quite clear how she felt last time we were all together, and she was right. I don't want to drag you two back into this.'

His face burned at the recollection, but this wasn't the time to be going back over old ground. Now that they were together again, there would be plenty of time to talk about that later.

'Julia won't be a problem. It's a long story, but, honestly, it's fine.' This wasn't the time, the place, or the circumstance to go into the saga of his marriage to Julia Fieldow. All he wanted to do was get his mum out of here.

'Look, let's go to the St Kentigern. It's only ten minutes away,' he said. It was the first place that he thought of, the hotel that she'd taken him to every year at the beginning of December when the city's Christmas lights were switched on. They would have hot chocolate and sticky toffee puddings, and then they'd walk along to see the spectacle of festive decorations at George Square and stay there until their feet and hands went numb with the cold.

Even when he was an adult, they'd continued the tradition, right up until his dad had gone and destroyed everything for them all.

'No!' The abruptness of her rejection shocked him, until... 'Son, I don't have that kind of money and I'm not letting you pay for it.'

Of course. She'd always been way too proud for her own good.

'I won't. The company has an account there. I think they can afford one night, don't you?' Mental reminder to send a text to Roger Fieldow, adding a night in a swanky hotel to his severance package.

'Come on, Mum. There's so much to talk about and I don't want to do it here.'

To his relief, she stood up, and the smile on her face was tentative and maybe still a little sad, but at least it was there. 'Okay. But I'll need to stop by the ward and let them know that I'm going.'

'That's fine...'

'Rory, I need to ask, do you want to see your dad?'

Crap. Rabbit. Headlights. Did he want to see his dad? It hadn't even occurred to him that she would ask. He'd only got as far as getting out of here and making things right with his mum.

He wanted to talk over the decisions they'd made, the road they'd chosen that had taken them apart and that had now brought them to this point. He wanted to tell her how much he regretted it. And he wanted to come up with a plan for what they were going to do next.

'No, Mum, I don't think I do. I'll wait outside while you go in.'

He wasn't going to be a hypocrite and pay homage to a man he despised. He was going to focus on the people he loved.

His mum had sacrificed her life to protect him.

Now it was time for him to repay her.

21

VAL

By afternoon, we had moved our gathering from our kitchen table to the picnic table in the garden, and it made me smile when I realised how well our outfits reflected our personalities.

Moi, a child of the sixties, whose parents couldn't spell SPF 50, had grudgingly slapped on some factor 10 and a pair of pink love-heart sunglasses to match my screaming fuchsia vest top. Even in times of emotional turmoil, there was no excuse not to wear life-enhancing colours. Carly had her dark blonde hair twisted up with a pencil holding it in place, was wearing a bra on the top, rolled-up jeans on the bottom, and in the middle was a muffin top that she absolutely could not care less about, because somewhere in her fifty-something years she'd become comfortable with her body and couldn't give a toss what anyone thought about her. Meanwhile, model, social influencer and all-round stunner, Carol, was so utterly paranoid about sun-induced wrinkles, she was wearing a thick lathering of factor 70, huge sunglasses, one of my floor-length kaftans and a hat that I'd only worn once to a wedding, because it could double as a manhole cover and was so huge I took out everyone in the row behind me every time I moved. It also provided shade for the laptop, on which she was furiously checking her social media comments, messages and shares.

There was no food in the fridge when we'd got back yesterday, because I'd thought I was going to be staying at Carly's for a fortnight, and we'd had no time or inclination to go to the shops, so we'd just had a very late lunch/early dinner of chips, mayonnaise, and two boxes of fish fingers we'd found in the freezer. Not that I had been able to eat much. I'd just filmed another one of those videos for Carol's Instagram, this time talking about the ring we bought Dee for her twenty-first birthday – a collection of diamonds that spelled out her initial. They weren't big diamonds, because Don and I didn't have that kind of money, but we'd ordered it from my catalogue and paid it up over a year. Our Dee had been so shocked and thrilled with it. She'd worn it every single day for the rest of her too short life. After she was killed by a drugged-up scumball who had no business being behind the wheel of a car, I'd taken to wearing it on my pinky, but the irony was that I'd stopped doing that because it was a little bit loose and I was scared I'd lose it. Instead, I'd put it in my jewellery box and I'd wear it at home every year on Dee's birthday, at Christmas and every other special occasion. It was my way of making sure my girl was with us and part of the family's good times.

The last thing I'd felt like doing after talking about that was eating. My stomach had been twisted into seventeen knots of devastation and self-reproach. How could I have been so stupid? How? Why hadn't I just put the rings in the back section of my bag and zipped the bloody thing up? Why?

I turned my face heavenward, eyes closed, sending up a silent message to my girl and my man. He always could read my mind, so I told myself he'd hear it. *Dee, my darling, I'm so sorry. I hope your dad is sitting up there with you now, but please forgive me for being so damned careless. I feel like I've lost the last little bits I had of you both.* I let that one float up into the ether before adding, *And, Don, if you know where the rings are, can you send me a sign, love?*

Eyes still closed, I saw his face, and that cheeky grin as he answered, *Aye, pet, but it'll need to have flashing lights and a bell, because you're hopeless with a satnav.*

The sight of him faded away, and I missed him even more than I had ten minutes ago. I couldn't imagine a time when that would subside enough to let me breathe again.

The only thing that was keeping me upright was that the girls were here and they were the very best kind of distraction.

Beside me, Carly groaned, 'I think I'm getting a migraine.'

Carol glanced up from the laptop. 'Are you though? Or is that just an excuse for more wine?'

'You know me too well. Red or white?'

'Neither,' Carol said with an edge of mischief. 'Aunt Val, is there any cider in your drinks cupboard?'

'I think there's some in the fridge. Nancy and Johnny brought it round just a few weeks before... before... Anyway, Johnny and Don were going to watch some cup final on the TV. Or maybe it was darts.'

I honestly didn't think I'd have got through the last couple of years if it wasn't for the incredible support system I had around me. I'd known Nancy my whole life, and after Josie died, she'd stepped in and kept me standing. And then, a few years ago, when her husband, Peter, had been taken too soon, I'd made sure I was there for her too. We'd become partners in caramel wafers and crime, and I'd been delighted when she'd rekindled her teenage romance with another old pal of Don's, Johnny Roberts, at a school reunion the year before last.

I saw Nancy most days, especially since we were unofficial joint aunties and childminders for our friend Tress's little one, Buddy. At least once or twice a week, Johnny and Tress's partner, Noah, would come round to keep Don company. Sometimes Don recognised them, and sometimes he didn't, it depended on the day, but they never minded either way. They'd chat away and sometimes even take him out for a run in the car or a walk down to the chippy, if Don was able. You really saw who the good people were when you were dealing with an illness like that, and it turned out that I was surrounded by them. In the weeks since he'd passed, they'd done everything they could to make sure I was okay and help me get through it, along with my son, Michael, and these two sweethearts here. One of whom was still giving a drink request to her sister-in-law.

'I'll have a cider then, please. I want to relive my teenage years,' Carol decided, before trying to jog Carly's memory with, 'Do you remember we got drunk on Strongbow when we were about fifteen, and then I got concussion because I was dancing on your bed and fell off? I took the knob right off your door.'

'Yep, but I'll forever worship at the temple of Kajagoogoo,' Carly said, laughing as she climbed off the bench. 'Two ciders coming up. Aunt Val, what would you like?'

I considered having a gin and tonic, but I still felt like my nerves were on the outside of my skin after telling the world about our Dee's ring, so I didn't want to add gin to the river of sadness that was already crashing against my heart.

'I'll stick to my tea, thanks. But bring out the packet of Hobnobs from the cupboard. I might take a notion for one in a wee while.'

Carly disappeared inside and came back out a few minutes later carrying refreshments. She deposited the two glasses of cider on the table, then took the Hobnobs from under her arm and put them in front of me.

I'd just begun to open the packet when Carol, her eyes still trained on the screen, murmured, 'Oh God, oh God. Oh God!'

Carly's cider was halfway to her mouth, so she paused. 'Has something shocking happened or have you found religion?'

'Shocking,' Carol exclaimed, and I felt my heart begin to pound, all notions for a chocolate-coated oaty biscuit lost.

'What is it? Has something slid into your PMs?' Even in my rising state of anxiety, I was sure I was getting good with the lingo.

'DMs, Aunt Val,' Carly corrected me with a grin, but I was only listening to Carol.

'All day we've been inundated with comments and messages, but they were all just either good wishes or advice on how to track the rings down. Or a few from blokes that wanted to buy replacements if I'd wear them naked, but I've blocked them. Anyway, I've just seen this one from someone called... Hang on, let me check, SophiesBackpack. Yep, that's her. Anyway, I'm going to read it out. It says... "Hi, this is going to sound like the maddest story ever, but I think I found your rings on the floor of a taxi in Glasgow."'

I jumped forward so violently, I nudged Carly's elbow, sending cider everywhere. 'That could be them! What else does she say? Where are they now?'

Sweet lord, I'd just asked Don for a sign and now here it was. That man of mine never let me down when he was on this earth and now, he was still taking care of me.

Carol was already on it, saying aloud what she was typing in the message.

'Hi, yes, that could be them. Can you give me any more information? Do you have them?' Send.

She turned the laptop around so that we could all see the screen, so now all three of us were staring... and staring... and staring... and I thought my heart was going to burst out of my chest, so I stared some more when... Ping.

Carol read out the new message.

'"No. It's a long story, but I don't know what happened to them."'

With a loud groan, Carly deflated beside me. 'Crap. This might be one of those cranks that thinks it's funny to wind people up. I swear to God, if this is a joke, I'm going to track them down and punch them.'

'Is it fake, Carol?' I asked, fearfully. 'Or do you think it could be real?'

Carol was reading it all again. 'I don't know. I can see her profile and she doesn't look like a troll. All her stuff is fairly normal and we follow a couple of the same brands. Not that an affinity for Mulberry bags and Warburton bagels makes someone an angel.'

Carly jumped in again. 'There's no point asking her what the rings looked like because they're all over our socials, but what's something we haven't said on the podcasts or the videos? Anything you can think of?'

'Did we say what kind of car the taxi was? I've talked that much today that I can't remember.'

'Me neither,' Carol agreed, and Carly shrugged.

Carol started typing, saying the words aloud again, 'Can I ask what kind of car the taxi was?'

'It was a red Skoda,' I whispered, as if I didn't want the person on the other end to hear the answer.

We were all staring at the screen again. Pause. Long pause. Longer pause. Ping.

'"It was red. I'm not sure what kind. A Skoda, I think. I got into it at the airport."'

The three of us shrieked so loudly that every dog in the street started barking.

When we'd got that out of our systems, Carol put her hands up, 'Hang on, though. Maybe you did say that earlier. Give me something else.'

I racked my brain. Racked my brain. Racked my brain. Got it. 'Ask her if there was anything with the rings.'

While Carol was typing, I whispered to Carly, 'My brush was with them.'

The computer pinged, and Carol's eyes widened as she read, '"A gold brush. The strings of the pouch were tangled in it."'

This time, the squeals lasted even longer, and Carly threw her arms around me. It took me a few moments to calm down enough to think, and then, almost instantly, a searing wave of dread came in. 'Aye, but that taxi driver was an arse. He could have sold them by now. Or pawned them. Or his wife could be down the bingo flashing them to her pals.'

Carol's fingers were already flying. '"I think that's them! Can you tell me anything else to help find them?"'

Ping.

'"Yes, but I wasn't kidding when I said it's a long story. Happy to help but maybe better if we meet. I'm in Glasgow but leaving tomorrow."'

Despite her excitement, Carly had doubts. 'Do you think this could be some kind of scam? A ransom demand?'

I shrugged. 'I'd give her my last pair of American Tan tights if it gets my rings back. Let's go meet the lassie.'

'"Yes! Where and when?"' Carol said as she typed.

Ping.

'"Could you come to me as I can't leave where I'm sitting. It's part of the long story. I'm at the George Square Grand Hotel. I'll be in the bar with all the windows at the front overlooking the Square."'

Carol's eyes came up, questioning.

'Tell her we'll come,' I blurted. I knew I should be worried that this was some twisted ploy, but, honestly, I didn't care. Besides, the lassie's picture looked nice and she seemed to have a good few friends on the Instagram thingy, so hopefully she wasn't a deranged criminal waiting to pounce.

Carol's fingers were away again. '"We can be there in half an hour."'

Ping.

'"Great. I'm wearing a white top and blue trousers. See you then."'

Sitting back, exhausted, I tried to take it all in, but I was almost paralysed with desperation at the same time. This had to be it. It had to be true. It had to be the first step on the path that would end with me getting my rings back, so that I could hold a bit of Don, Josie and my girl again. I wanted to stand up and move, but I wasn't sure my legs would hold me.

Carly leaned over and squeezed my hand. 'Right, Auntie Val, fire up the Jeep and let's get going.'

22

SOPHIE

Still holding her phone, Sophie went back to the bucket chair over at the window in her hotel room, where she sat down at her vantage point looking over George Square and pulled her legs up underneath her, wincing as something tugged in her shoulder and sent an ache right down her arm. Note to self, move gently for the rest of the day.

She took her mind off it by concentrating on how beautiful the view was. She'd only been in Glasgow for a month with Ash, but they'd done all the touristy stuff and the stunning architecture of the square made it perhaps second only to the Botanic Gardens on her list of favourite landmarks. Ash had given her the rundown on the significance of everything she could see now. He'd proposed to her in the corner of the square, next to a statue of Robert Burns. She remembered wondering if anyone was watching out of the windows of the stunning buildings on all four sides of the square, which included the City Chambers and the old Post Office HQ, which had apparently now been converted into flats and sat directly across from the hotel.

She replayed every detail of his proposal and felt a descending cloud of sadness.

In a perfect world, she'd have come back to him. But then, in a perfect world, her mum's treatment would have worked, instead of going on for month after gruelling month. And in a perfect world, she'd have maintained her relationship with Ash and allowed him to support her through her grief. But this wasn't a perfect world, and she couldn't go on beating herself up for letting him go.

It had all just been too much for her to deal with. All she'd wanted to do was focus on her mum, the woman who'd been her best friend all her life and she couldn't explain it to Ash, couldn't take his disappointment or his needs into account. In her head, she'd told herself that if they were meant to be together, then somewhere down the line it would work out.

Now she wanted to find out if that was true. She could still hope that there might just be a tiny chance that he still felt the same way about her, that he was open to seeing her and that they could rekindle their relationship. Two years ago, on that last day with him, right over there in that square, in front of Robert Burns, he'd said he would ask her here every year until she said yes. All she wanted was to know if he meant it, but, so far, there was no sign of him.

She peered down again. There wasn't even two old ladies sitting on a bench. Just loads of people lying on the grass, or wandering around, some taking photos, some chatting to friends, some focusing straight ahead, like they had somewhere to go and just wanted to get there.

Sophie wanted to be lying down there, without a care in the world, instead of fretting about Ash or thinking about that poor woman from the podcast.

She really hoped she wasn't making a mistake getting involved with the search for the missing rings, but after she'd watched the last video, she'd been in pieces. Sophie knew what it felt like to lose someone, and she could see how devastated that poor lady was. If her info was of any use at all, she was happy to share it. Plus, it took her mind off the fact that there was absolutely no one down in that square who vaguely resembled a tall, dark and oh so fit Ash clutching an engagement ring.

With a sigh, she straightened out her legs, stretched up her arms, then yelped as pain shot through her shoulder. If Ash didn't turn up, at least she'd have something to show for this trip. A fricking great big bruise and a nervousness in taxis.

There was a moment's hesitation as she thought about changing, then remembered she'd told the women what she was wearing. The white top and blue trousers would have to do. She brushed her dark waves and put a loose bobble low at the back, making a messy ponytail with some highlighted strands framing her face. Ash had always loved her hair when she wore it like that.

She wasn't sure when she'd get back to the room, so she texted her sister with an update.

Hey how's the hangover? Ash is still a no-show. I may be your spinster sibling for ever. Will keep you posted if there's any change.

The reply came back almost immediately.

We can be spinsters together because no one is marrying me in this state. I'm eating cold pakora in bed and the sauce went missing five minutes ago. I'm scared to look under the covers.

Another one came straight after it.

PS. If he doesn't show, it's his loss because you're fricking amazing (that was my sisterly encouragement for the month). Love you xx

Love you back... but am worried about the sauce.

She was so, so tempted to tell Erin that she'd spoken via text to one of her favourite influencers, Carol Cooper, but she decided to keep that to herself for now. It was too complicated. She'd need to explain about the accident and the hospital, and she didn't have time to cause all that inevitable drama right now. Maybe she'd ask Carol to take a selfie with her later to send to her sister after she'd told her the full story about how and why they'd met. Perhaps the photo would make Erin's day and would stop her sister from killing her for keeping the crash and the aftermath to herself.

While she was covering bases, she texted her dad too.

Hi Dad, just letting you know I'm great. Heading out now. Will text later to let you know I'm back safe. Xx

Okay, family taken care of, hair brushed, time to go downstairs and meet the ladies she'd contacted about the jewellery – via one last look out of the window.

She scoured the square. For a second, her heart began to race, when she saw a tall, dark guy in a white T-shirt passing the statue of Robert Burns. Despite her aching muscles and bones, she got ready for action. See Ash. Run really fast towards him. Hope he still loves you. Restart incredible relationship. Marry him and live happily ever after. Sometimes, bullet points were the way to go.

Sophie held her breath as he got closer, but as soon as he came into focus, she could see it wasn't him. Crushing disappointment, but she wasn't giving up hope. There was still time.

After picking up her phone and her Coach wristlet purse (a birthday present from Erin), she headed downstairs. The bar at the front of the hotel was almost as iconic as the building itself, with its floor-to-ceiling windows stretching out into the street over-looking the square.

After she'd exchanged messages with Carol Cooper, she'd called down and asked to reserve a table at the window, and she was shown to it straight away. Of course, the first thing she did was scan the square again, in case Ash had made an appearance during the thirty seconds she'd been in the lift. Nope, not there.

It was impossible to say the exact time he'd proposed, but she was sure it was around now, because she'd left immediately to get her teatime train.

She was so engrossed in the scene outside the window that she almost missed the three women coming into the room, one of whom was now speaking to the waitress and pointing in her direction. She recognised them immediately. One was the lady from the video, Val, the one who'd reduced her to tears. The woman speaking to the waitress was Carol Cooper, and Sophie remembered her now from the collab she'd done with Erin's company for their men's boxers range, which mostly consisted of Carol and her husband wearing matching pants, playfully arguing over who looked best. Her sister had been so proud of it because it had been a viral hit and increased sales by 17 per cent that month. It was the other woman from the podcast, Carly, who reached her first.

'Sophie?'

'Yes!' She stood up, unsure whether to hug or shake hands or neither. What was the etiquette in these situations?

The older lady took it out of her hands, by rushing her and clutching her into a bear hug. 'Oh pet, you have no idea how happy I am that you contacted us.' Sophie could see the dark circles of tiredness and the lines of stress around her lovely blue eyes.

'So much for playing it cool and not terrifying you,' Carly added, smiling. 'Actually my aunt does that to everyone – the postman avoids her street.'

Sophie recognised when someone was trying to break the ice and it worked. She immediately liked them and beckoned to them to grab chairs. 'I've just realised that I saw you,' she said to Val, an image dawning on her. She hadn't picked up on it when she watched Val on the video, but now that she saw her in person, the moment came back to her mind. 'You got out of the taxi right before me, at the airport. You were walking away when I went to speak to the driver and asked him to bring me into the city. You had two cases and you were rushing.'

'Yes!' Val responded. 'That's why I was so flustered.' Before she could say more, she saw that the very smiley waitress was waiting for their drinks order.

Sophie added to the other ladies' requests for glasses of wine, but Val asked for a tea, and then got right to it.

'First of all, before I make it all about me,' Val began, 'are you okay, lovely? I saw you wince when you stood up there, and that's some bruise you've got.'

Sophie followed Val's gaze back to her own body, and yelped. She hadn't realised that her T-shirt had slipped down to expose a swirl of black and blue on her shoulder. She hastily pulled it up. 'I'm fine now. So that's one of the things I wanted to explain in person. After I found the rings, our taxi was in an accident.'

'Dear God, you poor thing! Was it serious? Were you badly hurt?'

Sophie gently shook her head and, as she did so, shot a glance out of the window. Still no Ash. 'I'm fine, thanks. It was a crash on the motorway. Our car hit the central reservation and spun around, but luckily nothing else hit us. I had to spend a night in hospital with a mild concussion, but they let me out this morning.'

'What?' Carly gasped. 'You poor thing. Okay, I need to understand this, because I'm putting it my next book. You came to Glasgow for a trip...'

'A weekend. I arrived yesterday and I leave tomorrow,' Sophie clarified.

'Right. And you got into a taxi at the airport and then you were in a crash on the motorway? How long had you been here?'

Sophie tried to calculate it. 'Erm, about forty-five minutes.'

'Oh sweet Jesus, I'm going to need my drink for this,' Val said. 'I'm so sorry that happened to you. And thank God you're fine. You are definitely fine, aren't you? I just want to check you're not going to keel over because, to be honest, not one of us will be any good at first aid.'

'I'm definitely okay,' Sophie assured her, grateful for the concern.

Val went on, 'Right then. Well, if that just happened yesterday, the last thing you need is the three of us babbling on, so we're going to shut up...' she fired a warning glance at the others, who both nodded '...and let you talk instead. Right, on you go, pet. Start at the beginning.'

23

ALICE

Alice lay in the bath so long that her fingers and toes were like prunes. Luxury. She used to take it for granted, but now it felt spectacular. The two-person tub in the suite at the St Kentigern was like a swimming pool compared to the tiny, indelibly stained burgundy bath at home. Not that she'd ever bathed in that one. She hated that bathroom so much that she'd become a strictly shower-and-go person since they'd moved in, and besides, with the boiler only switched on for ten minutes a day to save money, there would never have been enough hot water for a bath.

This, however, was a different story altogether. White marble. Brass taps. Three-wick candles on the double vanity, under the ceiling-height art deco mirrors. And her favourite thing of all, Classic radio, down low, piped from a sound system in the other room, playing a concerto she couldn't name but that transported her to another world when she closed her eyes.

And yes, she could see that anyone looking down on her lying there like Julia Roberts in *Pretty Woman* (not physically – there was no salon, no make-up, and no reversal of the aging process that could make her look like that) would think it incredibly crass that she was in this bubble of bliss while her husband was fighting for his life in hospital, but right now she didn't care. This was the closest she'd been to heaven in a very long time and the last three decades of her life had been the price that she'd paid to enjoy this.

Every single aspect of this bliss, however, was enhanced by the knowledge that after more than a year of zero contact, her son was in the next room. She wasn't alone. She had someone here. Someone who cared. For all that time she hadn't had a single human connection deeper than a cold exchange with her husband, or a superficial conversation with the ladies she worked with. Now, having Rory here was worth more than all the luxury in the world.

She'd been hesitant about leaving the hospital, even with him. Actually, his presence had made it even more stressful, because detaching him completely from all the potential carnage that could affect his happiness had been her life's mission for so long. The last thing she wanted was for a journalist or photographer to spot him and drag him back into the whole bloody mess. However, once again, the hospital staff had been exceptional.

When they'd gone round to let the ward staff know that she was leaving, Bernadette, the lovely nurse she'd spoken to in the family room earlier, had welcomed her in. Rory had stayed outside in the corridor, and she hadn't challenged him on it. Given his non-existent relationship with his father, Alice understood his reaction. His path with Larry was his to choose and he was more than entitled to his feelings, whatever they may be.

From the nursing station just inside the ICU, she could see him though, still in the same bed, still lying in the same position, beeping machines and monitors surrounding him. It hadn't been within visiting hours and she hadn't wanted to seem like she was trying to get special treatment, so she'd chosen not to go to Larry's bedside. 'If you'd like to go over, it's fine,' Bernadette had told her, but she shook her head.

'Thanks, but it's okay.' Bernadette didn't push, and Alice had such a feeling that the woman could see into her soul, that she somehow knew what she was thinking. 'I just wanted to let you know that I'm heading out now to go change and freshen up. My phone is out of charge, but my son will be with me, so I can give you his number,' she'd offered. Her phone had been dead since a couple of hours after she'd arrived and she wasn't sure when she would have time to charge it again.

Before they'd come in, she'd asked Rory to write his new number on a piece of paper, and she handed that over now.

'Bernadette, I don't want to be an imposition, because you've all been so kind and done so much for me already, but do you think we could have someone's assistance in leaving without meeting any issues at the front door?' She didn't have to spell it out.

Bernadette had summoned a guard from the security office, who had escorted them downstairs and back out the way Rory had come in, through the staff entrance. Rory had pulled on a baseball cap and glasses at the door, before guiding her around the perimeter of the car park, to a very flash Audi.

'Here, Mum, put that bag in the boot,' Rory had beckoned her, gesturing to the blue plastic bag that she'd brought with her. It was the bag the police had given her, containing Larry's things from the car. Not that she wanted them. She'd have been quite happy to go over to the skip in the corner of the car park and toss it in there, but that would have run the risk of being spotted by the photographers. Grudgingly, she'd thrown it into the open boot, then climbed into the passenger seat, ducked down until the coast was clear, before driving for ten minutes, until they'd pulled into a parking space in Bath Street, in the city centre. On the corner was a large department store, and she'd gone in there and bought the first suitable clothes she could find. She was embarrassed to admit that she'd taken Rory up on his insistence that she use his credit

card, but the truth was, she had no other option. Of course, she'd
stuck to basic choices, unwilling to take advantage of his generosity. A cream, short-sleeved, turtle-neck top and black capri pants
that would work fine with the sandals she was already wearing
went into her basket, along with underwear, pyjamas, then some
toiletries. In less than fifteen minutes, she was out and back in
the car.

Rory had been wide-eyed with surprise. 'Bloody hell, Mum,
did you speed-skate round there?'

She didn't like to say that when you hadn't bought yourself a
single thing for two years, even a plain top and a pair of plain black
trousers felt like a treat.

Now, in a sea of bubbles soothing her body, his voice from the
other room snapped her out of her contemplations. 'Mum, room
service is here.'

Room service. She'd forgotten that it even existed, and she
hadn't thought that she'd ever experience it again, because she'd
knew that even in the future, when she'd broken free of Larry, she
would have to live very frugally and within her means. Not that she
would mind that. Her freedom alone was priceless.

'I'll be right out,' she shouted in reply.

Slowly, reluctantly, she stretched up out of the bath, catching
her reflection in the mirror opposite. It was the first time she'd
seen her full-length naked body in longer than she could remember. She'd always been slim, but now she could see the outline of
her ribs. Her breasts were small, but they hadn't lost the war with
gravity and were still in roughly the same place that they'd been
when she was younger. All cerebral connections to her body had
been switched off for decades. It had been a means to an end. It
had allowed her to work. To earn money. To function day in and
day out. She'd never contemplated whether a man would ever see
her naked again. Never allowed herself to wonder how good it

would feel to be held. To be kissed. She'd shut down every thought of a physical relationship because that way she didn't miss what she didn't have. But maybe... maybe one day that could change.

Out in the living area of the suite, a door banged and snapped her out of her thoughts. For goodness' sake, how ridiculous. One bubble bath and suddenly she was off down a path that had way too many roadblocks in place. *Get a grip, Alice.*

She dried off, then pulled on her new underwear, before covering herself from neck to ankles with the most fluffy, luxurious robe she'd ever touched. She closed her eyes. Inhaled. Exhaled. Life was an absolute shit show, but right now, she was clean, she was warm, she was safe, and she was with her son. She didn't need anything else.

White hotel slippers on her feet, she padded through to the other room to see Rory taking the silver cloches off two plates of pasta at the dining table by the tall windows that overlooked the garden square in front of the hotel.

She slipped into the chair opposite him, picked up the open bottle of wine and poured a glass, almost giddy with the anticipation of it. For over a year, there had been no wine. No alcohol. No takeaways. No treats. Because every time she spent ten pounds, that was ten pounds less that was going in her escape fund.

'So, tell me... and I want to know everything. How's work, how's Julia? How's your life? Are you happy?'

'Yeah, everything's fine.'

She froze. He was lying. He did it so rarely, and he'd always been so bad at it, that it was impossible to miss.

'And yet you're lying to me,' she said calmly, putting her napkin on her lap.

He put his glass down, shook his head, a rueful smile. 'You always could do all that mind-reading stuff. You're like a human lie detector.'

'Motherhood,' she said simply. She wasn't ready to eat now. Not until she knew the facts and the churning in her stomach had stopped.

'You want the shit stuff or the really shit stuff?'

She could, however, have a large sip of wine, before replying, 'All the stuff.'

'Okay. Yesterday, Roger Fieldow decided it was time for me to move on from Fieldow Finance. Of course, it's all been wrapped up in a very civilised way, but the bottom line is two years' salary and goodbye.'

Alice felt the beginning of a little eruption of rage starting in her gut, and she attempted to push it back down.

'There's no way Julia will let that happen,' she argued. 'We had an agreement.'

Their agreement. The discussion that had determined every single thing that would come after it. The night Alice had proposed breaking off all contact, Julia had agreed to protect the life she and Rory were building together: marriage, career, their future family. Alice had kept her side of the bargain.

Now, she was about to find out if her daughter-in-law was keeping her promise.

'Have you told Julia? Does she know? Is she going to speak to her father?'

Rory's body language immediately told her that he had. 'The reason I was fired is because she's divorcing me. We never really recovered from everything that happened with Dad and I guess she decided that our agreement was no longer worth it. I'm sorry, Mum.'

Alice's first reaction was to acknowledge the wave of fury bubbling inside her. So much for Julia Fieldow's promises. How could she? But then she immediately redirected her ire. It wasn't Julia's fault. Yes, Alice wished that her daughter-in-law had kept to her side of the deal, and loved her son enough to weather the storm, but Julia hadn't asked for any of this. No. Every bit of the blame for this was laid at the feet of the man who'd caused the storm in the first place. Even now, years after it had all blown up in their faces, and despite everything she'd done to prevent it, Larry's selfish bastard actions were destroying Rory's life and his happiness. She had despised that man for more than half of her life, but never more than now, in this moment.

She took a sip of her wine, her taste buds so numbed by anger that it barely registered. 'Don't you dare apologise,' she said.

'I need to. I should have been there for you for the last year and I wasn't.'

'No, that isn't true. Rory, you need to remember what I told you a year ago. It was only knowing that you were detached from your father's name, protected from the fallout, seeing that your life wasn't getting dragged through the press every day, that made it possible for me to go on.'

'I know but...' His words drifted off into an exasperated sigh. They both knew that right now, regrets were a waste of time.

Her chest began to hurt as she tried to regulate her breathing, tried to process his news, tried to see a way forward.

'What's going to happen to your house, your job, when will the divorce be actioned?'

Over the next half-hour, she listened as he outlined it all, right up until the point that the first thing he'd chosen to do when all was gone was to come find her. That one gesture told her that she'd raised a good man.

They'd picked at their food, but now she pushed the plate away. She'd polished off her wine, and refilled the glass, but Rory had stuck to water, in case, he said, that he needed to drive again later.

'So, what are you going to do with your life then, son?'

'I don't know. All I know is that my time here is done, Mum. Maybe Julia is right. Maybe it would be better to go somewhere that nobody knows me. Somewhere I can start all over again.'

The wine swirled in her stomach as the devastation of that hit her. All that she'd done, staying away from him for the last year, had been for nothing, because now, she was going to lose him again.

Before she could object, talk it through, try to change his mind, his phone began to ring.

He stretched over to retrieve it from the desk beside them. As he picked it up, she saw him check the screen, then he read out the digits on the display.

'That's the hospital,' she told him, recognising the number they'd told her to call if she wanted to get in touch.

He answered immediately, and she saw him hit the red speaker button, then hold it out so she could hear too.

'Hello?'

'Hello, Rory?'

'Yes.'

'Rory, it's Richard Campbell. Sorry to disturb you this late. Is your mum with you?'

She leaned forward so he would be able to hear her. 'Yes, I'm here, Richard.'

'Hello, Alice. As I said, sorry to phone you this late, but I thought you would want to know. The ward has just called me. There's been a change in Larry's condition...'

24

RORY

It was excruciating trying to stick to the speed limit on the way back to the hospital, but the alternative held no appeal. The last thing Rory needed was to be pulled over for speeding and someone catching it on their phone, especially with his mum in the car. That was what was so frustrating about Julia's decision to divorce him and the reasons she'd given him. The reality was that the press hadn't hounded them, because his mum's plan had largely worked. They'd become a footnote to the story, but not the story itself.

However, that said, people's memories were long, and stigma stuck around. Julia hadn't been delusional when she'd said she still felt that eyes looked at her with judgement when she walked into a restaurant. Or that she had to be careful of everything she said or did, because, God forbid, something could be taken out of context and spun into a story. He'd hoped their break would give her a chance to recalibrate, find a way to build a bulletproof vest so that she repelled the shots and learned not to give a damn what people thought. Turned out she had. But 'people' were him. She no longer gave a damn what *he* thought. She didn't care that he'd loved her, married her, promised to be with her until the end of time. And the truth was, there was no point in fighting it. He'd spent his whole life watching a woman trying to survive an existence that she hadn't signed up for. He wasn't going to do that to someone else.

When they reached the hospital car park, he slowed as he searched for a space. 'There's one right there,' his mum pointed out, and Rory turned to get to it before a white Mercedes further down the lane. As the Mercedes drove past, the driver gave him the finger and mouthed, 'Wanker'. He was just winning fans all over the place today, but this wasn't the moment to waste time being overly polite.

Richard's phone call had made that perfectly clear. 'The ward has just called me. There's been a change in Larry's condition,' he'd said, and Rory had held his breath, waiting to hear if his father was alive or dead. 'Larry has come round, he's managing to speak and he's asking for you.'

Rory couldn't bring himself to wish someone dead, even his father, but there was a sinking feeling of dread that this chapter wasn't over. Rory wouldn't have blamed his mother if she had decided not to come here, and if he were being perfectly honest, he could live a lifetime without another encounter with his dad. However, Alice was unwavering. She wanted to come. She needed to know exactly how Larry was doing and there was no way Rory was letting her deal with this alone. Not any more.

Richard Campbell met them at the staff entrance that Rory had tried to sneak in to earlier, so this time there were no objections from security.

Rory let his mum go first, walking while listening to Richard's update. 'He woke up about an hour ago. I've already been up to see him and we've run preliminary tests, which are all looking remarkably good considering what he's been through. We're monitoring him and we still need to keep a close eye on him – we're not out of the woods yet – but if he continues to gain strength and shows no significant deficits, then there's no reason to think he won't make a full recovery.'

'That's great, Richard. Such a relief,' he heard his mum say, but even from behind her, he could see by the tightness of her jaw that her smile was fake and he knew she was having to summon all her strength to say the right things. She went on, 'And all being well, if he continues to recover, when would he be able to come home?'

Rory was pretty sure Richard Campbell thought she was asking that because she was eager to see her husband well again. Again, Rory knew better. She was trying to work out how much time she had before she had to deal with that bastard again. His heart broke for her. She didn't deserve this.

'It's impossible to say for sure, but if there are no further complications, there's no reason to keep him in any longer than a few days.'

His mum's shoulders immediately tightened, as if every nerve in her body had just snapped to attention. Rory had exactly the same reaction. A few days. It was way too soon.

They reached the lift, and Richard stopped, pressed the button, then glanced around to make sure that he couldn't be overheard.

'Alice, Rory, there's something else I have to mention to you, and I'm sorry, because I know you've been through so much.'

Rory felt his teeth clench. Holy shit, what now? Hadn't his mum dealt with enough in the last two days? They'd clearly pissed someone off up in some cosmic realm of the frigging universe.

Richard took a pause, then a breath before he went on.

Rory felt his jaw clench with dread. Crap, this must be really bad. Richard was giving off extreme discomfort vibes, and he was a doctor who'd seen dead bodies.

'The police have requested to speak to Larry when he's well enough to do so.'

'The police?' Rory asked. 'But I thought it was an accident? Or is it about something else?' On the inside, he was groaning. What the hell had his dad done now? Hadn't he fucked up enough?

'Something else, I'm afraid. The initial results of his toxicology came back and there was alcohol in his bloodstream.'

'Oh no,' his mum whispered, brow furrowed. 'He'd been drinking when I went out to work on Thursday night. It must have still been in his system. I'm not defending him though. He should have known better.'

Richard was shaking his head. 'It wasn't from the night before, Alice. He was more than three times the legal limit.'

His mum gasped. 'So he'd been drinking that morning? When he was driving?'

'It seems so. Look, I'm probably breaking all kinds of rules here, but as a friend, I just don't want you to be blindsided, because there's something else. The test results indicate that there was cocaine in his system too.'

Rory turned, faced the wall, rested his forehead against the pale blue surface, only barely managing to resist the urge to bang his head until he slipped into unconsciousness. Fucking cocaine again. His father's drug of choice and the one he'd been caught with when the scandal broke. And this time, he'd done it while he was out driving a taxi, picking people up, taking them to their jobs, or the shops, or to see their families. The booze too. The guy was walking, talking, breathing scum.

Another thought struck him. His mum had told him how frugally they'd been living. She'd been on the breadline and that bastard had been splashing his wages on cocaine and booze. Forget what he thought earlier about not wishing someone dead – that was what that prick deserved.

His mum, however, retained the same poise and dignity that she'd shown all her life.

'Richard, I appreciate your candour. And, as a friend, I'm going to be completely honest with you too. I'm disgusted by my husband's behaviour. Not just in this instance, but on far too many occasions before now. I'm truly sorry that you and your staff have had to give their time and their expertise to care for someone who behaves in this way.'

The lift doors opened, and Rory pulled his head off the wall. The three of them got into the lift, as Richard continued the conversation. 'You don't need to apologise. This is our job and we're not here to make judgements on people's actions, just to pick up the pieces afterwards. Like I said, I just didn't want any of this to come as a shock.'

'You're a good man, Richard. Thank you,' Rory said, meaning every word. He wondered if twenty-nine was too old to revisit the dad lottery, put his ball back in and pick out one like this man here instead. Not for him, but his mother deserved someone like this: decent, intelligent, caring, with a moral compass that didn't point south.

When they got out of the lift, Richard led the way to the ICU, holding the door open for them to enter first. Rory's gaze immediately went to the bed that the ill, sunken-cheeked man had been in earlier, but he was gone. In his place was his father, propped up a few inches with pillows, the mask removed from his face and his eyes open and swivelling towards the sound of their footsteps. He saw them and the corners of his mouth turned up, but Rory couldn't be sure if it was a smile or a grimace.

'You can go on over,' Richard encouraged them.

Rory met his mum's gaze and he knew what she was thinking – exactly the same as him. There were few places he wanted to go less than the bedside of that man over there. Still, he could see she was intent on doing this, so he put an arm around her shoulder for moral support and walked with her. His dad didn't take his eyes off them until they were standing by his side.

Rory took the lead, determined not to put his mum in the flames of the fire. 'Hello, Dad.'

His father's first words to him in years came out in a contemptuous sneer. 'Well, well, the prodigal son. I must be dying, right enough.'

Rory had a brief contemplation as to whether or not there was any etiquette around when it was permissible to punch a recovering patient in the face.

Instead, he managed to hold a neutral tone as he replied, 'Sadly, not this time, Dad. Looks like you got lucky.'

His dad groaned as he tried to move his shoulders, his face flinching with the pain of it. 'Aye, son, I feel very fucking lucky.'

'Close your mouth, Larry, and don't you dare swear in this ward,' his mother said quietly, but in a tone that left no room for doubt that she was furious.

The flash of rage on his father's face was instant. 'Who the fuck do you think you're talking to?'

'Don't you ever speak to her like that,' Rory hissed, but his mum put her hand on his arm to stop him, then turned back to his dad.

'I'm talking to you,' she said, still quiet, still deadly.

Rory wanted nothing more than to walk away. This was his whole childhood. His whole life. His father, hotshot gregarious personality to the outside world, his mother handling him with fearless dignity on the inside. He used to wonder if she was scared of him. It would be understandable, because he was a pretty terrifying guy. But by the time he'd reached his late teens, he knew she wasn't physically fearful or intimidated by Larry, she was just terrified of what he could do to Rory if she riled him.

Rory was his mum's Achilles heels and his dad used that every time.

Enough. This pathetic, arrogant old bastard was getting no more control over either of them. But before Rory could speak, his mum got in there first.

'The staff said that we only had a couple of minutes because you need to rest. They also said to keep you as calm as possible. So I'm going to leave now. But before I go, I'm just going to tell you that the police will be here to speak to you soon, probably tomorrow. There was alcohol and drugs in your system, you despicable piece of crap. I hope they lock you up for ever.' With that, she smiled, as if she were saying something sweet to him, then turned and walked away.

Rory stepped back, ready to go with her.

'Aye, on you go, son. You know your problem? You're too like your mother. Too fucking high and mighty.'

Rory stopped, turned back, leaned down so that his lips were almost touching his father's ear. Anyone looking on might think that he was whispering words of love or tender encouragement.

'You know what, Dad? Mum and me are too fucking good for you. I hope you rot in hell. And I hope you get there soon.'

With that, he stood up, gestured thanks to the nurses over at the desk, and he walked out.

He caught up with his mum in the corridor, and his throat was so paralysed with guilt that he could barely speak. He should have persuaded her to leave his dad a long time ago. He should have taken better care of her. Time after time, she'd told him that she could take care of herself, but that was no excuse. Time to change that. Time to put her first. Make up for everything she'd been through.

They weren't going to be able to do that living in this fish bowl. And his mum wasn't going to be able to do that if his dad was out in a few days, even if he was taken into custody on drugs and alcohol charges. No. She was never going back there. Hell would freeze over before he would let his dad insult his mother one more time.

The plan formulated in his mind in the seconds it took to put his arm around her shaking shoulders.

'Mum, I've been thinking. There's no need to stay here. You've given enough of your life to him. And I've been dumped, so I'm slightly at a loose end,' he said, with a hopeless shrug that made her smile. 'So... there's only one plan that makes any sense to me. And I'm completely serious when I say this... Why don't we go back to the hotel, grab our things and then go straight to the airport and get a flight out of here?'

25

VAL

I could barely believe the story that was coming out of this poor lassie's mouth. She'd arrived in Glasgow, got into the taxi with the same nasty git of a driver that I'd had, and there, on the floor, were my rings. Next thing the lass knew, she was waking up after an accident, then carted off to hospital with concussion. Carol and Carly's jaws were both dropped, listening intently to the story, and I was fairly sure the two of them had never been silent for this long in their lives. Meanwhile, I was waiting for the straw to clutch at, desperate to take in every single detail in case it threw up the vital clue that would lead me to my wee black pouch.

'The thing was, though,' Sophie was saying. 'I remember asking the nurse if the driver was going to be okay, because I thought the accident was my fault.'

'How could it possibly be your fault? You were in the back seat and he was driving,' I pointed out.

'Yes, but we wouldn't even have been on the motorway if I hadn't got into his cab at the airport. And now I remember that we were arguing. I wanted to hand your rings in to a police station, and he just kept insisting that he would take care of it. But there was just something that made me think he was lying... I don't know what it was. I'm not usually very confrontational like that, but there was just something about him.'

'Aye, he was an arse. Rude as can be. I was for wiping the floor with him, but I was in a bit of a state that morning, so I didn't have it in me. I'm glad you stood up to him though, pet. I'm grateful for that.'

The lass blushed and my heart went out to her. My life was full of smart-mouthed, take-no-nonsense, bold-as-brass females – Carol and Carly were a case in point – but this young woman wasn't that. In fact, she reminded me of Tress, who was one of the most caring, sweetest people I knew.

'Maybe the argument distracted him. But then he got angry because someone cut him up, maybe overtook him or something, I'm not sure.'

'And he rammed into them?' Carly asked, still clearly riveted.

Sophie shook her head. 'No, he just shouted at them, and then – again I only remembered this earlier when I was trying to think it all through again – he slumped forward first. The nurse said whatever happened to him wasn't caused by the crash, so I think that he maybe had a funny turn, or some kind of medical episode, and then he lost control of the car and we crashed.'

I sat back in my chair. I didn't go for all the modern lingo, but if I did, I would say I was... what was it they called it on *Criminal Minds*? Triggered. Aye, that was it. This lassie could be dead right now if that car had hit something the wrong way, her life snapped away in a heartbeat. Just like my Dee. One minute, perfectly fine, the next minute gone.

'I'm so sorry that happened to you. It must have been terrifying.' Carly told her, and then she must have noticed that I was getting teary in the eye department, because she reached over and tangled our fingers together.

I cleared my throat and told myself to pull it together. What right did I have to be sitting here crying when it was this lass who'd been through all the trauma? And she was obviously really nervous, because she kept looking out of the window and checking her phone. Maybe waiting for her parents to call. 'I wish you'd had people up here to take care of you afterwards, but you do now,' I reassured her.

Sophie smiled. 'Thank you. That's really kind of you.'

I wrapped both my hands around my tea.

'I'm sorry too.' Carol said. 'You're not much older than my daughters and I'd be devastated if they had to go through that.'

'Thank you,' Sophie said again. 'I just wish I could tell you where the rings are now. My backpack was returned to me by the police after the accident, but it only had my stuff inside. Last I remember, I was holding the pouch in my hand, so I guess it's either still in the car or the police have given it to the driver.'

Carly, always the pragmatic one, took over the conversation next. 'When you got out of hospital, do you think the driver of the car was still there?'

'I think so, yes. It sounded like he was in a pretty bad way, although I don't know for sure.'

'That'll be why the taxi company were so cagey and wouldn't tell us anything,' Carly said. 'They were probably just covering their backs and didn't want to reveal that their driver had been in an accident. Maybe privacy policies and employer protection kind of stuff.'

I had no idea what she was on about, but I went along with it. 'Maybe. But you'd think they'd have at least told us the gist of what was happening so that we could have had all the information. I mean, I don't know where we go next. We're at a bit of a dead end now.'

Silence fell as we all pondered that.

'What if we tried to find out more about the driver ourselves?' Carol suggested. 'I mean, it was an accident on the M8. Maybe there's a record of it somewhere, maybe something that would give us the driver's name. I'm not sure what that gets us, but it's somewhere to start.'

'Wait!' Sophie's exclamation was so sharp, I nearly spilled what was left of my tea. The lass was on her phone again, clicking like fury.

'I know his name! I took a photo of his ID badge when I got into the car, because it was a private pick-up with no booking or records, and I was concerned that it was a one-way ticket to human trafficking. Sorry. My dad fills me with all these stories because he's always overanxious that something awful could happen to me.'

Dee came into my mind again, but I decided not to mention that her dad wasn't wrong.

'Here it is!'

She turned her phone around, and held it up, first in front of Carly, then Carol, then... Offft!

This time, I did splutter my drink.

'In the name of the holy Mary! That's Larry McLenn.'

Three blank faces stared back at me.

'Larry McLenn!' I said again, as if repeating it would make his moniker instantly recognisable to the others. However, a poshlooking bloke at a table further along was now staring curiously in our direction, so I hushed my voice, and leaned in conspiratorially so I couldn't be overheard.

Still, I couldn't hide my exasperation. 'Larry McLenn!' I said for the third time.

'The only Larry McLenn I know was the dodgy MP – and that doesn't look anything like him.' Carly replied.

'An MP?' Sophie asked, and no wonder she was confused. There weren't many of them driving taxis.

I tried to fill in the blanks. 'That's right, He was a Glasgow councillor, and then an MP, until he got caught up to no good, lining his pockets with bribes of cash and drugs. Oh, he was a nasty one. Fought it all the way, arrogant as anything, even though they had photos and videos of him doing it all. It was in the papers for months.'

Carol stepped in with a nonchalant but honest, 'I never read newspapers. Although, I do pay attention to Scottish news if it involves Sam Heughan or Lewis Capaldi. But I did see something about a crash on some of the Scottish headlines today – I just didn't give it any thought because we've been so busy trying to get the rings back.'

Sophie was wide-eyed now. 'So you're saying I was in an accident with a guy who was an MP? And now he's a taxi driver? This is crazy.'

'I can't argue with you there, pet. I can't believe I didn't recognise him in the taxi. But then, I was mostly staring at the back of his head and I didn't have my specs on. And I was mighty distracted too.' I rewound to the taxi yesterday morning, pictured what I'd seen. 'He looks so different now though, even from that picture. Much heavier. Long straggly hair. When he was in the papers, he always had that hair slicked back and the Marbella tan. Always thought he had a look of smarm about him, to be honest, but, by God, he's let himself go.'

Carly didn't say anything because she was on her phone now too. 'Holy fricking crap, it's here. I just googled him and it's everywhere. Like you said, Carol – top story on all the Scottish news websites. Look!'

She held up her phone and began scrolling with her finger to let us see how many stories and pictures there were, while reading snippets from the headlines. 'It was a heart attack. Non-fatal.'

Pulling my glasses on, I peered at an image of a mangled car on the motorway. I recognised the background, and I could see a sign for ASDA, so I reckoned it must be somewhere round Govan. 'Yes! That's the car!' I exclaimed, just as Sophie leaned forward, nodding furiously.

'It is. That's the car and that's where it happened. Oh God, I hope I'm not in any of the photos. If my dad sees them, he'll go nuts. He'll be on a flight up here before I've finished this wine.'

Carly was still scrolling through. 'Nope, there's one that kind of shows a second person, but they've pixelated the face. I don't think they're allowed to show pictures of people in accidents in case their families see them or the person dies before their families can be notified.'

That sobered the mood for a second, until there was a realisation on Carly's face of what she'd just said, and she whispered, 'Sorry!' to Sophie. 'I didn't mean to traumatise you there.'

'It's fine. I was more traumatised at the thought of my dad seeing me on a stretcher. Honestly, it would kill him. Anyway, does this help? That we know who he is?'

'Well, definitely. But the only problem is, we can't ask him anything if he's ill in hospital, can we? That would be awful. So tactless,' Carol pointed out.

'She's right,' I agreed. 'Absolutely. That would be terrible...'

Carly read something on her phone. 'A Twitter post just went up from one of the newspapers. It says he's out of danger and expected to make a full recovery. Still crass to try to contact him, though. Definitely. Absolutely. Not the done thing.'

We all fell silent again, before I cracked. 'Although, he was a total arse to me, a nasty tosser to Sophie and he did nearly kill her.'

'He did,' Sophie agreed, seeing where I was going.

'Okay, sod it,' Carly blurted. 'How are we going to get to him though? There's no way the hospital will let us speak to him.'

'Do you think we could ask the police what happened to the car? My rings might still be in there. Maybe we could try that?'

'I don't think they'll give us any information without his agreement,' Carly countered and I knew she was probably right. I just didn't like it.

'Does he have family?' Carol asked. 'Maybe we could find a way to ask them?'

Carly was typing again. 'He has a wife.'

'We can't contact her. If her husband has had a terrible accident, the poor woman will be distraught.'

'He has a son too. Rory Brookes McLenn,' Carly read aloud. 'Sounds very posh. Apparently they're estranged. Might be worth a try? Look, Rory Brookes is on Instagram. He must have dropped the McLenn, but it's definitely him because it's the same guy who came up on Google. I could send him a DM. In fact, Carol, send it from you. The entire population of the free world follows you, so he's more likely to think you're legit.'

Despite my vague understanding and recent encounters with the Instagrams and the social medias, I had less than zero clue about what they were hatching here. However, they seemed to be making progress because Carol was on her phone now, and suddenly gasped, 'You're never going to believe this, but he follows me. Yassss!'

I couldn't contain myself any longer. 'What does that actually mean?' I wailed. 'How does it help us?'

Carly tried to explain. 'It means that he's one of the five and a half million folk that follow Carol's account, so if she sends him a message, it will go straight into his inbox and he'll probably get notified that it's there. It just increased our chances of him reading it by a thousand per cent.'

Nope, still none the wiser.

'Okay, I'm going to start gentle. I'll see if he replies and try to strike up a conversation before I go right in with questions about the rings.'

'"Hi Rory."' Yet again, Carol was speaking as she typed. '"Sorry if this seems like a strange message, and if this is a sensitive time, please ignore it, but I've seen reports of your father's accident and both my aunt and my friend were in the taxi with your dad this morning. They just asked me to reach out..."'

All three of the others froze, then I watched as they turned towards me.

'What?' I genuinely had no idea.

Carly raised an eyebrow of reproach. I'm pretty sure she learned that from me. 'You just sang that line from the chorus of "Reach Out" by the Four Tops.'

'Sorry.' I blushed furiously, sending Carly into fits of laughter. 'Didn't even realise I'd done that. It's a habit. Me and Nancy do it every time we hear someone say that on the telly. I mean, on all the American TV shows, everyone seems to be reaching out.'

'Anyway...' Carol got us back on track, then went back to her 'reading out loud' voice. '"And pass on their good wishes. My aunt is particularly upset and would like to enquire as to how your dad is doing? We understand, of course, if this isn't a good time for you to respond. Hope the news is all positive. Thanks and take care, Carol."' Pause. 'Send.'

'Okay,' I said, looking at the others expectantly. 'So what do we do now?'

Carol put her phone on the table.

'Now we wait.'

26

SOPHIE

It had been ten minutes since Carol – who was TOTALLY gorgeous – had sent the DM to the taxi driver's son and Sophie still couldn't quite take it all in. From what she could gather, it went along the lines of this: a politician had got busted for some illicit dealings, he'd beat the charge, but he'd gone broke, started working as a taxi driver, and she and Val had both been unlucky enough to have stepped into his taxi. This weekend just was not turning out the way that she'd hoped. Up until an hour or so ago, she'd have said she was beginning to wish she'd stayed at home, but she was having the most entertaining time with these women. If Erin was here, she'd be having palpitations right now.

New friends aside, however, it was beginning to look like the romantic aim of the trip was as much of a bust as the politician's career. There was no sign of Ash. No man in the square, looking around to see if his love had come back to him. And now, the daylight was fading outside, so she doubted she'd be able to see him anyway. Although, she could swear she just saw Tilda Swinton jogging past in neon green leggings and a matching crop top. Maybe not.

Anyway, it was fair to say he was a no-show. And it didn't look like he was going to just reuse last year's photo and send it to her tonight either.

She checked her phone again. Nope, definitely no photo.

'Can I ask you something, pet?' Val hijacked her thoughts. 'You keep checking your phone. Are you supposed to be somewhere or need to call someone? Honestly, we won't be offended if you can't stay. You've already done so much and got me so much closer to finding my rings. I'm so grateful. Without you, I'd still be thinking they could be anywhere between here and London. At least now I'm on the right trail.'

'No, there's nowhere else I need to be,' Sophie answered honestly. She wasn't going to tell them. She just wasn't. They'd think she was mad. Bonkers. Because let's face it, this whole idea and this trip both fell firmly into that category. But then... Val had one of those faces that made you want to pull up a chair, put your head on her shoulder and tell her all your woes while she stroked your hair. Her mum had been like that too. Same energy. Same vibe. Same aura of kindness. And anyone who'd watched Val's video where she talked about her daughter knew that her heart was huge. 'No, no, it's not that,' she tried to brush it off.

Don't say anything. Don't. Mouth zipped.

But they were all now staring at her expectantly. All they needed were CIA badges and an interrogation light.

She suddenly broke and confessed all, gushing, 'I was hoping that I'd meet my ex-boyfriend. That's why I came to Glasgow for the weekend.'

'Wait a minute, he stood you up? What kind of cretin is that? Outrageous!' Val was obviously incensed, so Sophie felt she had to clear it up before she called in a SWAT team to hunt Ash down.

'No, he didn't know I was coming.'

They were now all visibly confused, and Sophie could feel

herself beginning to flush. Sod it, she should just tell them. But if she didn't do this in one go, she'd never get it out, so she inhaled until her lungs were about to burst and then went for it.

'Two years ago today, my boyfriend proposed to me out there in George Square, but I had some awful stuff going on because my mum was dying so I asked him to wait and then I got so wrapped up in taking care of my mum and ended up really down and ghosting him and then my mum died and I was missing her so much I couldn't face any kind of romantic relationship but then exactly a year after he proposed he sent me a photograph of my ring sitting in George Square again but I missed the message and by the time I called him back his number was out of service so I came up here and went to his flat today but he's moved so my only hope of finding him is if he comes back to George Square tonight on the second anniversary of the proposal or even if he's just thinking about me today and maybe sends me a picture of the ring again from his new number and then I'll be able to speak to him and tell him I'm sorry and see if there's still something between us.'

And yes, she said all that without taking a breath or punctuating a sentence, so now she felt giddy.

The pause as they all stared at her, dumbfounded, made her squirm even more.

Eventually, thank God, Carly broke the silence. 'I think that might be the best story I've ever heard in my life.'

'You don't think I'm completely mad?' Sophie checked.

Carol was grinning now. 'Tell her, Carly...'

'By the time I was not much older than you, I had been engaged six times and when I turned thirty, I went round the world tracking down all my ex-fiancés to see if they were Mr Right. And that was the days before social media, so I had to do it in person.'

Sophie felt the giggle coming right up from her trainers. 'Suddenly I don't feel so bad. That's brilliant! Six? At least I'm only on my first one.' She wasn't sure if it was the wine, the stress of the weekend, the craziness of the story, or the fact that it was the first time she'd had fun with another human being in days, but she'd caught a fit of the giggles and couldn't stop. She spluttered out the burning question, 'Did any of them turn out to be the right one in the end?'

Carly made a 'meh' face. 'Not exactly. I married someone who wasn't on the list.'

'So it was a waste of time?'

'Not quite. I had almost twenty happy years with that one, then we got divorced and I married someone from the list the second time around. It's a complicated story. But I did write a book about it, and it launched my career, so it was all worth it. Anyway,' she switched tracks, 'what are we going to do about you and this man?'

Sophie hadn't realised it was going to be a group effort, but she was enjoying herself, so she went with it.

'Can you not put something out on social media?' Carly asked the obvious question.

Sophie just wished it was that easy. 'He doesn't have social media. He always said it just sucked away his time and when he started working as a teacher, he binned it altogether.'

Carly wasn't giving up. 'Yes, but someone he knows might see it and hook you up.'

'I have about forty followers and several of those are dogs,' Sophie said. 'Somehow, I don't think that'll win the day.'

She thought that was the end of that, but Carol wasn't letting it go. 'However, if, say, you happened to know someone who had a gazillion followers, would you be interested in, say, letting her work her magic? That someone being me?'

A flip of something happened in Sophie's stomach, but she wasn't sure if it was excitement, dread or terror at the prospect of putting herself and her disastrous love life out into the world. She wasn't the kid who'd wanted to have fame and fortune as an actress or a singer or the wife of one of the blokes from One Direction. Actually, she might accept that last one if it was Niall Horan. She'd always had a thing for him. But centre of attention wasn't her happy place – that had always belonged to Erin. Sophie much preferred mild obscurity and general disinterest. At the same time, though, hadn't Ash taken a risk when he'd asked to marry someone he'd only known for four months? Hadn't he shown how romantic and inventive he was with the photo he sent on the one-year anniversary?

Screw it, she'd almost died yesterday (a touch dramatic, but in this moment, she was going for it), so it was time she took life by the balls and stopped being so fricking afraid. She had absolutely nothing to lose.

'Okay,' she murmured, half hoping that she hadn't actually said that out loud.

'Pardon? Louder for the old aunties at the back, please?' Carol joked, and was immediately countered with a snippy, 'Less of the old aunties please, madam,' from Val.

'Okay!' Sophie repeated, louder this time, giggling at the absurdity of it.

'Yassssss, she's one of us now,' Carly announced gleefully.

'But please don't use his name in case he gets bombarded with people trying to track him down,' Sophie back-pedalled a little. 'I don't want him to be pissed off. Maybe just use a photo?'

Carol got right on board. 'Do you have a pic? Airdrop it over to me.'

It took Sophie three attempts because her fingers were shaking, but she managed it eventually. It was a photograph of her and Ash, on the Star Ferry in Hong Kong at sunset, impersonating Kate and Leonardo in *Titanic*, both of them laughing as their hair blew in the breeze. It was one of her favourite images of the trip.

'Aw, I love that,' Carol said when it pinged in. 'Okay, let's do this.' Her voice changed to keep in time with her typing. '"Chums, Carol's Detective Services is back in business. We're still on the case with my Auntie Val's rings, but, in the meantime, a lovely friend of mine would like some help to find this sweet guy. Do you know him? If so, comment below or get straight to the DMs. And in case you need to hear it today, you're gorgeous and I love you."' Pause. 'Post to Instagram stories.'

'How many glasses of wine have you had today?' Carly asked Carol.

'Two wines and a cider. Why?'

'Because you normally start telling randoms that you love them after four drinks.'

Carol nodded ruefully. 'It's been a long day. I'm overwrought. Right, Sophie, brace yourself. Let's see what we get. Are you excited?'

'Terrified.'

'Close enough,' Carly decided.

On the table in front of them, Sophie's phone suddenly sprang to life with several pings.

'Is it him? Is it? Is it?' Carol was desperate to know. 'Has he cut me out and contacted you directly? Does he know how invested we are here?'

'She's definitely had more than three glasses,' Carly commented.

The phone was face down, but fingers trembling even more now, Sophie picked it up. It had to be him. He'd somehow seen the post and called her immediately. She hadn't been wrong about him. Their story wasn't over. They were meant to rekindle their love. It was happening. It was really happening.

She flipped the phone over to see the screen and...

OH MY FUCKING LORD WHAT ARE YOU DOING ON CAROL COOP-
ER'S INSTA?

Erin. And all caps. Carol's post must have blown the cobwebs
off her hangover.

Sophie texted back.

She's my new friend. I'll call you later. Just in the middle of something.
Love you xx

The phone rang, and Erin's face flashed up. Sophie was about
to decline it. 'I'm sorry. It's my sister. She's just seen your post and
she's a huge fan. You and your husband once did a campaign for
her company's knickers.'

'Yes! Ah, I loved those photos. My husband is a sex god,' Carol
joked, and Carly immediately covered her ears.

'Noooo. Please don't call my brother a sex god in my presence.'

Carol ignored her, and gestured to Sophie's phone, grinning.
'Want me to answer it?'

Sophie realised that could come with a hiccup. 'It'll be the
shortest conversation ever because she'll faint. She's dramatic that
way.'

'I love dramatic.' Carol took the phone and answered the Face-
Time call, speaking quietly so they didn't disturb the other
customers scattered around the bar.

'Erin, hi!'

Looking over Carol's shoulder, Sophie could see her sister's
astonished face. Hungover. No make-up. Hair greasy. And what
looked suspiciously like pakora sauce speckled on one cheek. Oh,
and her chin was on the floor.

'Lovely to see you,' Carol said, 'but Sophie is kind of tied up
with something at the moment. Can we call you back?'

Mouth still open, eyes still wide, Erin nodded, and as Carol ended the call, Sophie gave in to the giggles that she'd been holding on to.

'I bet she's still sitting there, right now, just staring at the phone, convinced she's hallucinating and swearing that she'll never drink again.'

Carol was still laughing when she went back to her own phone. 'We have comments!' she said, then started scrolling down them. 'Couple of people mention his name but no contact details, so we're no further forward. Cancel that, hold on, someone says they've messaged me.'

Sophie couldn't bear the suspense of watching Carol click through to her Instagram messages. Okay, this could be it.

Suddenly Carol's shoulders slumped, as she groaned, 'Oh no. Shit.'

Sophie's stomach collapsed. 'What is it?' It was already clear that whatever it was, it wasn't good.

Slowly, clearly reluctantly, Carol turned the phone around so Sophie could read it.

Hello. I saw the photo you posted of Ash Aitken. Can you please tell me why you're looking for my husband?

27

ALICE

For the first time in longer than she could remember, Alice felt something like excitement. Happiness. Like there was something worth living for, instead of just surviving every damned day. More than that, she felt that maybe she had a future, one that was a world away from the miserable existence she'd been trapped in for so long. One that was right here, beckoning her to come along.

'Why don't we go back to the hotel, grab our things and then go straight to the airport and get a flight out of here?'

That's what Rory had said. And her first reaction had been to come up with a million reasons not to do it. Maybe he should stay and fight for his marriage. Or start trying to find a new job. She didn't have enough money saved yet. She didn't want to depend on him. She didn't want to pull him back into her cesspit of a life.

But then...

It was as if the person she used to be, the one who had allowed herself to feel, and laugh and cry and love, had somehow resurrected from the dead and was now charging in with answers to every objection.

It seemed like his marriage was definitely over. That saddened her, because if the scandal hadn't happened she truly believed he'd have had a long, happy, successful life with Julia. But then, maybe it was better to find out now that Julia's love wasn't strong enough to survive tough times.

On the career front, he'd said that his termination package for his job would be through in a couple of weeks, so he could hang off on starting a search for something new and a break was what he needed to get some breathing space.

She might not have enough money, but she had some. If she blew it all on a week or two weeks away with her son, then, right now, in her mind, it would be worth it. She could start saving again when she got back.

And… This was the kicker that did it. What if she didn't pull Rory down into the cesspit? What if having him back in her life gave her the strength and the support to climb out of it?

'Okay,' she accepted, not quite believing her own words.

'Okay?' he checked. 'Yes! I'm so glad because kidnapping you to get you out of here and away from him would have been way harder to pull off.'

If there was even a tiny bit of her that was concerned about the optics of leaving her husband in hospital to fend for himself, she squashed it. She'd just seen that he was in full control of his faculties again. He could handle his own life from now on. She never wanted to see his face or hear his voice again.

That thought raised one issue in her mind, though.

'The only thing is, I need to go home first. I have some things there that I need to get. My passport, for a start.' She did a quick calculation. She'd renewed it right before everything imploded, so, yes, it would still be in date. 'And a suitcase that has everything that matters to me. I can't leave without it.'

He nodded. 'That's fine. We can go get it now and then work out what we're doing from there.' He checked his watch, grinning. 'Although, I think I might just have been going for dramatic effect with the "straight to the airport tonight" thing. I don't think there are many flights leaving this late in the day and, if there is, we probably don't have time to book them. How about we go get your things from home, then go back to the St Kentigern as planned, and book something for tomorrow.'

'Oh, the hardship. I don't know if I can cope,' Alice teased, making him laugh. This was it. Breaking free. Both of them. Now that the decision was made, she just wanted to get on with it.

She picked up her handbag and followed him out, down the warren of corridors to the lift. They waited for a few moments, then got impatient and took the stairs, making their way back out the staff entrance. Silently, they crossed the car park, scanning warily for press, before making it safely to the car. As soon as they pulled away, Alice exhaled. She was done. Done with it all. She felt like throwing her arms out and cheering for her freedom, but the last thing they needed was another accident.

It only took twenty minutes or so in the late-evening traffic to reach her home, and she asked Rory to circle a couple of times, to make sure no one was waiting there. In previous times, she'd literally had photographers hiding in bushes, looking to catch a photo of the person who was pretty much universally scorned for being the woman who'd stood by the vile politician. She couldn't argue with the judgement. She'd seen it too many times before too. These men, caught having affairs, or taking bribes, paying hookers or falling out of sex dungeons, and there they were the next day, giving fake, repentant speeches to the press, while the dutiful wife stood by them. Alice had always reserved her opinion because she knew there had to be a story behind the woman's decision to stay.

Maybe it was for the kids. Or for security. Or even for love. Or maybe, just maybe, it was because they were terrified for themselves or their families, because the man with the power said that if they left, he'd destroy them. That had been her. Not any more.

'If you go round to the back, there's an alley you can pull into. We can go through the hedge.'

Rory turned to look at her, his expression amused and incredulous. 'Through a hedge? I have no idea who you are right now. Are we storming the building?'

'It's that or commando crawl up the path in case one of the neighbours tips off the press. Take your choice.'

'Back alley it is. I'm not ruining these trainers.'

Argh, this felt so good. It was the same light-hearted sparring that had got them through his teenage years and into adulthood. There were no words to say how much she had missed it.

They pulled into the alley and he stopped just a couple of metres in, between a long row of wheelie bins and the huge hedge that ran along the back of her garden. To her surprise, Alice felt an overwhelming sense of dread. She didn't want to go into that house ever again. It had Larry in every room. In every corner. On every floor.

She took a couple of deep breaths to steady herself.

'You okay, Mum?' Rory asked her, concerned.

She steeled herself. *Come on, Alice. Just get it done.*

She reached for the door handle. 'Let's go.'

Strength gathered, she climbed out, gently closed the door, then led the way to the point in the hedge that was sparser than the rest, where there was just enough room, if you knew exactly where, to squeeze through it.

Rory had a slightly harder time, given that he was six foot four with the shoulders of someone who went to the gym every day, but he managed it with just a few exclamations of discomfort.

By the time they went up the path, and the security light at the back door flicked on, she already had the keys out, so she had them inside in seconds.

She closed the door behind him, held on to the counter for a second, until the sudden urge to throw up passed. She didn't want to be back here. Every cell in her body was rejecting it.

Meanwhile, Rory was scanning the room. 'I always wondered what it was like in here,' he said. Of course. He'd never been. She'd cut off all contact right after they'd moved in.

She could hear the sadness in his voice. Not because of the location of the house – despite the labels of deprivation and poverty this estate attracted, there were plenty of good homes and good people in this street and this area. But it was the state of this one. The cracked window that Larry refused to spend money to fix. Probably blowing it all on cocaine instead. The ancient cooker that was blackened with use and rust. The lino on the floor that was ripped and tatty. The net curtains that were grey and frayed. The sheer bleakness of it all.

But this wasn't the time to reflect or to chat. All she wanted to do was get out of there.

'I'll need you to lift my case downstairs, is that okay?'

'Right behind you, Mum,' he said, getting on board with her urgency.

The heels of her sandals clicked on the bare wooden stairs as she practically ran up them, and when they reached the bedroom, she couldn't even bring herself to look at his reaction. Instead, she reached under her bed, pulled out the empty suitcase she'd left there when she'd first unpacked.

She opened it on the bed, then went to her wardrobe, flicking through the clothes that she'd meticulously preserved from her former life. She pulled out hangers, passing them to Rory, who immediately understood the assignment and folded them into the case. As soon as that was done, she moved to the shoes in the ottoman at the end of the bed, then packed underwear and pyjamas into a linen bag and put that one in the case herself. She got her passport out of her bedside drawer and put it into her handbag. Okay. That should be everything she would need for a trip. Or a lifetime away from here. Except…

Her eyes went back to the wardrobe, where she could see the other case. She reached in and pulled it out, but as she did so, a sickening thought made her stop. This was the case that contained her savings. Her photographs. Everything that she still had left that had value, either financially or emotionally.

Most importantly of all, her insurance policies.

There was more than just physical baggage in here. There was a lifetime of memories and there were secrets. If Rory ever looked inside, what he would see there would shatter him – evidence of so many things his father had done that had never come to light. Every detail of everything she'd witnessed over the years, written down in notebooks. She'd started compiling it after she got here, while he was out at work. Hours after hours of remembering and writing it down. After she'd saved enough money to leave, this was what was going to keep Larry away from her. These were her insurance policies.

But it was the other things that were there that could wreck everything with Rory. The original photos and videos that had brought her husband down. And the letter that had come with them. She'd never told Rory the truth about them, and she could still keep it to herself, but if she'd learned anything, it was that secrets had a way of coming out.

She couldn't go away with Rory, have a fresh start, rebuild their lives, if there was always a loose brick in the bottom of their wall of trust. It was time for no more secrets. Even if it cost her all she had left.

She turned to her son. 'Rory, I need to talk to you.'

'Here? I thought we were rushing?' he said, locking the first case and pulling it off the bed.

'We are but...'

Her legs started to shake and she realised that she couldn't do this standing up, so she sat on the bed.

Rory crouched down beside her. Waiting.

She sighed. This was it.

'The person who took the video and pictures of your father accepting bribes and doing drugs wasn't a journalist, Rory. It was someone who was trying to blackmail him. Someone who wanted something from him. A contract. Power. Influence. I don't know who or what it was.'

She saw his forehead dip into a frown, exactly the way it had done since he was a kid when he was focusing on trying to work something out. 'And he didn't give them what they wanted?'

Alice could feel the nerves under her skin begin to prickle with cold rivers of dread. 'The package with the evidence was left on the doorstep here and I got it before he did. There was just a letter with it saying copies would be sent to the press if he didn't give them what they wanted.'

Rory's frown deepened. 'And when he didn't answer them, they went to the press?'

'Not exactly,' she said. This was it. She could back pedal now, lie to him, but hadn't there been enough lies in this family. She forced the words out. 'He never saw the threat. I assume that if he did, he'd have given in to them. But it wasn't them who exposed your father.'

He stopped. Lifted his gaze, locked it on hers, as if he was seeing someone he didn't recognise for the first time. That's when she knew he'd got it.

'*You* sent the video to the press? You exposed him?' His voice now had an edge of disbelief as he realised she wasn't jumping in to contradict him. 'You caused all of this?'

Alice nodded slowly, the terror of admitting something aloud for the first time making her tremble. It had been her. If she'd given the blackmail communication to Larry, he'd have found a way to squash it. It would have been just another thing he'd got away with. But that day, that minute, she couldn't stand that thought. So yes, she'd done it. She'd sent copies of it all to a journalist who'd covered the story. Blown the whole thing apart. Alice McLenn had been the architect of Larry's destruction. And of her own. And despite everything that had happened since, she'd do it all again.

Rory was pacing back and forwards now, speechless for a few moments until he found the words. 'Look, Mum! Look what happened to your life,' he gestured around the room, to the ridiculous oversized furniture packed into the tiny crumbling space. To the damp patches on the ceiling. The mould on the wall at the window, that didn't come off no matter how much she scrubbed it. His voice was raised now in agitation and disbelief. 'Why would you do this to yourself? No, no – to us! I haven't seen you for over a year, Mum! This wrecked our family.'

Alice snapped. 'I didn't do this, he did!'

The sharpness of her voice stopped him dead, and now he was absolutely still, just staring at her.

'It was always going to happen. He was careless. Reckless. It was only a matter of time. The drugs, the money... He was out of control and he thought he was untouchable. So yes, I was the one who exposed him. I sent the video to the press, because I wanted him gone. It was the only way I could see to escape him, to get him out of our lives forever. And I would have happily lived with the shame and embarrassment of having been married to him because it would have been balanced by the knowledge that he was rotting in prison somewhere. We would have been free of him.'

'But he got off...' Rory said quietly, restrained now. She could see he was processing the sequence of events, and he'd just hit on the brutal twist to the whole story. Larry McLenn hadn't ended up in jail. Instead, they'd all had to serve a sentence.

'Yes, he got off. It was the worst day of my life. He got off and I had to let you go. I felt the way you feel right now. That it had all been for nothing.' She sighed, suddenly feeling light-headed, the exhaustion catching up with her.

'But then I saw that this...' She repeated his gesture to their surroundings. 'This is a prison for him. No money. No power. No one to control. The only thing that wasn't right was that I was still here with him. So I've been saving... just waiting for the right time to leave.'

'Mum, I could have given you money. I could have helped.'

'No, because if he thought we were in contact, if he'd discovered there was a way through me to you, then he would have been banging on your door with his hand out, dragging you back into this. No. I had to do it on my own. And I would have. I just needed more time.'

There was fear, and anxiety and dread that this could destroy them for ever. But there was also relief. It was out. He knew the truth. Now she was about to find out if he really was the son that she had raised, the one who would see that she had done the right thing, or if he would only be swayed by how it had affected his own life.

'So there it is, Rory. Now you know everything. Your dad put a grenade in our lives, but I pulled the plug. I really hope you can forgive me, but if you can't, then please leave now because I can't have another man in my life who hates me.'

Deathly calm on the outside, but fear exploding in her heart, Alice watched as the son she adored stepped back, turned and walked towards the door.

28

RORY

Rory opened the door, as a spray of bullets ricocheted of the inside of his skull.

It was his mum. She'd turned his dad in. Let the whole world know what he was doing. She'd caused this. But then...

'Come on, Mum, let's go.' Fuck it, his dad deserved every single moment of his spectacular downfall. And as for the consequences the rest of them had faced? The honest truth was that if Julia had loved him enough, she would have stayed. And Roger Fieldow, in some ways, was just as bad as his own power-wielding, ruthlessly self-aggrandising, manipulative father. It's probably why they'd got on so well when they'd met – recognition of kindred spiritship and how they could use each other for mutual gain. Fieldow could shove his job. Rory's stomach was in knots and he was pretty sure it would take a whole load of time and more conversations with his mum to process everything, but right now, all he wanted to do was get out of here and he wasn't leaving his mum behind.

'Are you sure?' his mum asked, and the worry was all over her face.

This was what mattered, he decided. She mattered. She'd given everything for him, made every decision, good or bad, because she thought it would be best for him. This was the person who needed to be protected and taken care of now. There was no question. And besides...

'I'm sure. If I thought there was a way I could have landed his arse in jail for years, I'd probably have given it a shot too. That or a hitman.' It was an attempt to lighten the mood, to wipe her expression clean of the searching anxiety, and it worked. Then he watched another transformation as she slumped, exhaled, as if all the air had left her body, then almost instantly inhaled again, sat up straight, pulled her shoulders back, stood up and smiled with a calm, dignified bearing. This was her. He saw it now. The shell of a person he'd met this morning was gone; this was the woman that he'd grown up with.

'Then, as you say, let's go.'

It did cross his mind that he should still be miserable. Divorce. Career screwed. But somewhere in the craziness of today, he'd realised his life wasn't over. In fact, he'd been so miserable since Julia had told him she needed a break, that there was actually a sense of relief. And maybe, just maybe, some happiness about having something to look forward to.

His mum went first, carrying her handbag and the smaller trolley case, while he went behind with the larger one. Jesus, what had she put in here? This bloody case was a workout in itself.

At the back door, she stopped, glanced around the kitchen again. 'I swear to you, son. No matter what, I'm never coming back here.'

'Good. Because no matter what, I'm never letting you. Even if you have to sleep in Albie's spare room, and I'll move to the bath.'

They reached the hedge at the end of the garden and Rory forced the big case through the hole, then went after it, before reaching through for his mum's smaller one. By the time he made it to the car and pressed the button on the key to open the boot, she'd caught up with him.

'Erm, slight problem,' he observed, resisting the urge to laugh. Or groan. He wasn't sure which.

All his possessions that couldn't fit in Albie's flat were in the boot, including several sports bags, an ab trainer, and a dozen random refillable water bottles. Bugger. The back seat was populated with four footballs, a paddleboard and a snorkel set because he'd been planning to go down to Loch Lomond this weekend.

'Two secs, I just need to reorganise this.'

There was no way the big case could go in the back seat, so he had to make space for it in the boot. He pulled out the sports bags and the ab trainer and was just about to try to fit the case in when he noticed the other bag. Blue. Plastic. But fairly opaque so he couldn't see inside.

'What's this again, Mum?'

She leaned in to see. 'It's your dad's belongings from the taxi. The police gave them to me.'

'Ah okay. I'll squeeze them in the back seat.'

His mum surprised him by blurting, 'No.' She looked perturbed. 'I don't want them. I don't want anything that he's touched.'

'But there might be important stuff, maybe his wallet...'

His mum was having none of it. 'I don't care. I don't want a single thing that he possessed. Nothing. Put it all in the bin.'

'You mean, in the house?'

'Nope, in the wheelie bin there. Why should we go out of our way even one more time to help him? Here, give it to me.'

Surprised, but fairly impressed by her new kick-ass, take-no-prisoners attitude, he couldn't help but grin as he handed it over. She promptly turned to the row of wheelie bins behind her, lifted one of the lids, and dumped the whole bag inside.

'If there are journalists raking through our bins like last time, they're in for a treat. Although, the druggies round here have set fire to these bins twice this month, so they'll have to be quick.'

Rory didn't stop laughing until they pulled out of the alley and hit the road. They were just leaving the estate, when a song came on the radio and his mum leaned towards the audio system. 'Do you mind if I turn this up?'

He could barely hear it, so he wasn't sure what it was. 'Go ahead. But if it's George Michael's 'Freedom', I'm going to give you top prize for soundtracks that would be in a movie of this moment.'

It wasn't. But it was close. They sang Bruce Springsteen's 'Born To Run' at the top of their voices all the way to the motorway.

When they reached the St Kentigern, they were hoarse, but just a glance at his mum was all it took to see she was happy. He lugged the cases up the steps to the front doors, then stopped by reception to see if there were any messages, half expecting a note to say his company credit card had been declined. Nope, there was none. Happy days.

As soon as they got into the suite, he put the cases in his mum's bedroom and then grabbed a beer from the minibar and poured a can of gin and tonic for his mum. When she came out of her room, he handed it over, then clinked the glass. 'Here's to a different life, Mum, one that starts right now. And here's to finding a flight to somewhere fricking fabulous tomorrow. Where do you want to go?'

'Son, until yesterday morning, I thought the furthest place I'd go for the rest of my life was the school that I clean in every morning, so I'm good with anywhere.' She rethought that. 'Make that anywhere we can lay low and be completely anonymous. With sun.'

'Anonymous and sun. Got it.'

He sat down and picked up his phone, ready to check his flight apps to see what the options were for tomorrow – Glasgow Airport to Anonymous and Sun. Before he even opened it, he saw the Instagram notification on the bottom of the lock screen.

Message from @CarolCooperMiddleAgedModel.

It took Rory a moment.

'Something wrong?' his mum asked him, sitting down on the sofa beside him, and curling her legs up beside her, gin and tonic in hand.

'No. It's just I've got a message from an account I follow on Instagram, but it's someone pretty well known. Carol Cooper. Julia made me follow her... I can't remember why. Hang on, I do. It was last Christmas and Carol was doing a rundown of the top ten designer gifts for women – Julia wanted numbers one to six, and only because she already had the other four. It must be a mistake that she's messaged me, though, because I've never met her.' He thought for a moment. 'Although I did meet her husband in the hospitality suite at a football match once.' He shrugged. 'It must just be some kind of sales text for one of the products she's punting.'

His thumb was on it, and he was about to swipe left to delete it, so that he could get on with his holiday search, when he had the sudden thought that maybe it was a travel promo. She did loads of those. Amused at the thought that the universe or the Instagram algorithms might be telling him where to go, he clicked on the message.

Hi Rory, sorry if this seems like a strange message, and if this is a sensitive time, please ignore it, but I've seen reports of your father's accident and both my aunt and my friend were in the taxi with your dad this morning. They just asked me to reach out and pass on their good wishes. My aunt is particularly upset and would like to enquire as to how your dad is doing? We understand, of course, if this isn't a good time for you to respond. Hope the news is all positive. Thanks and take care, Carol.

He couldn't have been more surprised if Carol Cooper had knocked on his door to deliver the room service.

He read it through again. Nope, still bizarre. He turned the phone so that his mum could read it. She scanned it twice too.

'What do you think?' she asked uncertainly. 'Do you think they were in the car when he crashed? They said only one woman was brought in with him though.'

Rory shrugged. 'I haven't a clue. Maybe the other one wasn't injured? I suppose that would explain it?' He took a sip of his beer. 'Normally, I wouldn't want to answer it in case it's some journalist trying to get info, but it's clearly from the real Carol. This is the weirdest thing since I got a friend request from Salma Hayek. I thought all my dreams had come true until I put my specs on and realised it was a spam account called Thelma Hijack.'

His mum was peering over, reading it again.

'What do you think I should do?' he asked.

His mum hesitated, then: 'Answer her. Maybe she's just being genuinely nice. Or maybe her aunt and her friend are hurt and want to sue your father. In which case, they deserve every penny.'

He clicked on to the message and replied. '"Hi Carol, thank you for getting in touch. My father is... is..."'

He turned to his mum. 'What should I say?'

'Recovering.'

'Recovering. Okay. This is like when you used to dictate my English homework because I'd forgotten to do it and it was due in twenty minutes later.'

'"Recovering, thanks. I hope your aunt and friend are okay? Were they in the car when it crashed? Please pass on my best wishes to them both and thank your aunt for her concern. Cheers, Rory."' He pressed 'send', then shrugged it off and closed the app, fairly sure he'd never hear from her again.

Right. Holidays. He wasn't one for lying in the sun all day, so maybe New York? His mum had loved to wander around Central Park last time they were there.

Ping! One new message: @CarolCooperMiddleAgedModel.

'Go on,' his mum encouraged him. 'I'm curious now.'

He opened it. '"Thanks for your reply, we really appreciate it. Glad your dad is doing well. Our friend was in the taxi when it crashed. She was taken to hospital, but she's out now and she's okay. My aunt had just left the car before it happened, so she's unscathed. Although, she's very upset because she left something very precious behind. You'll see what I mean if you look at my profile. Perhaps when all is well again, and honestly no rush, we could speak to your dad? She would be so grateful to have her belongings returned. Thank you so much, Cx".'

His mum had been reading it at the same time as him. 'What did she leave?'

He went on to Carol's profile page and clicked on her Stories. Every single one had a link to a podcast, with a photo of Carol and an older lady, with headlines like PLEASE FIND AUNT VAL'S RINGS. And RIGHT, SQUAD, WE NEED HELP TO MEND VAL'S BROKEN HEART.

He clicked on the first one. It began with Carol introducing her aunt and saying they were trying to track down jewellery that meant a lot to her.

'Earlier today, we told you about two of the rings on the podcast and the Instagram live. Now, Aunt Val, tell us why the third one means so much to you.'

The camera panned to the other lady, whose eyes were filled with tears, and she seemed to be finding it difficult to speak because she was so upset. She blew her nose, then finally spoke...

'Our Dee was the most incredible young woman. She had a good job, a lovely husband, a smashing future all mapped out. And she was funny. Lord, she could make us laugh. Most of all, though, she loved her friends and her family. She would sit here, at this kitchen table all afternoon, drinking tea and gabbing, like she had all day just to keep me company. If you were lucky enough to be loved by Dee, well, you knew it. And I knew it every day until she was thirty years old. That's when she died because she ran on to a road to save a little boy who was about to be hit by a car, driven by a guy who was high on drink and drugs. Dee managed to get the child out of the way, but there was no time to save herself. That bastard hit her with such force that she never stood a chance. He killed my girl.'

His mum gasped, her hand went to her mouth, as if she couldn't bear the woman's pain and he understood why. It was gut-wrenching. And there was way too much synergy between what had happened to the woman's daughter, and the fact that his father had just been caught driving someone around while off his face on drugs.

They carried on listening, as Val told the rest of the story, about how they'd grieved, how she missed Dee every day, how the most precious thing she'd had left of her daughter was the ring they'd bought her for her twenty-first birthday. White gold. Little diamonds in the shape of a D.

'The ring was in the pouch that I lost yesterday,' Val was saying now, her voice hoarse. 'And I really hope you can help me because I can't replace it. Just like I can't replace Dee.'

The two of them just stared, absorbing the horror of what they'd just heard. Rory's mind flicked back to Carol's message. 'My aunt had just left the car before it happened... she's very upset because she left something very precious behind.' His thought process hit the conclusion and he groaned, 'Oh shit. Oh no. No. Don't tell me...'

He rushed straight back on to the messages to check he was reading this all correctly. '"Carol, we just watched your post. Was it the pouch of rings that your aunt left behind? And do you think it was in my father's car when it crashed?"'

Please say no. Please say no. Please say no.

'"Yes. It was. But I didn't want to pressure you by mentioning it earlier. I know it's a terrible imposition, but we wondered if you could tell us where the car is? Or give us any help to track them down. Again, totally understand if this isn't a good time."'

Rory groaned again, then turned to his mum. 'That blue bag. Did you say it was the personal effects from the car?'

His mum was biting her lip when she nodded with visible apprehension.

'And we put it in the wheelie bin?'

All the colour that had come back into her cheeks earlier was now gone. 'We did. I didn't even check what was inside. Oh God, Rory, that poor woman.' She was already on her feet and he could see she was thinking and fretting at the same time. 'We have to go back and get it.'

Rory was on exactly the same wavelength and was reaching for his car keys when she said, 'Son, ask them to meet us here tomorrow morning. Whether the rings are in the bag or not, we have to help find them. And given that your father nearly killed their friend, she deserves to hear the truth about the state of him.'

Christ, his dad was just the toxic gift that kept on giving.

Rory fired off a quick reply. '"We are going to try to locate them. Are you in Glasgow? Would it be possible to meet both your aunt and your friend? Say 10 a.m. tomorrow at the St Kentigern hotel?"'

The response was instant. '"Yes! We will see you there. And thank you."'

'Okay, let's go, Mum,' he said, already on the way out of the door.

They were back in the car in five minutes, and in his mum's street twenty minutes later.

'So much for not wanting to ever come back here again,' she sighed. 'We didn't even make it until the end of the day.'

'It'll be the last time, I promise,' he told her, meaning every word, before he was distracted by a noise, a siren and then lights behind him.

At first, he thought it was the police, but he quickly realised it was something different altogether. 'Oh no. No. Shit, no.'

The fire engine pulled right up behind him and he quickly veered to the left to let it pass.

'Mum, what did you say about kids setting fire to the wheelie bins?'

'They might not be here for that,' she said, but there was more than just a hint of doubt and dread in her voice. 'We'll know if they turn left up here...'

He was right behind the fire engine, only fifty metres or so from the road that would take them up the side of his mum's house to the back alley. He willed the fire engine to go straight on. Thirty metres from the house. *Go straight on.* Fifteen metres from the house. If psychic pleas could make something happen, he needed it to be now. They reached the front of his parents' home. *Go straight on.*

The fire engine turned left.

'Oh no,' his mum whimpered beside him.

Rory followed the flashing lights, sticking right behind the vehicle. *Don't stop at the alley. Do. Not. Stop.*

He already knew that he was going to lose this one. Even with the car windows closed, he could smell the fire, and he could see a big cloud of smoke coming from the left.

The alley.

The fire engine stopped and there was a chaotic rush of bodies as firefighters jumped out and started pulling out hoses from the side of the vehicle, while two others ran into the alley, presumably to see what they were dealing with.

Rory slammed on the brakes. 'Stay here, Mum!' But he was wasting his breath.

Alice was already out of the car and running towards the end of the alley, where a small crowd of youngsters and adults – presumably neighbours – had formed.

A firefighter had blocked the area and wasn't letting anyone past, but Rory could see the flames about thirty metres behind him.

'What's going on?' he shouted to the elderly gent he'd spoken to earlier in the day.

'Och, some wee buggers have set fire to the wheelie bins again. It's like *Chicago Fire* up there. Whole lot of them have gone up in smoke.'

SUNDAY

29

VAL

'You might have warned me that it was this posh in here. I would have worn my sequinned mules instead of the fur ones. Much more elegant,' I whispered to Carly, pointing to my blue, fur-clad toes.

'Och, I don't know,' Carly replied. 'I think nothing says elegance more than wearing emus on your feet.'

I didn't dignify that with an answer. For about twenty seconds. Then I said dryly, 'There's a reason I've always preferred Carol.'

Which did, of course, make all four of us sitting at a round booth-style table for six in the very beautiful bar at the St Kentigern Hotel dissolve into very inelegant laughter. These lassies could dish out the jibes – a survival skill taught in childhood in their world – but oh, they made my heart soar.

I leaned over and left a kiss of pink lipstick on Carly's cheek. 'You know I'm kidding, love. I adore you both equally and could never choose between you. A bit like Ariel and Daz.'

'What time is it?' I asked Carol, and argh, my nerves were on the outside of my skin again. I didn't want to take my eyes off the door for long enough to rummage in my bag for my specs so that I could see the time on my watch.

'Well, you know how two minutes ago you asked me and it was ten minutes to ten?'

My jaw settled into a clamp and I stared at Carol, then quickly shifted my focus. 'Sophie pet, you've always been my favourite.'

'Yassss,' Sophie exclaimed, punching the air.

That set them off again and it was a relief to see Sophie laughing too. She was such a lovely lass and the poor soul was bearing up well, all things considering. Heart-breaking that she'd lost her mum. Nobody should have to deal with that kind of pain at that age. And then to come all the way up here, almost get killed, and then find out the lad she'd come to find was married? Oh sweet Jesus, the calamity of it.

Carol reached over and playfully squeezed my hand. 'You know we're only messing with you to distract you. We're worried your head will explode if they don't get here soon.'

I rubbed my chest bone. 'I don't think it'll be my head. Can you die of heartburn? It's always terrible when I'm anxious, and right now it's on fire.' I slipped a couple of Rennies out of my bag and popped them in my mouth.

'They'll come. I can feel it.' That came from young Sophie again. She'd been happy enough to come along with us today after the McLenn lad asked to meet us here this morning. And then, the ex-boyfriend said he wanted to speak to her before she left Glasgow, and we weren't letting her do that on her own, so she'd arranged to see him here later too. We'd appointed ourselves her official Scottish best pals, but she didn't seem to mind.

'Has that Rory lad messaged again, Carol?' I asked, rubbing the middle of my chest again. Lordy, I'd be through the whole box of Rennies before the morning was out.

Carol shook her head. 'Still not since last night.'

Uch, this was excruciating. The previous night Larry McLenn's son had come back, said he was going to go and try to track down his dad's personal belongings from the car. We hadn't had a chance to ask if he'd found them because there had been no contact since. It was late at that point, though, so he probably hadn't wanted to text again in the middle of the night. When we didn't hear any more from him this morning, I took that as a positive. Maybe. Almost definitely... Or maybe not. Perhaps he just felt he had to deliver bad news in person. Or if the lad was anything like his dad, he'd probably sold them and buggered off with the proceeds.

'There they are,' Carly whispered urgently, and I swivelled round to see a very tall, very handsome bloke walking into the bar. I recognised the woman immediately, from the news on the telly and also from the papers. It had been the biggest political story in years and the press had milked it to death. I had paid no notice to it whatsoever because I was disgusted by the whole thing, but I remembered having a conversation with Nancy about the fact that the wife had stood by him. Not that we were judging. Actually, aye, we were definitely judging. You had to wonder what would possess a woman to stick by someone like that, someone who'd committed that level of betrayal. My Don would have been right out the door, not that he'd ever have done such a thing.

Carol waved over and the tall guy returned the gesture.

'Remember his name's Rory,' Carly whispered, reminding me just in time. I was so overwrought, I'd struggle to name my own son right now. 'And the woman is...' Too late.

'Hello, I'm Alice. It's very nice to meet you. This is my son, Rory. You must be Val.'

'I am. And these are my nieces, Carol, Carly and our friend, Sophie.'

At the other end of the booth, Carol had got up and she was already giving Rory a hug, while saying, 'Thanks so much for returning my messages last night. It honestly means the world to us. Please, sit down with us.'

Carol shuffled around the booth, so that they all fitted in, Rory at one end of the semicircle, then Carol, Carly, Sophie, me, and I'd budged up to let Alice sit right next to me.

'Thank you for coming,' I said, and I felt the croak in my voice as I spoke. 'And I'm sorry to get right to it... but did you... did you...' Suffering Moses, I was so utterly terrified of the answer, that I couldn't get the words out.

Alice could apparently read my mind though, and I saw a sad smile loaded with so much sympathy that I knew immediately that they hadn't been found. My chest tightened even more, my whole body began to shake, and I felt like maybe my head would combust after all. I couldn't take my eyes off Alice, couldn't speak, couldn't move.

But just when I couldn't take it any more, Carly, on the other side of me, nudged me. 'Aunt Val,' she murmured. I couldn't bear to listen to her trying to make me feel better right now. Not when every bit of me was dying of disappointment.

'Aunt Val, look,' Carly said again, more urgent this time.

It was like the whole world slowed down, like one of those films where the action heroes run in slow motion. Somehow, I found the strength to move my head round and...

A black velvet pouch.

Sitting in the middle of the table.

And a lovely big smile on that lad, Rory's face. 'I think this belongs to you. Sorry, we didn't find it before you contacted us, but we hadn't checked my dad's belongings.'

Still feeling like I was in slow motion, seeing that all the eyes around the table were staring at me, I reached over and picked it up. It felt lighter than I remembered.

I sent up a silent prayer to the patron saint of friendship and sweary sarcasm. *Josie, love, if I ever needed you, it's right now. Please let them be inside. Please let them be inside.*

Slowly, terrified, hands shaking, I loosened the strings, pulled open the top of the bag, and tipped it over, then watched as one, two, three rings fell out and on to the table.

My lungs were still refusing to inflate, when a fourth one fell out and rolled right off the marble surface, and Rory, had to chase it under the next table.

When he stood up, he was clutching a gold band with a rectangular emerald on the top. Josie's ring. That woman always had to have the last laugh.

My teary gaze returned to the table, where I saw my original engagement ring, Dee's magical diamond D ring, and – a gasp of sheer joy escaped me – Don's wedding band. I hadn't had the strength to tell the world about that one yet. I couldn't say out loud that he'd worn it every day of his life. That one day, years ago, before Alzheimer's had robbed his brain, we'd agreed if something happened to one of us, the other one should wear their ring on a chain around their neck until the end of time. Of course, I'd agreed. That's why, on the day before he was buried, I'd taken his ring from his finger before his coffin was closed and I'd slipped it on to my gold chain. But that night, the chain had broken under the weight of the ring, and that was when I'd put it in my jewellery box, telling myself I'd buy a thicker chain when I felt up to going shopping. Just another thing that had gone out of my head in the last few weeks.

The thought of sharing that story with the world had almost broken me. And now I wouldn't have to. Don had sent it back to me. And for the first time since I closed that casket, I felt him here, felt him touch my hand, the one that held the ring he'd worn for over forty years.

No one spoke. No one said a single word. And then, I felt something crack and I burst into torrents of unstoppable sobs that robbed me of any words other than, 'Thank you. Oh thank you. Thank you. Thank you.'

Carly's arms came around my shoulders and squeezed me, and I took a moment to let my niece's support calm me, to breathe again.

Breathe in. Breathe out. You've got this, Val, I heard him say.

Still trembling, I picked up all four rings, and held them in my clenched fist like I was never going to let them go. Which I wasn't. Not bloody ever. I was even going to wear them in the bath.

'You know, it's strange, because just touching them makes me feel all of them here. It really does. I can hear Josie telling me I'm a daft cow for losing them in the first place. And I can feel Don, those big arms of his, wrapping round me. And Dee... well, she's telling me to go to the ladies' room and fix my mascara because all this crying has wrecked it.'

The sobs turned to laughter.

I turned to Alice, and before I could remind myself that I'd only met this woman five minutes ago, I grabbed her hand and squeezed it tight. 'There are no words that can express how thankful I am for this. These rings are all I have left of the biggest pieces of my heart and I'll never stop being grateful to you for bringing them back to me.'

As she listened to me, I could see the tears in Alice's eyes too.

'And you too, son,' I added Rory into my gratitude. 'Thank you for not ignoring our Carol's messages and tracking these down. You're a credit to your family,' I added, instinctively throwing in one of the biggest compliments in the Glasgow vault of really big compliments.

'Just to my mum,' he said, with the most handsome smile directed to the woman sitting next to me. Och, that was lovely. He reminded me of my son, Michael. That was a lad who was never slow to make me feel loved and appreciated either.

'Well, son, not to sound like one of those emotional old aunties that gets all sentimental after too many sherries at Christmas...'

'Although, you are one of those,' Carly interjected and got a dig in the ribs.

'But there is nothing that swells the heart more than looking at the ones that come after you and seeing that they're good people. I've got that with these two,' I gestured to Carly and Carol, 'and I wouldn't have got through the last few days without them. I love the bones of both of them.'

'See. Emotional old auntie, but we love you too,' Carly said.

'We sure do,' Carol murmured, and I couldn't miss the glistening in their eyes.

One more stop on the thank you tour.

'And you, Sophie, I will always be so grateful that you contacted us, because none of this would have happened without you. You gave us the answers that helped get us here.'

Before Sophie could reply, I caught sight of a dark-haired gent coming down the stairs into the restaurant. I recognised him immediately from the photo Sophie gave Carol last night.

'There you go, lass,' I gestured in his direction. 'Time for you to go and get some answers for yourself.'

As I watched her go, I hoped that despite everything, somehow there would be a happy ending in store for Sophie too.

30

SOPHIE

At first glance, Sophie saw it was him. Ash. Yet, somehow not him. He looked different from the guy she'd fallen in love with. Two years older, obviously. But her Ash had always been in shorts and T-shirts, maybe occasionally jeans, as they'd travelled around Asia with rucksacks on their backs. His hair had been long, and his skin tinted a few shades darker with the sun. This man was in a polo shirt and smart trousers, he was paler, and his hair was cut short and neat. If she saw him in a bar, she'd think he was handsome, but she doubted she'd have the same instant connection that she'd had when she met that carefree spirit on that beach in Bali.

Or maybe all her feelings right now were being skewed by the fact that she'd spent all night and morning, processing the news that he was now married.

Married.

To. Someone. Else.

She still wasn't sure what feelings she had about that, other than sadness. Although, there had definitely been a big bit of foolishness and embarrassment thrown in last night in the bar of the hotel when the reply to Carol's post had first come through.

Hello. I saw the photo you posted of Ash Aitken. Can you please tell me why you're looking for my husband?

Sophie had immediately replied from her own account.

Hi. The message on Carol's Instagram was on my behalf. I'm...

She'd stopped typing.

'Who shall I say I am?' she'd wailed, panicked.

'An old friend!' That had come from Carly. She'd recommenced typing.

...an old friend of Ash's. I'm in Glasgow this weekend and was hoping to catch up. Apologies. I'm sorry if I upset you. Thanks for replying.

She'd sent that and then slumped back in her chair. So that was that then. Over. Done.

'He's married. He's bloody married. How did that happen?' she'd asked the other women, cognisant that they wouldn't actually have an answer.

'Three more wines please.' Carol had ordered another round of drinks, then rubbed Sophie's shoulder sympathetically.

Ping. She'd almost jumped out of her skin when her phone burst into life again. A reply hadn't been expected.

Hey Soph, it's Ash. Can we meet?

'Oh crap, oh crap. What do I say?'

'Say yes! Tomorrow. Ask him if you can text him where and when later, because we don't know where we'll be yet,' Carly had suggested.

Sophie wasn't quite sure what Carly was saying. 'We?'

'Yep, don't even think about going alone,' Carol had argued. 'Nope, anything could happen. It could be a scam. You could get jumped...'

'I'm absolutely sure nothing will happen to me,' Sophie had laughed, despite the anguish of the moment. 'I'll be absolutely fine.'

Carly was undeterred. 'You were in Glasgow for forty-five minutes and you almost died. We're coming with you. We'll watch from a distance though. If you see a large plant moving, that's us.'

That was so like something that Erin would say that it almost ached.

She'd texted...

Tomorrow morning? If it's okay, I'll text you time and place later.

Here, right now, was the time and the place and her stomach was swirling like it was on a spin cycle as she approached him. His face broke into a smile, but he didn't open his arms to hug her, as he'd have instinctively done two years ago.

She thought about shaking hands, but then just went for a non-contact wave and a nervous, 'Hi.'

There was a free table just behind them, and she knew they'd be in view of the others. Somehow that felt reassuring. She wasn't alone. They were rooting for her. 'Shall we sit?'

As he nodded, she could see he was just as nervous as her.

They sat down and did that really clichéd thing where they both started to speak at the same time.

'Ash, I...'

'Soph, I...'

They both stopped, but it had been enough to break the ice.

She was smiling when she said, 'Sorry, you go first.'

Now that he'd relaxed a bit, she recognised the gorgeous shape of his jaw and the very sexy creases around his eyes as he grinned. Okay. This was the Ash she remembered. Despite the circumstances, she felt the spin cycle in her gut slow down.

'I was just going to say you're looking great. Which I know is a really shallow thing to kick off with, but I panicked.'

'I was about to lead with that too,' she admitted honestly. 'I'm not proud.'

The creases around his eyes were back again.

'How have you been?' he asked.

Well, my mum died, and I was broken for a long time, but then I decided to come find the only man I've ever loved, and it nearly killed me because I was in a car crash on the way and when I did find him, turns out, surprise! He was married.

'Fine. You?'

'Fine...'

'Your mum?' he asked, and she appreciated that it was said with genuine concern.

'She passed away. Just over a year ago now.'

His brown eyes saddened, and the Adam's apple on the neck she'd kissed a thousand times moved as he swallowed. 'I'm so sorry, Soph.'

'Thank you.' She had to change the subject if she was going to hold it together. 'And you, you're...' She got stuck. Okay, she probably shouldn't have changed the subject to focus on the very obvious bombshell news.

She saw his gaze go to the gold band on his finger. '...Yep, erm...'

'Married?' she helped him out.

'Yeah, married. Sophie, I feel shit that you found out this way.' The genuine sorrow in his voice did make her feel a tad comforted.

'No, no, don't feel bad. I was the one who didn't come back. I'm the one who should be feeling crap and apologising to you.' Inside, she'd been holding a bottle of regret for how she'd treated him and now it cracked, and everything spilled out. 'When my mum was sick, I just couldn't contemplate leaving her, and in a weird way, I felt guilty every time we spoke. As if I shouldn't be chasing a new future when she didn't have one. After my mum died, I was... lost for a while. It's only in the last couple of months that I've started to feel normal again. Optimistic. Happy, even. Look, I didn't come here thinking we would just fall madly in love again and take up where we left off...' Okay, there was a part of her that had definitely been open to that, but now wasn't the time. 'But I thought you deserved an explanation. And an apology. I really am sorry. And I really am pleased that you're happy.'

It felt surprisingly good to get that out and now she sat back, feeling the tension in her shoulders slacken and the spin cycle stop altogether.

'I am,' he said softly. 'The year after I proposed, when I sent the photo, I really hoped... Well, I really hoped that you'd see it and come back. When I didn't hear anything, I was gutted, but then...' His eyes flickered in the direction of the bar, just for a split second, but Sophie spotted it. 'Then I met Emily, she came to teach at the same school, music and drama...' He filled in the facts, and she decided not to point out that they weren't strictly relevant. 'And that was it. Maybe not first sight, but pretty close. We were engaged six months later, and got married last week.'

A week. She was one week late. But then, she could see by the way he spoke about his wife that it wouldn't have made a difference. He was madly in love with his Emily. Sophie knew that, because once upon a time his face had looked like that when he'd talked about her too.

And going by the slightly anxious but intent glances firing their way from the pretty girl sitting at the bar, it was reciprocated.

'That's Emily?' she asked, her eyes guiding him to where his wife was sitting.

'Yes, sorry. She wanted to come along. I think maybe she was worried that there were still feelings...'

'There aren't,' Sophie told him gently, surprised to realise that she meant it. At least a little. There definitely weren't 'you're the one for me and I need to steal you away' feelings. There was just acceptance. And a little bit of sadness. And a feeling of closure.

'I'll always be happy we met, Ash. I truly will. But I think maybe you should go take your lovely wife out for lunch somewhere and then have a truly fab life. I mean that.'

They both stood up at the same time, and he hugged her. 'I'm really glad I met you too. Take care, Sophie.'

'You too.'

With that, she watched him go over to the bar, take the hand of the pretty woman and then walk towards the door. Sophie couldn't resist a glance at his wife's wedding finger. A diamond solitaire. It couldn't be more different from the silver ring he'd proposed to her with. For some reason, that made her happy. She managed a cheery wave, and at that moment, her gaze met Emily's and Sophie nodded and gave her a smile that she hoped said, 'Take him, he's yours. And I'm wishing you the most amazing life together.'

As soon as they went through the door, she stopped waving, paused to take a breath and then went back to the other table, where everyone sitting there, even the two strangers she'd only met an hour ago, were trying to pretend they hadn't been watching the whole thing.

'Are you okay, love?' Val asked her, oozing sympathy. 'I'm so sorry you had a wasted trip.'

Sophie looked around the table at the three women whom she'd had the absolute pleasure to meet, people she knew she'd stay in touch with, and she had the overwhelming feeling that it hadn't been wasted at all.

At the end of the booth, Rory stood up, to let her back in, then stayed standing.

'Sophie, my mum and I just wanted to say we're so sorry about the accident. Truly. And we hope you're okay, but if there's anything at all you need, please let us know. It's the least we can do. My father isn't someone that we're proud of.'

Sophie shook her head. 'I appreciate the apology, but it wasn't your fault. And there were no injuries that won't heal, so I'm sure I'll be fine.'

Alice leaned forward to speak. 'I just need you – all of you really – to know that it seems he'd been drinking...'

'No!' Val gasped. 'At that time in the morning? It was the crack of bloody dawn.'

Alice nodded, her expression distraught, and Sophie thought that this had to be having such a dreadful effect on her. 'I know. Just defies belief. Actually, it doesn't. I wouldn't put anything past my husband, to be honest. There has been no love between us for almost our whole marriage, because I see who he is.'

Wow. Sophie had so many questions about that, but she didn't know this lady anywhere near well enough to ask. Before anyone else could say anything, Alice went on. 'And the other thing I need to tell you is that he had drugs in his system too. As far as we're aware, the police will be charging him with both. Rory and I just wanted you to know that, Sophie and we hope that Larry pays dearly for his despicable behaviour. I'm so, so sorry that it affected you.' She glanced at Rory. 'We both are.'

Sophie had no idea how she was meant to feel about this news. Angry. Disgusted. Relieved that it wasn't worse. Grateful that she'd been given the information. Even more sure that someone up above had been looking out for her.

That's when she realised that Val was still stuck at anger.

'I could kill that man myself,' Val whispered. 'What an evil bastard.'

Alice nodded sadly. 'I feel the same way. Rory cut him out of his life a long time ago, and I'm about to do the same. I can't tell you what a relief that is to say out loud.'

Rory pulled a pen out of his pocket and jotted his number on a napkin, then gave it to Sophie. 'Thanks for being so understanding. I can only imagine how terrifying it must have been. Just in case you ever need to speak to my mum or me, this is our number.'

How could a dickhead like that taxi driver have such a nice son?

Alice reinforced his words. 'We truly mean that. Any issues at all, please call us.'

And such a nice wife! It was truly baffling.

'Thank you,' Sophie said, taking it and tucking it in her bag, thinking how sorry she felt for them. It must be horrific to have someone like that in your life.

Rory was still standing and now Sophie realised why. He pulled on his jacket. 'I know the circumstances have been awful, but it's been really good to meet you all. I'm afraid I have to shoot off. My mum and I have decided to take a trip and I have to go back to my flat to pack.'

Sophie realised she was sad he was going. She also spotted that he could follow up on that promise to help her out in any way. 'Is your flat by any chance in the city centre?' she asked him.

'Yes. Merchant City.'

'Is that anywhere near George Square?'

'Right next to it,' he replied.

'Perfect!' she probably exclaimed that too loudly. 'Do you mind if I tag along? I need to go back to my hotel to grab my things because I'm flying home tonight.'

She wondered if he was looking at her strangely, or if she was imagining it. 'You're flying home tonight?'

'To London. Yes.'

This time, she caught the look that flew between Rory and his mum.

'What time is your flight?' Alice asked, curiously.

Sophie quickly checked the app on her phone. 'Eight o'clock. To Heathrow.'

Alice smiled at her. 'I think you'll see two familiar faces on there. That's the flight we've booked too. We're staying at a hotel at Heathrow tonight, then flying out to New York in the morning.' A thought must have crossed Alice's mind, because her demeanour instantly changed. 'I mean, as long as it won't be uncomfortable for you, after what Larry did. The pain he caused. We could change our flight.'

Sophie didn't hesitate. 'Not at all. Look, I'm angry and slightly terrified now about what could have happened, but the thing is, it didn't. I'm okay. And I promise I don't resent you in any way for his actions. In fact, the opposite. I'm very grateful to you for giving me all the information. My mum used to tell me all the time to live in the present, so that's what I'm going to do today. I'm just going to enjoy my last day in Glasgow and be happy about the good things that have come out of it. Especially you bringing Val's rings back to her.' She had a sudden thought about how she could prove that. 'Actually, after I've grabbed my things, I'm coming back here and we're all having lunch. If you're not leaving until tonight, maybe you could join us?'

Val spoke up, doubled down on the offer. 'We're going to keep Sophie company until she leaves and we've promised her a smashing afternoon. We're planning lunch, lots of chat, maybe a walk round the park outside. Another chat. Then afternoon tea, and a chat. And maybe dinner if we can squeeze it in among the chatting. We'd love you to join us. You did say you're staying in this hotel anyway, didn't you?'

Sophie saw the hesitation in Alice's demeanour. 'Yes, we are. And thank you for the very kind invitation, but I'm afraid I can't stay. I have some unfinished business at the hospital. Rory, will you give me a lift there on your way home too? I want to go alone, so you don't have to come in. I'll get a taxi back to save you hanging around. That'll let you go drop Sophie and take your time getting your things.'

There was something very definite and final about the way Alice said 'unfinished business'. She almost spat it out.

Val might have been thinking the same thing, because she wasn't taking no for an answer. She'd put her bag on her lap and now she was saying, 'Alice, how about if I take you? I'll wait outside, so I won't invade your privacy. You can take as long as you want and then I'll bring you back here and we can have that lunch. It's the very least I can do after what you've done for me today and it will make me so happy if you agree.'

Sophie thought Alice was about to object, but then Rory intervened.

'Mum, that's a good idea. Be nice for you to have some company that isn't me.'

His words were said with obvious kindness, and seemed very casual, but Sophie was sure she detected a deeper meaning to them.

His mum seemed surprised at first, but then, after a few moments, she agreed.

'I would appreciate that, thank you. As long as you're sure it won't inconvenience you.'

'Great. All sorted then,' Rory said.

They all stood up and she watched as he said goodbye to the others, hugging them one by one.

When he got to Sophie, there was no goodbye hug, but he gave her the friendliest smile she'd ever seen. Wow.

'Let's go, shall we?' he asked her.

Sophie felt her voice was a little higher than normal, when she replied, 'Ready when you are.'

31

ALICE

'This was really very kind of you,' Alice said, as she pulled on her seat belt in the passenger seat of Val's Jeep. She'd been surprised when Rory had gone along with this suggestion, encouraged it even, but it didn't take a genius to work out his motivations. He was well aware that since the scandal, all her friends had cut ties with her. Not that she blamed them. They had families and reputations to protect. She also had a recollection of saying to him that there had been no friendly interactions, no interesting conversations, no hint of care or concern from anyone. She took her share of responsibility for that too. Shame and survival had completely shut down that side of her personality. However, this lady, Val, despite all she'd been through, just radiated kindness and care and affection for everyone. And even though the stories behind her rings showed that she'd suffered unimaginable heartbreak, there was still joy there, and definitely humour. Alice hadn't felt this kind of connection with anyone in a long time. It was very obvious why her son thought she would enjoy getting to know this lady and Alice didn't disagree.

But first, there was that unfinished business to conclude.

'I'm so sorry you've had to deal with all this. Sounds like you've been through the wars,' Val interrupted her thoughts, as they pulled out of the parking space and began to drive the ten minutes to the hospital.

'Thank you,' Alice replied politely, then immediately felt a smack of remorse for leaving it there and not engaging further. No, not remorse. Guilt. Irritation. Fury with herself. Hadn't she kept her mouth shut for all these years, despite everything that bastard had done? Hadn't she cut herself off from the rest of humanity, just so she could protect herself and survive from one day to the next? How was she going to change that if she continued to keep the whole world at a distance and refuse to share even a tiny bit of her soul?

'Actually... To be very honest with you, Val, and I hope you will keep this in confidence, but I have been married to that man for thirty years and I've detested him for almost all of that time.'

Val kept her eyes on the road, but her voice was full of compassion. 'Alice, love, I could have shut my eyes and stitched them together and I'd still have been able to spot that. I just didn't want to overstep by mentioning it. The lassies have been teaching me about boundaries and I'm trying to get the hang of them.'

'You're doing very well,' Alice told her, amused despite the weight that was pressing down on her shoulders.

'Thank you. Plus, and please don't take offence to this... I know who your husband is and that was a terrible business he was involved in a couple of years ago as well. That said, I try to judge folk on my own experiences, so I don't pay much notice to what they say about people in the news.'

She paused for breath, and Alice thought how polite and diplomatic she was being. Until...

'However, I met him in the taxi and that man was an arse. I

have no idea how you manged to tolerate being married to such a pompous, arrogant horror of a man for that long.'

That would be the diplomacy and politeness gone then. Not that Alice minded in the least.

'It's hard to explain, really.' Years of repression were screaming at her to stop speaking, but she turned their volume down and continued.

'Our marriage was over almost before it began. Rory is his son, but I had him out of wedlock, much to the disapproval of my parents. I found out afterwards that Larry would even have married me if he hadn't decided to go into politics. We were the instant happy family image that he needed. Of course, I was too young and stupid to realise it at the time, but it didn't take long for it to become crystal clear.'

'So why didn't you leave him?' Val asked.

Alice could sense that it came from genuine curiosity, not any kind of accusatory judgement.

'Because it also quickly became crystal clear that he was a cruel man. A ruthless one. And he got even worse as he got more and more power. When I threatened to leave, he said he'd destroy me, that he'd take Rory, that he'd make sure we suffered, and I didn't doubt that for a second. That probably sounds very weak to you...'

'It truly doesn't. I'm not in your shoes, Alice. You did what you thought was right for you and your son. That's all anyone needs to know and it's nobody else's business to judge.'

'Thank you.' The words got caught in the lump that was in her throat, caused by the validation, the support, the solidarity from the only other woman she'd ever told about this. Val was practically a stranger, yet she'd shown her more kindness than Alice had ever shown herself. She gave off the same air of care and encouragement that she'd felt from the nurse, Bernadette, this morning.

'That must have been an awfully hard life to live, though. I hope you had friends to lean on. To get you through it.'

It was as if Val was reading her thoughts.

'I actually... I never told a soul. Not ever. I just built a world around Rory and me, a shell that protected him as much as possible from his father, and I filled it with love, and encouragement and wonderful times with just us, and with his friends too.'

'And anyone can see what a great job you did. You can tell just by meeting him that he's turned out to be a good man.'

Alice saw that they were pulling into the hospital car park. 'Would you mind going round to the side there? There's a sign that says, 'Staff Entrance'.'

'No problem,' Val said, heading in that direction.

'Thank you.' Alice fell silent, trying to process how it felt to crack open that shell, even just a tiny bit. Strange. Scary. Liberating.

'But, Alice,' Val was saying now, 'that's a long time to live a life of unhappiness and struggle. What about you? When do you get to be happy? At what point do you call it quits and find your own happiness?'

The car pulled to a stop and Alice unbuckled her belt, exhaled, steadied herself. 'I think that point is right now.'

She needed just a tiny bit more courage to get her over the line and Val was right there with it. 'You go do it, Alice. I'll be right here waiting for you.'

She got out of the car before she changed her mind. As she entered the building, the security guard recognised her and waved her through. The walk to the ward passed in a blur, and it seemed like only seconds later she was standing at the door of the ICU. This was it. She could do this.

Push the door, Alice. Do it right bloody now.

Her hand connected with the door, she pushed it open, her

eyes went to his bed and there the bastard was. Sitting up. With that horrible leer on his twisted face. But there was something else...

Or rather, someone...

Sitting next to him was a woman that Alice had never seen before in her life.

Nurse Bernadette, just a few feet away at the desk, shot her a look that said so many things. None of them good. And it was impossible to miss the support in her tone as she said, 'Hello, Alice. Larry has a visitor. Sandra Vickers. He asked us to let her in. Apparently, they work together at the taxi office.'

Steady, Alice. Stay steady. Her first urge was to turn around and go right back downstairs into Val's car, but no. There were things she needed to say.

Calmly, head high, she walked over to his bed. Larry and Sandra both saw her at the same time, and as the woman jumped up from her seat, Alice could see that they'd been holding hands.

'I'll... I'll... wait outside,' Sandra blustered, and she couldn't meet Alice's gaze as she passed her.

Their actions made it very obvious that they were more than just colleagues or friends. If it wasn't so tragic, it would almost be funny. Some poor, manipulated soul had fallen for his crap. It was easy to think that the woman was a fool, but a lifetime with Larry had taught her otherwise. He was vile to everyone, except when he wanted something from them, and wow, then he could turn on the charm. It was why he'd won elections and served two and a half terms as an MP. If he'd been attracted to this woman, he'd probably bowled her over with charisma and affection and pulled out every big-shot tactic from his past to impress her. It had obviously worked.

'Don't fucking start...' Larry warned her.

Alice shrugged. 'I'm not here to start anything. I think you'll find it's the opposite.'

She sat down on the seat Sandra had just vacated, then leaned forward so there was no danger of anyone hearing a word.

'I'm here to tell you it's over, Larry. I'm leaving. I won't be back. But I just needed you to know something in case you ever decide that you don't agree with that decision. There is a case of photographs and videos of countless immoral and illegal things you've done in your life. And not just the ones that are already out there. There's more – some of them downloaded from your own phones when you were asleep. And then there's the ones I took too. The drinking. The drugs. Every single person I've ever heard you boast about lying to or screwing over. There are records of the deals I witnessed, that I've now discovered were dodgy. The promises you shouldn't have made. The rants you spewed about everyone who's ever crossed you. The endless freebies that I know now you didn't declare. And notes. Books and books of notes that I've kept every single day of the last two years, documenting every memory I have of your miserable, evil life. And if Rory or I see you or hear from you again, I'll make it all public. Every. Last. Word. Of. It. And it will bury you under so much shit you'll never breathe again. So I'm going to get up from here and I'm going to walk away. And Larry? You can rot in hell.'

She was already on her feet when he snarled, 'I was tossing you out anyway. Sandra is moving in with me.'

Alice stopped. Turned. 'You know, I think that's the first time you've made me happy in thirty years.'

Nothing on earth would make her stick around, but it would also have made her happy to see his face when the police came to arrest him and when he realised that he wasn't going to dodge those charges. Medical evidence this time. She doubted any lawyer could get him off this one.

Steadily, chin still up, she walked back towards the door, speaking to Bernadette as she passed. 'Can you please take Miss Vickers' number? She'll be Larry's point of call from now on.'

'I certainly shall,' Bernadette said with upmost professionalism, but there was an unmistakable expression of pride on her face.

'Thank you, Bernadette. For everything.' She was absolutely certain that they both knew what she was referring to.

Bernadette hugged her. 'You're so welcome. You take care, Alice.'

Alice walked on by, through the doors, and there she saw Sandra, standing against the opposite wall, sporting a look of what appeared to be scorn.

Many thoughts went through Alice's mind all at once, but two of them stuck longest. This woman knew that Larry was married yet she was clearly having an affair with him. However, on the flip side, Alice wouldn't want another living soul to be subjected to the horrors of that man.

'Sandra?' Alice said, as she stopped in front of her.

The other woman nodded, not even giving her the courtesy of a 'yes'.

'Thirty years ago, my family and friends warned me against that man in there and I didn't listen. I've never stopped wishing that I had. He's controlling, abusive and his narcissism ensures that he destroys everything he touches. Please don't let that be you too.'

'It won't. He's not like that with me.' She said it with such superior smugness, Alice almost felt sorry for her and the reality that would undoubtedly come. She'd learn.

'It's only a matter of time. And, Sandra, he's about to have no job, no income and there's a pretty good chance he's going to jail. Good luck with that.'

Sandra didn't react, but Alice didn't care – she could live with herself now that she'd warned her husband's mistress. It was up to Sandra what she did with that information.

Every step Alice took all the way back to the car knocked another chunk of that weight of fear, of unhappiness, of dread, of misery, of loathing, of sadness from her shoulders. When she got back into the car, she was so stunned, but so incredibly happy, that she couldn't speak.

'Done?' Val asked her.

Alice nodded.

'It's over?'

She nodded again.

Val pulled away, out of the hospital car park, then veered straight into the Tesco car park across the road. She drove to the deserted far corner, where there were no cars or people, then she stopped.

'Right, Alice, love, I'm going to step outside for a second and you're going to scream. As loud as you can.'

At any other time, Alice would think this woman had gone mad, but right now her mind was still too stunned to function.

Val opened the door. 'Remember, as loud as you can,' she said, before climbing out, closing the door, then leaning down and nodding through the closed window.

Alice just sat there. Looking straight ahead. Frozen. Then something strange happened. She felt her mouth open, her vocal cords tremble, and then a bomb of rage, relief, and a million other emotions, exploded and she screamed and screamed and screamed until there was nothing left in her and the car fell silent.

A few seconds later, Val climbed back in and hugged her.

Alice clung on, then, slowly, when she was ready, released her.

'Me and my pal, Josie used to do that when we needed to get something out.' Val told her.

Alice wasn't sure if she had any voice left, but she found a whisper. 'I think I would have loved your pal, Josie. Thank you, Val.'

Val pulled her seat belt back on and started up the car.

'So, just let me check I've got this. You're leaving that arse, and your home?'

'Yes.'

'And where are you going to live?'

Alice shrugged. 'I haven't got that far yet.'

'Right. Well, I've got an idea about that. Until you get back on your feet, how would you feel about a lovely wee spare room in Weirbridge?'

32

RORY

Rory had felt a little guilty pushing his mum into accepting the lift from Val, but the woman they'd met this morning was lovely and she'd obviously been through a lot of heartache and low times in her life. His mum could definitely relate to that. And how long had it been since she had spent time with someone who could be a friend? If they were going to start over, it might as well be now.

'Nice car,' Sophie said, as they left the hotel and reached the Audi.

'Company car. Or, at least, it was. Since it was part of my termination package, I guess it's just mine now. I got fired on Friday.' He unlocked the doors, and they got in. He was glad he'd put all the junk from the back seat in the boot last night after they'd taken out his mum's cases.

'No way.'

'Yup.' Before he could even press the ignition, he felt an irrepressible need to apologise again. 'Sophie, I really couldn't be sorrier about what my dad did. I can't even stand the thought of what could have happened.'

To his surprise, she put her hand up. 'Nope, not doing that. No what ifs. My dad is the kind of person who is full of worries and worst-case scenarios, and it drains the life out of him, so let's just focus on where we are now. Like I said, I'm fine. And I'm only accepting this lift if you promise not to mention it again.'

Her objection made him laugh and impressed him at the same time. 'Agreed,' he said, as he started the car and pulled out of the space.

'So anyway, you got fired. How was the rest of your week? Bet it wasn't as eventful as mine,' she countered, and he immediately warmed to the teasing in her voice.

'So... I travelled up from London, got in a car crash, almost died, and as you saw, the ex-boyfriend that I did all that for just made it clear I'd wasted my time.'

Rory nodded, seriously, as he drove.

'Okay, I'll take that.'

'See, I win.' Sophie sounded playfully triumphant.

'Eh, not quite,' he stopped her victory lap, before going on, 'My wife told me she's divorcing me, I got fired from the only job I've ever had, I told my father I'd never speak to him again as long as I live, and my back really hurts because I've been sleeping in the most uncomfortable bed in my pal's box room for the last two months.'

Sophie's laughter was so utterly contagious. 'Okay, you win. But only because my bruises will fade, but you're completely screwed. The Shit Stick Of The Week is officially yours.'

'Thank you. I'll put it in the boot with the rest of my worldly goods.' There was a pause before Rory pivoted to a new subject. 'So, did I hear you say that you met that guy backpacking? Where were you?'

They chatted about her trip for the next few minutes until they reached her hotel. When he stopped, she picked her bag up off the floor and turned to face him.

'Thank you. It was so nice to meet you. Even in the week you won the Shit Stick award.'

'And you. You were a pretty close runner-up.'

She'd just put her hand on the door, when he had a realisation. 'Wait a minute, are you going back to the St Kentigern after you've got what you need?'

'Yes. But I need to go pack up my stuff. I was in a rush this morning, so I didn't have time.'

'Well, I can give you a lift back there. I only live five minutes from here and I'm just going to throw things in a case, then head back to be with my mum.'

There was a hesitation, and Rory hoped he hadn't over-stepped.

'Are you sure? That would actually be great. My experience of taxis hasn't been the best this week.'

He checked the clock on the dash. 'I'll probably be about an hour – is that okay?'

'Sure. I need to check out and call my sister too. That'll add half a lifetime to the wait. She demands details. Also, she's in love with Carol, so we'll have to discuss that too.'

'Collect you in a week and a half then?' he laughed.

'I'll cut it down to an hour. I'll tell her she's getting it in instalments.'

She was still laughing when she closed the door, and he watched her bound up the steps of the hotel, thinking sometimes in life you just met people who made you smile. She was definitely one of them.

Rory worked his way around the square, then along Ingram Street and managed to get a parking spot right outside the door of Albie's building. First lucky thing that had happened to him all weekend. Maybe things were turning around. Actually, that wasn't true. Reconnecting with his mum had been the best thing to happen to him since he'd driven away from her that night a year ago, knowing he had to do what she begged of him.

If he could go back, he'd do a lot of things differently, but hindsight wasn't available then, so he had to let it go. All that mattered was where they were now. His mum was going to speak to his father, to tell him he was out of her life, and Rory was where he was. Both of them with clean slates and now it was up to them what they did from here. He couldn't wait to get started.

He galloped up the stairs to the flat, and as soon as he walked down the hallway, he could hear the music. In the living room, he could see the carnage from yesterday morning was still there. In the kitchen, he was almost knocked out by the fragrant aroma of Friday night's kebabs.

'It's a social experiment,' Albie croaked as he walked in behind him, omnipresent cigarette dangling from his mouth. 'I'm trying to establish whether those kebabs or my blooming relationship with Belinda will go bad first.'

'I think the kebabs are already there, pal,' Rory said, laughing as he used a spatula to scoop them all into the bin. There was no way he was touching them for fear of botulism.

'Is Belinda back?'

Albie's expression transitioned to one of both surprise and pride. 'She sure is. She's next door right now. I think I'm in love. I'm even developing a liking for flowers on leggings.'

'Definitely love. I'm happy for you, mate.'

'Cheers. So where have you been then? Not to sound all parental, but you didn't come home last night. Did you get lucky, get arrested or sleep in a gutter?'

'Are those the only possible explanations?' Rory asked, laughing.

Albie shrugged as if it was obvious. 'In my life, that's the usual choices.'

Rory realised that Albie had no idea about his dad. Or the accident. Or his reunion with his mum. Or any of the other batshitcrazy stuff that had happened to him since he'd left here yesterday morning. Albie didn't read newspapers or have any interest in news sites. He'd always lived in his own chilled-out lane. Sometimes, Rory wished he could have the same level of oblivion to the outside world.

He thought about filling him in on everything that had taken place, then decided against it. He didn't have the time and he loved Albie too much to burst his bubble today. The updates could wait until he got back.

'Lucky, mate. I got lucky,' was the only explanation Rory gave him as he went to the big cupboard in the back of the kitchen, where he engaged in face-to-face combat with a hoover, an ironing board, a set of gold clubs, three guitars and the front wheel of a bike, to get to his suitcase at the back.

Albie watched him fish it out. 'Woah! So lucky you're leaving me?'

'Just for two weeks. Going on holiday with my mum. Please don't let anyone have sex in my bed when I'm away, because I might need it for a couple of nights when I get back, just until I find a new place.'

Albie immediately threw his arms around him, wailing, 'I feel like my kid is going off to university.'

Rory was choking with laughter as he peeled him off. 'Yeah, but Daddy Albie gets to have loads of private time, so you can go get back in there with Belinda.'

'Good point. Take care, mate. Call me if you need anything.'

And then, leaving only a trail of carcinogenic fumes, he disappeared back off into the bedroom.

It only took Rory half an hour or so to pack, so he was back in the car and drawing up outside Sophie's hotel five minutes early.

She was already there waiting for him. He opened the door for her, and she threw her backpack in the back seat and then jumped in.

'Thank you. You're packed?'

'Case is in the boot,' he said, pulling off.

'So, tell me, what's the plan then?' she asked. 'I mean, after you get back from the holiday.'

'I've got no idea. Haven't got that far yet. I was thinking about your trip around Asia though. I've been this corporate machine for almost ten years now. Into a job straight out of university, then marriage, house, commitments. The company is paying me for two years, so I think I'll start by taking some time off after the trip with Mum. Maybe travel to places I've never been. Get lost on a beach somewhere.'

'Yes! You should definitely do that! There's nothing like a sunset on a Thai beach to make you think about what you want out of life.'

He didn't answer because he'd just stopped at traffic lights on Bath Street as she said that, and he was distracted by a car across the road. Parked. A red Ferrari. And two people were walking towards it. One was a guy he recognised as another accountant in his company. A senior manager. Bit of a dick. And the other was Julia. His arm was slung across her shoulders, and they were laughing and it couldn't have been more obvious that they were a couple. Fuck. So this was what it had come to. The woman he'd loved, adored, promised to be with forever, only to get booted out and cancelled when it got too rough to handle. And there she was, with someone else, and without a fucking care in the world. If Sophie hadn't been in the car, he'd probably have pulled over, punched the steering wheel, then tortured himself by watching them for longer. It would achieve nothing, but maybe it would be the bat around the head he needed to begin moving on.

In fact, maybe he didn't need to stop to cut those ties. They'd been fraying for months, so the threads were already bare. All he could do now, for the sake of his heart, was cut them completely.

'Are you okay?' Sophie said. Then she must have spotted where his eyeline was fixed, because she asked, 'Someone you know?'

Was it? He'd never been more sure that he didn't recognise that person at all.

'No,' he said, and strangely, he didn't feel one bit of regret as he heard it out loud.

'Just someone I used to know. Not any more.'

Not any more. Now he was only looking forward, not backwards. And also to the side, to the smiling face in the passenger seat.

'So tell me where you think I should go then. Map it all out for me.'

And as the lights changed to green and he drove off, that's exactly what she did.

EPILOGUE

ONE MONTH LATER

'Are you ready for the podcast, Aunt Val?' Carly asked, that big beaming grin of hers on her face as usual. I couldn't believe they were still here, but, God love them, they were.

A month ago, on that day we'd got the rings back, we'd got home late at night from the St Kentigern Hotel. Carly had made us all a cup of tea, and we'd sat down right where we were now, at the kitchen table.

Before I'd even unwrapped my caramel wafer, Carly had reached for my hand. 'I need to say sorry, Aunt Val.'

I'd had no idea what she was talking about. 'For what, pet?'

'For relentlessly persuading you to come down to my house so soon after you lost Uncle Don. I thought that maybe a change of scenery would be a good thing for you, especially as so many of the people in your life up here were away. I thought I could take care of you and that the different surroundings would be a way… well, not to forget, but to make the memories a little bit quieter. But if I'd stopped to really think it through, I'd have realised that what you needed wasn't new memories, it was to have us take care of you while you came to terms with the old ones. We should have come here, to you. For as long as it took.'

Carol was nodding in agreement. 'She's right, Aunt Val. We're so sorry.'

I'd put down my biscuit and grabbed a paper towel from the counter behind me. 'Holy kitchen roll, just when I thought I had no more tears to shed. Listen, you two, you have nothing in this whole world to apologise for. I'm thankful every day that I have you both and I know you were coming from a place of doing your best and thinking you were doing the right thing. I didn't think it through either. The pain of losing Don... I don't think I've thought straight since, to be honest with you. And anyway, your lives are far too busy to be trekking up here at the drop of a hat.'

'Actually, that's something we wanted to talk to you about. We've been thinking that we could stay for a wee while?'

'Nope!' I'd blurted. I wasn't having that. I had déjà vu from that first morning in Carly's kitchen when they'd insisted on coming to Scotland with me. 'I will not take you two away from your own families to stay here and look after me. I'm quite capable of...'

Carol had stopped me. 'We know that, Aunt Val. We know. But this isn't that. Everything that's happened this weekend has got me thinking that maybe I need to spend some more time with my mum, so I'm going to go stay there for a while. They've even agreed to turn the gym back into a bedroom for me. Cal can come up when he's not slammed at work. And maybe the kids too, although they've all got their own busy lives going on, and that's okay.'

Carol's mum was only a few streets away, so I could practically see what they were having for dinner.

'And as for me,' Carly had cut in. 'I'm on my own anyway. Sam and Mac will be on location for another month, and Benny doesn't have leave until October. I can work from anywhere, just like Carol...'

'We can do the podcast from this table, just like we did earlier,' Carol had added. 'Besides, people love you on my Instagram. The post I put up with the video of you sharing that your rings had been found went viral and it got the most likes and shares of anything I'd ever done. You're the star now.'

I couldn't think of anything worse. 'I'll send you my invoice,' I'd joked, still trying to process their news about staying.

Carly had sealed the deal. She'd wrapped her arms around me, the same way she'd done since she was a kid. 'So we'd really, really like to stay. If you'll have us.'

I had been overcome with pure unadulterated love for these two magnificent women. 'I'll have you all day long,' I'd told them, meaning every word.

Since then, they'd kept to the plan, and now, four weeks had flown by and the month was up. They were leaving tomorrow, but I knew that I'd be fine. I was in a very different place from when I'd walked out of my front door and stepped into Larry McLenn's taxi. Nancy and Johnny were back from their holiday. Tress, Noah and little Buddy were home too, and Nancy and I were back to two childminding shifts a week with the gorgeous wee button. I'd even managed to wander up and down the high street a few times. Once everyone got past the first encounter and gave their sympathies, it had got so much easier. And I was strong enough now that I didn't crumble at the very thought of my darling big man.

Maybe the biggest factor in that was that I wasn't sitting in my own thoughts all day and night, because I had other company in the house now. It had taken a bit of persuasion when I'd picked her up from the airport after her trip to New York with Rory, but Alice had moved into our Dee's room and it was lovely to have someone around the house again.

I glanced over at Alice, who was also a different woman now. It was like the whole world had been lifted off her shoulders. She looked ten years younger now that her eyes were sparkling and all that stress was off her face. She'd added a few blonde highlights to her newly styled grey hair, and she always had lovely bright colours on. I had asked her how she always smelled so gorgeous, and Alice had told me that she lathered on loads of that Chanel No. 5 body lotion. Apparently, she'd bought a couple of new bottles of it in the duty-free on the way back from New York. She'd had a wonderful time there with her lad. She'd told me how they'd gone to the fountain in Central Park on their first day and they'd both taken off their wedding rings and tossed them in there. She said she felt like punching the air as she realised she was free. Truly free. Maybe for the first time ever.

I was glad for her. She's a good woman. Although, given that rings are a touchy subject with me these days, I was a wee bit perturbed that they'd thrown them away. Apparently, though, the fountain gets dredged regularly and all the coins and everything else of value gets donated to local charities. That would be a wee bonus for them this month then.

Rory and Alice had spent the rest of their trip just walking in Central Park, strolling around the streets, eating in cafés and doing whatever the notion took them. Alice said it was like a decompression chamber and now she was coming out the other end, ready to face the world again. I was glad she was doing it here with me, especially since that arse she married was never out of the papers these days. As soon as he got out of the hospital, he'd been arrested, charged with driving under the influence and something about endangering lives. According to the *Chronicle*, he was up in Barlinnie on remand, and the chap that writes their legal stuff reckoned he'll get at least a couple of years for it. Alice wasn't fussed in the least when she told me that daft bint, Sandra, had started a petition online to free him. Nobody signed.

Meanwhile, I'd offered to share the Jeep, so every day Alice goes off to her cleaning jobs and she comes back with a smile on her face. She says they saved her when she was at her lowest, and she isn't going to give them up just yet.

We've never discussed how long she'll stay for, but I hoped she wasn't in a rush to go anywhere. The two of us are good for each other – especially since Rory hadn't taken the second flight on the trip back from New York. He'd got off in London, because he'd made an arrangement to meet up with Sophie. Two weeks later, he still hadn't come back and given their big soppy grins when they FaceTimed last week, I don't think he'll be getting on the plane back up to Glasgow any time soon. Sophie has a few weeks off in the school summer holidays, so last I heard they were thinking about spending it travelling around Asia. Or maybe it was America. Or Europe. Or all of the above. Not that they'd be backpacking. That company he used to work for paid him all of his severance package, so they'd probably be in five-star hotels with shag pile carpets and minibars. I told him Alice and I are available for weekend visits.

Oh, and Sophie did tell her dad and her sister what really happened that weekend, because she might have to come back up to Glasgow to testify in Larry McLenn's court case. This time, her dad says he's coming with her. They're going to stay here with me and Alice, and you never know... maybe there could be a spark between Alice and Sophie's dad, two souls who've been to hell and who are just trying to build new lives. Carly says if that happens, she's going to write a book about it.

'Right, Aunt Val, are you ready?' Carol asked as she slid the microphone towards me.

I patted my hair, dabbed on a bit of lippy, pulled my shoulders back.

'I'm ready, love.'

The camera started recording, and Carol and Carly said their greetings before giving me a lovely introduction. I jumped in right on cue.

'Hello to all the Instas and the Podcasts!' I added a wave to the camera and I could feel my cheeks hurt with the width of my smile but I didn't care. 'A few weeks ago, you all listened to my stories about losing my most precious possessions and hopefully you saw my wee clip that was filmed the day I got them back. And aye, since then I've invested in waterproof mascara because those big black lines of happy tears down my face weren't my best look. You'd think my nieces might have pointed that out to me before they showed it to the world, but I'll forgive them,' I said, nudging Carol on the shoulder. 'Anyway, I just wanted to come on here and tell you myself how grateful I am. The number of comments and messages we got was just incredible and I've had time to read them all now. I've always known that despite all the awful things that go on, most of the people out there are just kind and decent, and now I know that all those good folks listen to our Carol and Carly's podcasts and video thingies. There were a few individuals who were directly involved in getting these back to me, but I'm respecting their privacy by keeping that to myself.' I winked at Alice, over at the other side of the table, out of shot. 'But I will say, Sophie Smith, if you're watching, I now consider you part of my family, so you'd better hurry back to visit me soon. Anyway, I've taken up enough of you terrific folk's time, so I'll just say, thank you all for listening, for sending your good wishes, and remember, tell your people that you love them. Tell them every day. And don't forget to lock up your valuables.'

Carol and Carly took over, the camera back on just the two of them as they wrapped up the broadcast. I felt another wave of gratitude for them both and as they spoke, I squeezed the ring on the chain around my neck, closed my eyes for just a second to thank the others that I knew had a hand in this today.

My silent thoughts went upwards.

Josie, I can hear yer cackling laugh from here, ma darling. Yer the best pal a woman could ever have and I hope you're raising hell up there. Dee, sweetheart, I love you and I'll never stop being grateful that you were mine, even if I didn't get to keep you forever. And Don... oh my big darling Don. Give our girl a hug from me and hold her tight until I get there. You know I'll love you in this life and in every life to come. But aye... next time I'll leave my rings in the house.

AND FINALLY...
THE BIT WHERE I TELL THE REST OF MY OWN STORY

Me again! This note is the continuation of my tale of woes and lost rings from the start of this book, so if you skimmed that, apologies. Now might be the time to pop back or the rest of this chapter won't make sense.

So I left off as I rushed to the waiting taxi. Fast-forward to sixteen hours later, after flying Glasgow–London, switching from Terminal 5 to Terminal 3 at Heathrow Airport, then soaring through the skies until I landed in LA, finally snatching a few hours' sleep somewhere over the Atlantic. That's when I flipped up the flap on my overstuffed handbag to grab my hairbrush and realised the little black pouch containing my most treasured possessions was no longer there. It took a few seconds for a horrible blanket of fear to descend. I frantically searched the bag, emptied it, turned it upside down, but they were gone.

In the devastating hours afterwards, I would arrive at my best guess, that, as in Val's story, the bristles of my brush had become entangled with the strings of my little jewellery pouch, and when it had fallen out of my bag, it had taken my rings with it. And nope, no barrage of recriminations, criticisms or words of wise hindsight could make me feel as awful, as idiotic, as heartbroken as I did at that moment, or in the stomach-churning hours, days and weeks afterwards as I made dozens of calls, filed endless reports and wrote countless emails and even some social media posts, trying desperately to track them down.

The search for them consumed me, as did the guilt, the self-recrimination, and – it gets worse – the realisation that I'd vaguely noticed my handbag's magnetic catch popping open a couple of times during the journey, but in my distracted rush, I hadn't even considered that anything could have fallen out.

So did I find my rings? The answer is... drum roll... No. I didn't. I spent the next month absolutely heartbroken, while emailing and calling every lost property office between Glasgow and London, berating myself for losing them. There were three of them that stung the most. The smoky quartz was the only physical thing I possessed that connected me to my beloved gran, Betty Murphy. I adored her, not least because she was a truly wonderful woman who loved fiercely, laughed uproariously and revelled in the delights of a Sunday carvery, but also because she was never slow to say what she thought – I can almost hear the bollocking I'd be getting for being careless.

The other loss that hit hard was my engagement and wedding rings, bought about five years ago to replace the original ring my husband of thirty years gave me when we decided to get married, exactly one week after we met. I know. It's a whole other book. Back then, we were skint but oh so happy and I didn't need diamonds to show it. In 1993, I picked the ring, and he bought it – for a whole £54. Thankfully, that original one is still in my jewellery box, on its own velvet cushion, and it'll always be my very favourite thing I own. However, I adored the replacements almost as much, because of what they signified: our marriage, our family and the lives that we've had together.

I don't think there's any chance my little black pouch of gems will show up now, so, like Val, I'm trying to look for some kind of meaning in what happened. I've settled on this – I lost my rings, but I found this story, because, as always, my feelings consumed my writing too.

It gave me an opportunity to bring back Carly Cooper, the very first character I wrote back in 1999 when I sat down with an idea in my head about a woman who went around the world trying to track down her ex-fiancés. That novel, *What If?*, launched my career and it'll always be the book that I'm most grateful for.

This story also allowed me to hang out with my darling Val, who has been with me, popping up regularly in my novels, for over a decade. If you've ever heard me talking about her, you'll know that she was inspired by both my grandmothers, Betty Murphy and Sadie Hill, and a few other utterly spectacular women of that generation and the next.

This year, I needed Val's presence more than ever, because in July, the irreplaceable Sadie Hill passed away at the age of ninety-eight. She was a piece of my heart, and she is missed beyond words.

So this book is dedicated to Sadie, to Betty and all the other Vals in this world. Unapologetic forces of nature who love, laugh and show the rest of us how it's done.

With all my love, Shari xx

ABOUT THE AUTHOR

Shari Low is the #1 bestselling author of over 20 novels, including *One Day With You,* and a collection of parenthood memories called *Because Mummy Said So.* She lives near Glasgow.

Sign up to Shari Low's mailing list for news, competitions and updates on future books.

Visit Shari's website: www.sharilow.com

Follow Shari on social media:

 facebook.com/sharilowbooks

x.com/sharilow

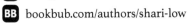 instagram.com/sharilowbooks

bookbub.com/authors/shari-low

ALSO BY SHARI LOW

My One Month Marriage

One Day In Summer

One Summer Sunrise

The Story of Our Secrets

One Last Day of Summer

One Day With You

One Moment in Time

One Christmas Eve

One Year After You

One Long Weekend

The Carly Cooper Series

What If?

What Now?

What Next?

The Hollywood Trilogy (with Ross King)

The Rise

The Catch

The Fall

Boldwood

Boldwood Books is an award-winning fiction publishing company seeking out the best stories from around the world.

Find out more at www.boldwoodbooks.com

Join our reader community for brilliant books, competitions and offers!

Follow us
@BoldwoodBooks
@TheBoldBookClub

Sign up to our weekly deals newsletter

https://bit.ly/BoldwoodBNewsletter

Printed in Great Britain
by Amazon